A Drop Of

Faerie's Blood

Summer Raine McLerran

Sea Shanties:
"Spanish Ladies"
"Blow the Man Down"
"Fishes Lamentation/ Windy Old Weather"
Collected by Roy Palmer, Oxford Book of Sea Songs from late eighteenth century, available by public domain

Quoting from the book for review purposes is allowed and encouraged.
Thank you for your reviews!

Publisher: North Coast Stories
Cover & Interior Design: Crissi Langwell

ISBN: 978-1-961240-06-3

This book is also available as an ebook.
Please visit the author's website to find out where to purchase this book.

Table of Contents

I. Lambið

She felt closest to me in the morning. Before the sun rose over the hills. When the world was still quiet, and this town, that I resented in so many ways, held the smallest space of peace just for us.

We came to the beach when she was still alive. When she needed time away from the ranch. I just enjoyed being with her, and as I grew up, I understood the need to see the Occidental Ocean after remaining on the ranch all week. It wasn't the sheep or the manure scent that suffocated me, but the people who seemed to forget there was a world beyond our borders.

The beach was quiet, apart from the rolling waves sliding over the vibrant pebbles and the tumble of water receding back across the pale sand. The air still had that lovely crisp feeling before the penetration of the sun left everything damp and heavy. I roamed across the hills from my father's ranch, around the town, staying on the lightly trodden path that led to the coast.

The once perfectly sculpted rock stairs were now brittle, and pieces fell as I scaled down the cliff. My feet could hardly fit on the steps, but I maneuvered carefully, unafraid of falling or slipping. I made this trip every week and had come to know the weakest points in the cliff wall.

Few ventured to this cove, which was precisely why Mateo and I chose it as our Sunday meeting point. The less people who saw us there, the better. There were already enough rumors about me as it was: the Hidalgo wretch, the daughter of the burned Spriggan, the failed heiress of el Don Hidalgo, and the one no one should show any kindness to unless they wanted to spend the rest of eternity in hell.

I say this with some humor. The extremities my father's tenants went to make me out as the villain were almost too incredulous to believe. But it's easy to tarnish those not understood. Most people of Port Villaviciosa had never been out of Playada. In fact, the vast majority had never been further than a day's journey from the town itself. So when my mother, an immigrant from the north, arrived and had me soon after, we were both looked at with suspicion. We were unknown and, therefore, untrusted. Of course, no one wishes to be the outcast of their community. But having lived this way my entire life, I didn't get much choice in the matter. Better to embrace it than to suffer beneath their labels.

Mateo, el Don Ries's youngest son, was preparing the rowboat when I made my way down the cliff, balancing on my toes, hoping no pebbles found their way down my tall, black boots. The silly dance across the sand was wasted because I still had to shake them out when I made it down to the small dock we spent a week building a few summers before.

Mateo grinned at me as he watched me shake out my boots.

"Mornin', Mayra. Told you they were too big on you," he chuckled.

"Well, they're better than my dress boots, aren't they?" I scowled. I was in my normal Sunday best which included Mateo's hand-me-down boots, a second-hand tricorn hat, a white shirt I had found in one of my dad's old chests, and pants that would have slipped right down had it not been for the leather belt tied around my waist twice. I looked no better than a court jester, but the goal wasn't to look like a lady, but as a sailor, so no one would tell my father or stepmother that they saw me rowing in the bay with a boy.

Mateo was more well-fitted for our outings. He too had a reputation to uphold, though his father was a master fisherman, and had earned his lordship from that role. Mateo could be seen upon the water in drabs and no one thought less of him. Had el Don Ries had a daughter, I am not certain she would be respected as much as Mateo or his older brother, Tomas. But who's to say?

Still, there was an obvious difference between males and females of noble birth. My father was lord of livestock, and yet it would be improper to see me herding our sheep.

We rowed out while the rest of the town attended church, just as we had for several years now. It was our one chance for some peace from being the children of los Dons and to speak plainly of anything on our minds, without rules of what was proper for young men and women of noble birth.

"Pa got a deal with a ship to the south. It's a much larger fishing ground and is promising three times what we make here. He sees it as an opportunity to expand his reach and double the value of his business," he said, paddling the boat out far enough in the bay that the water would settle and we could drift for a while.

I had laid back against a pile of nets and put my feet up. "Will you go with him?"

Mateo shrugged. "Tomas wants to. But Ma will stay. She thinks it's all a scam and that Pa's being cheated."

"Are you worried about her being here alone?"

Mateo nodded. "That's why I haven't decided."

"I can look after her," I joked. La Doña Ries hated me. Harlot, wench, whore, and Brannish scum were all her favorite words when she spoke of me. Never to my face, but women don't tend to speak their malice so directly.

"Ah, don't mind her," Mateo replied. "She's also got eyes for Javier Vasquez. I'm sure she's just waiting for Pa to be off so she can take her chance."

"But she's a married woman!" I exclaimed.

"If Pa don't know, she don't see it as being unfaithful."

I laughed theatrically. "Church-going women are a mystery. I am a sin for being Brannish and yet they step out on their husbands and are destined for heaven."

Mateo was the only person I could speak to frankly and not feel as if every word that crossed my lips would be twisted. There were many who would have loved to hear me blaspheme so openly, giving them a concrete reason to expel me from Villaviciosa.

"I also don't know if sea life is for me," Mateo admitted. "Months away from home. No real bed. Food's poor. Not really much opportunity to find myself a wife."

"You wish to find a wife?" I asked, straightening a bit. It wasn't all that surprising. Mateo was twenty, like me. While it was customary for a woman to be married at that time, men could enjoy their solitude well into their thirties. There were a few who chose to marry young, but many sought out matches for status and uniting families. Besides, Tomas had not yet found a wife, and Mateo was a second son. My friend would have to rely on love to give him a union.

"Doesn't everybody want to get married?" he asked in response to my question.

I raised an eyebrow. I didn't wish to ever marry. I had never loved anyone and certainly didn't want to belong to anyone in the village. Not that anyone would want me either. If la Doña Ries had her way, Mateo would not speak to me at all for fear he would marry the girl of Brannish blood. It was for this reason the other boys in town avoided me. Should they make me their wife, their babies would be scrutinized just as I always had been.

I didn't wish that fate on anyone. My mother never anticipated our ill treatment in this town, but had she known the prejudice of Port Villaviciosa and how they'd view us, I believed she would have raised me elsewhere.

But that wasn't the only reason. I just didn't see how a life being married could bring anyone joy. Mama had been complacent with my father, Lupe, but seemed happier when it was just her and me. Her eyes never lit up when she saw my father. He would sometimes kiss her cheek or tell her he loved her, but it appeared more conversational than sincere.

I had read enough books to know what love was meant to look like, and I was sure I had never witnessed it. I had never seen Lupe sweep Mama off her feet, kiss her hand, or whisper sweet words in her ear. They had addressed each other cordially, respectfully acknowledging each other. They slept in the same quarters, but I don't recall ever hearing any sort of enjoyment coming from their room.

"Well, I was thinking of carrying on Pa's business here," Mateo said. "He'll leave his smaller boat and I could man it. Hire a few men. Maybe you could join me?"

"Me? Work on your boat?"

Mateo nodded, not seeing how ridiculous that sounded.

"No one would buy from you if you did that." A woman on a boat was a curse. A working woman especially. No one would want to see me as a crew mate, and no one would buy from someone who allowed a woman to work if she wasn't mending or baking.

"Ah, I think they would. I'd bring on Jorge, Daniel, and Hugo. They wouldn't mind you, Mayra. And they're old enough that their mas don't hold onto their leading strings anymore," Mateo said.

But I knew their mothers' prejudice would be passed to them, and to their children and so on. They were our age, but still lived in a town that had held these beliefs for hundreds of years. Mateo was an anomaly, though I still had room for fear that one day he'd think me damned. Surely whatever girl he married would want me as far away as possible.

"Well, think on it," Mateo concluded. "I need a first mate."

It would be an adventure if I could join Mateo's crew. It would give me time away from home, some independence, a chance at a life beyond just marrying into wealth. But such things were not done in Villaviciosa. Mateo had to know that. We still lived in the town that paraded my mother around before they hung and burned her body under the accusation that she was a Spriggan.

Eight years earlier

Stories of Spriggan were known in all corners of the world. In the Aldinian corner, our neighbors diretly to the north, Spriggan were known as the fae people, mer-folk, the elves, the dwarves, the nature spirits, and anything else inherently magical or pagan. They existed plentifully in the old world, before civilized men rose to power and banished them to live in small tribes in remote places.

The Spriggan were not to be allowed within a stone's throw of the Playadan border. No town was willing to break that law, no matter the promise of riches. In this matter alone, Playada willingly followed the laws decreed by the rotten Aldinian king: *any who are or associate with a Spriggan will be hanged and burned for their blasphemy.*

The church in Villaviciosa had a sermon on the dangers of Spriggan once every month or so, particularly on the threat they caused to the common people and how they were all in league with the devil. Also, a Spriggan was not limited in bodily form as one of the wee-folk. To my knowledge, the wee-folk could not be found this far south.

I was raised hearing stories of Spriggan, of how they were tricksters who caused mischief to the human world. Most were benign, but they could never be trusted. My mother was sure about that.

"I do not agree with the slaying of small Spriggan creatures," she said while she braided my hair, "but I would not break bread with them. They'd end up with both halves."

She told me the stories of the fire sprite, of the lone siren, and the epic romance of the dwarf and the *Sjöfru*.

To a Playadan, each of these tales was a horror story. Their greatest pride was that their piousness kept the devils out of the south, but we were always reminded that we weren't truly safe. One's neighbor could be considered a Spriggan, especially if she hangs lavender above her door and sings below the full moon.

Like my mother did.

Vivanka Ogren-Hidalgo came from the northern country of Brannland. Aldina and Brannland did not get along, but the stronghold to the far north was not for Aldina to claim. Aldina claimed Playada as one of them through a bitter decade-long war. My birthplace was just one of the long list of countries Aldina claims to hold. They argued it was to unite two strong countries and that our forces would be impenetrable. But we had better trade access. We had more resources. Much of our land was unclaimed to the east because settlements stayed near the sea, so the Aldinians saw an opportunity to place more of their lords in power to govern these lands. Which meant my father's lordship, and los Dons like him, would be taken from power. It hadn't happened yet, but it was foreseeable in our future.

But Aldina left Brannland alone. The kingdom would argue that their lack of action was because of the severe weather and unfarmable soil. But the men of the north were brutal, savage, and unforgiving. It would be too great a risk to attack. Not to mention the wee Spriggan ran free over their lands.

When Vivanka came to Playada, she was looked at with suspicion and almost forced to leave. Everything about her set her apart from the southerners. Her pale skin. Her bright blue eyes. Her hair was as dark as theirs, but she wore it in intricate braids and not tucked away in scarves. And when she spoke, everyone shied away. The northern accent was often mistaken for a faerie's tongue.

But my father, el Don Guadalupe Hidalgo, proposed to her, making her la Doña of his lands and giving her safe refuge without scrutiny. She became a Playadan citizen. I came shortly after as their only child. There was speculation of a lord in power marrying someone from outside their borders, but he did his best to keep the peace.

It was expected of my mother to abandon her Brannish traditions, many of which resembled Spriggan acts. But she would not deny her heritage. Lupe allowed her to practice within the confines of our home, but these rituals were to be done in secret, and she was to attend church with us on Sundays. Vivanka complied. If she hadn't, her trial would have come a lot sooner.

The things my mother did were seen as sinful. However, I was mesmerized by her. She was smart in a well-traveled way. In her journey south, she had visited many places and expanded her mind. She read books in Brannish, the old Playadan language, and the common tongue. She could remedy a headache or a cut with pastes and pills she made from plants in our garden. She taught me to make teas and tonics that would allow one to rest or feel giddy.

It was all considered witchcraft, but I did not see the harm. I was taught as the Brannish lived—free of the minor aches and pains that Playadans suffered through for fear of being associated with the Spriggan by treating them.

"Why did you leave?" I asked this question endlessly. Everything Mama told me of her homeland made Villaviciosa seem dull and hopeless. I wished to someday see the enchanted forests and snow topped mountains of Brannland. I wished to meet the people who would take me in as their own, because the Brannish would not see me as wicked and damned as the Playadans always would for being of northern blood. I only held some fear for the wee folk, but I was sure the lords who protected the Brannish village would ensure none ever touched me.

"Love," she replied, each time I asked. "And now I have you and all of Brannland isn't worth you, *lambið mitt.*"

Her lamb.

Before Vivanka, my father merely raised his livestock and sold them off, whether it was to the butchers or the cheese makers or to artisans who used their skins for clothes. But Vivanka urged him to keep a few of the sheep for her to care for. Throughout the year, she used their wool to craft beautiful cloaks. They were thick and warm, unneeded for the warm Playadan seaside, but they still were nice on the chillier nights or when she would whisk me outside to tell me stories of the stars.

For my twelfth birthday, Mama had crafted me a juniper green cloak with a golden broach twisted in a knot. The edges were embroidered with golden thread and on the breast was a seven-point golden star. That day she braided both of our hair into crowns and adorned them with flowers. We sat by the creek and snacked on bread and honey, dropping crumbs for the birds. Mama sang little tunes in Brannish.

"Speak to me stars
dance with the birds
Lay with me among the trees
Keep far from the sea
stay here with me."

Someone cleared their throat as they passed us on the trail. It was el Don Alvarez, whose wife was a gossip and continued to deny tripping Mama as she walked by her in the pews many months before.

I was haunted at the sight of him. We were forbidden to speak Brannish unless we were on our property, locked away from anyone else who might hear. If anyone were to hear us speaking, they would immediately jump to the worst conclusions: that we were manifesting spells or that we were speaking ill of them. Lupe even seemed uncomfortable whenever we would speak Brannish, because he never cared to learn his wife's culture.

Mama stopped singing but didn't seem afraid. She put her arm around me and hummed the rest of the song.

"Let not the spirit of wild
capture your pure heart
and take my love away."

It wasn't long after that they came for her, binding her and keeping her locked in their hold for three days while the trial was conducted. Lupe and I sat in silence while so many of the town folks spoke against my mother. Many accused her of being Spriggan only for her Brannish heritage, but did not hold tangible evidence that she practiced the dark arts.

"The bitch is from the north. Can't trust them Brannish," el Don Alvarez spat in her direction when he was called as a witness.

"That's enough, Erik," the judge said to him. "No cursing in my court."

The statement was still logged onto the list of Complaints.

The harsh words didn't end there. They called her a whore. A witch. And a dirty Spriggan. I ached for her. I imagined myself running to the stand, declaring them all fools, freeing my mother so we could run away to the north and finally be happy.

I imagined boarding a boat, wrapped in our cloaks, sailing the northern seas back home. I began to feel more and more that I wasn't truly Playadan. I belonged amongst my mother's people. We would be welcomed by the chiefs and drink honey wine. We'd attend fire festivals and make garlands for May Day. But none of this could happen.

As much as it pained me to admit it, I didn't have the power to stop them from convicting her.

"You have to do something, Papa," I pleaded. "You have to tell them it's all lies."

"I can't," was all he said. It was against the law for a spouse to testify in court. It would be seen as biased since he would obviously lie about her practices. He would not tell them that she burned candles and incense and prayed to the old Brannish gods. He would not tell them that she spoke of fae-folk kindly and that she even read bedtime stories to me about how they grant wishes and leave charms. He would not tell them that we celebrated pagan holidays and did rituals involving ash and feathers in the barn.

Even though I knew Lupe could not testify, I hated him for not doing anything when they declared Vivanka to be guilty of performing acts of witchcraft.

Lupe was cleared of all charges. He was Playadan bred, owned land, and was friends with the priest, who testified that Lupe had not known of the practices of his wife. He claimed that she did them all in the barn, which had been entirely cleared out. They found her jars of herbs, her bones, her trinkets. It was all more than enough to prove her guilty. They took them away, so I would have nothing left of her.

Proving my innocence was more of a challenge. If I had been put on the stand, I would have lied to defend my mother. At twelve, while I was scared to die, I was not scared enough to not defend all that I loved. But the priest did his best.

"Mayra Hidalgo is of Playadan blood, was born on Playadan soil and was not manipulated by her mother. And if she was, she is a child and cannot be held responsible for her mother's deal with the devil."

The court was not convinced though.

"She has Brannish blood in her," el Don Alvarez said. "She's tainted with sin and will continue her mother's practice."

"She will not," Vivanka declared from the stand. "My daughter is not in league with the Spriggan as I am."

"So, you admit to the charges?" Alvarez asked. Everyone in the courtroom fell silent, holding their breath for her answer.

Her bright blue eyes found mine, tears running down her pale cheeks. Her eyes were like enchanted ice, resembling the cold lands where she was born. I had always wished my eyes were that bright, but I had my father's dull brown eyes.

"I do," Vivanka told the court, knowing her fate. "And my daughter, Mayra, is innocent."

Performing witchcraft may have meant a life in prison. Being in league with the Spriggan meant death.

The town treated it as a festivity. Everyone came to watch as she was marched to the noose. I had to be there to witness, to make sure the consequences of her crimes were understood. The message couldn't have been more clear. It could be me on that stage if I was not careful.

The people of Villaviciosa gathered in the town center, gazing up at the gallows, screaming obscenities at Mama. I stood near my father, whose grip was tight on my shoulder. Everyone was too distracted with my mother's execution to harm me, but things could always turn once she was hung. Even after she pleaded guilty, many were suspicious of me. I had been seen singing songs riddled with witchcraft with her at the creek. I did live in the house where she performed all of her spells. I was born from her. But my youth and the little bit of Playadan blood I had saved my life that day.

They read Vivanka's charges. Of hanging herbs. Of praying to the moon. Of serving Spriggan devils.

I wanted to scream that there were no Spriggan devils anywhere near there. My mother had never spoken to them. She only kept to the Brannish customs and continued her culture through her practices and teaching me of them. But I couldn't say anything. Because doing so would end my life, despite Lupe's protection.

"Any final words Doña Hidalgo?" the officer asked.

Mama looked at me and smiled. "*Ég elska þig, lambið mitt.*"

"She speaks in tongues! Hang the Spriggan!" someone cried from the mob.

I sobbed into Lupe's cloak, hiding my face as the executioner pulled the lever. Nothing could have hurt more than hearing the door drop and the cheers from the crowd that followed.

Nothing, except hearing Mama's last words.

I love you, my lamb.

Present Day

We paddled back home as the church bells started ringing. Once we reached shore. I walked up the hill to la Casa de Hidalgo to find Carla, my stepmother, standing by the window. Carla was a merchant's daughter whose father seemed all too eager to rid himself of her when he delivered her with her dowry. She was five years older than me, and thus capable of giving my father a son. Beyond that, I did not understand their union, nor did I wish to. She was vile. Whatever grip she had on Lupe was worse than Spriggan magic.

"I saw you with that boy," she said as I walked in and hung up my cloak.

Since Carla had become la Doña Hidalgo, my father hardly spoke to me or even looked in my direction. But Carla was sure to order me about and act as la Doña of the house. In truth, she did very little work and was only a Lady in title. It was I who carried on much of what Mama had once done, like mending and spinning cloaks, tending to the ewes, and keeping up on my guardians' accounts. Carla's only job, it seemed, was to remind the tenants when taxes were due.

"What boy?" It irritated Carla when I acted oblivious. Thus, I continued.

"The Ries boy," she said, putting her hands on her hips. Her swollen belly jutted out underneath her chemise.

"Which Ries boy?" I asked, concealing a smirk. "There is more than one."

"Oh, don't you play the fool with me, *puta*," Carla snapped. "That boy might be el Don Ries's son but if you're seen with him unaccompanied, the town will talk. And you know better than anyone what happens when the town talks."

Carla used my mother's trial as a weapon to keep me quiet. Sometimes it worked, but I grew tired of her brandishing my life before me.

"Let them talk," I shrugged. "I've been friends with Mateo since we were out of the womb. It's never been a problem."

"You're no longer a child, so stop acting like it. You will begin meeting suitors and eventually marry your way out of this house."

My impending marriage. Carla spoke of my marriage prospects more than she spoke of moving me out of my bedchamber into the smaller one when the baby was born.

And did Lupe stop any of it? No. He continued to brood in silence.

Conversations with Carla were often pointless because the woman just enjoyed talking. The only way to make it stop was to aggravate my stepmother to the point of storming off.

"I could marry Mateo," I mused, which, of course, was a ridiculous notion, but I knew it would dig a knife into Carla. "He's a Don's son. It would unite our families and our lands. And all this would become Ries land that I would be the lady of." I mimicked the lofty tone that Carla used whenever she was speaking as la Doña Hidalgo.

"Stop that, your father isn't dead yet."

"Doesn't matter. The Rieses have more money. They could easily buy the land from under Lupe for my dowry."

"How dare you speak about your father this way! As if you have any rights to the land at all." She put her hands protectively at her belly. I knew it was getting close to the point where Carla would storm off.

"Ah, yes, how could I forget? Your son will become heir. That is unless I marry. Then I claim my right as eldest."

"That's what you think," Carla murmured. "You have no claim. Not by birthright anyway."

"What?"

Carla always lied. She would do anything to stay in power. The shrew was speaking for her life. Except she was speaking of something I had wondered many times—if Lupe was not my real father and it was all a mistake.

When I was younger, I had sometimes hoped a Branman would come and collect me as his heir—but my father could not have been Brannish. I looked Playadan, like Lupe. I had desired nothing more than to do away with my mud brown eyes and copper skin but they were a part of me. That was always the realization that kept me from drifting away.

"You don't have a birthright," Carla repeated. Her eyes were shiny but there was an edge of amusement in her voice. "The Spriggan slut was involved elsewhere. Guadalupe could have thrown you out a long time ago. And Mateo isn't even an eldest son, stupid girl."

A smile tugged at her lips and she sauntered down the hall to her bed chamber, her words still echoing in my head.

No. No, she couldn't be right. Carla would do anything to hoard my father's wealth and land. She only said such things to challenge my claim, to make my life hell, to make me doubt my own right to el Rancho de Hidalgo.

Lupe was my father. He may not have been the same nurturing presence as my mother, but fathers rarely were. He would not have given me his name had I not been of his blood. Right?

The worst part was I had suspected such things after Mama had been killed. When she was alive, Lupe was there, but like a ghost. It was Mama who raised me, showed me how to interact with the world, taught me to read and to speak. Fathers rarely took a large role with their children. But Lupe kept an even greater distance with me. It was almost as if it hurt him to see my face at all, especially after Mama was gone.

I always assumed it was because I resembled her. Not in the eyes or skin, with her being so fair, but in small features we shared. Our heart shaped lips, our pointed chins, our high cheekbones. Sometimes, I would wear my hair in braids, the Brannish way. I often wondered if it was more than just appearing as Vivanka for Lupe to look at me with such regret and pain.

But if I wasn't Lupe's daughter, what was all this for? Me staying in Villaviciosa after Vivanka was gone? Enduring the loneliness that gripped me?

I would not accept it. Not without answers. I grabbed my cloak off the hook and made my way back to town to find my father in the tavern with the other Dons. They often got an ale following their weekly meetings.

"Papa," I said as I walked towards the bar without hesitation. If being seen with Mateo was scandalous, being alone in the tavern would be seen as outrageous. My father being present would be the only thing to shield my virtue from being questioned, as usual.

"Mayra? What are you doing here?" His eyes widened. "Is it Carla?"

"Yes, but not about the baby. I need to speak to you."

"Ah," he looked to Dons Ries and Alvarez. El Don Ries gave me a smile and Alvarez avoided my gaze. "Very well."

We went outside and sat on a bench. Lupe looked uncomfortable, but that wasn't unusual.

"I need to ask you something," I said slowly, "about Mama."

He shifted on the bench. "What about her?"

"Why did she come to Playada?"

"To flee Brannland."

That was the simple answer, but nobody had ever wished to tell me what it was beyond that, so I pushed. "But why? She always spoke nostalgically of Brannland."

"Must we speak of your mother now?" Lupe asked.

"Yes," I swallowed. "Carla said something about my birth. About me not having any right to your land. I need to know the truth, Papa."

"That woman speaks too much."

"But does she speak the truth?" I asked.

"You are my daughter," he said firmly.

"Through marriage or through blood?"

"You have my blood."

"And there was never another?" I hated asking if my mother had been unfaithful, but the feeling that there was more I did not know had not left me.

Lupe took in a deep sigh, pinching his eyes. He continued, "Yes. There was another. Vivanka fell in love with a soldier who was fighting for independence. He was from

Playada and fighting in the northern territory of Aldina. Vivanka was working as a healer there and she fell in love with him. They had a courtship. He was wounded and when she mended him, he was sent back here. To Villaviciosa. She followed, because the result of their courtship was you."

My heart quickened. Another man was my father. "Where is he? Who is he?"

"He got sick on the journey home. His wounds became infected when he arrived and the town didn't have a proper healer. But Vivanka did not know he died when she followed him here. By the time she arrived, he was already gone."

"But who was he?" my voice quaked. The truth of it all was settling. Not only was I a bastard, but I was also an orphan. Both of my parents were gone from this world.

"My younger brother," Lupe said, his voice flat. "His name was Francisco. Frankie. I agreed to marry your mother because she was pregnant with my brother's child and had no way of getting home. She spent all her money to be here with him. It was the honorable thing to do, and I grew to love her. Though I don't think she ever felt the same way towards me. I'm not Frankie."

I looked at the man I had always thought was my father. All this time he had been my uncle, claiming me as his own for honor. I knew why he always looked at me with pain and grief, why he couldn't just be there for me when my mother died. When he looked at me, he didn't just see Vivanka, but his dead brother as well.

"Why didn't you ever tell me?" I asked.

"It was bad enough to have everyone questioning you because your mother was Brannish. If they knew you were a bastard, I knew there would be no saving you. And it was the only good thing I could do for Vivanka. She could at least know I kept you safe."

"Because you did nothing to save her," I whispered. Tears poured over. I didn't say anything more to my father. No, my uncle. And he did not call after me when I walked away.

I went to the pier to sit and dip my feet in the water. I wrapped myself tightly in my cloak, but it wasn't enough to stop the shivering.

I felt like I knew myself well. I had grown up within myself all this time, so I knew how my body moved, how my mind thought, and how I felt each day. Knowing my father was another man did not change who I was at my core, and yet I felt at odds with my identity. I had lived life as el Don Hidalgo's daughter, following the rules to what that title meant, when all this time I could have been the daughter of a second son.

Yes, I was a bastard, but there was freedom in that. As a Don's daughter, I had to act and speak a certain way, and my mother's culture was watched even more closely. If she had found my real father alive and discovered he held no title, they could have sailed far away and started a new life. Maybe in Brannland. They would have raised me in my own culture, not having to hide our practices.

Perhaps I would not be pushed to marry. Or I would have seen what real love could be like instead of convinced it doesn't exist. Best of all, there would be no Carla to stir up trouble.

If Carla knew the whole truth, she would use it against me eventually. And Lupe was right—once everyone knew he was not my father, I would have no protection here. He was the only one who gave me the right to be in Villaviciosa, and that had all been a lie. But without him, I had nowhere to go.

I considered my options.

I could join Mateo's crew. But he had expressed that his plan would be to take over his father's business. He would not leave the Playadan coastline. My problems would not be solved. They would only worsen, as my supposed corruption got hold of him. No wife would take him, and I would never forgive myself for stealing his happiness. Plus, all las Doñas would still have their eyes on me.

No, I needed to get out of there.

Aldina could be safe, except I would never be free to reveal my lineage and I couldn't reclaim the Brannish traditions my mother passed to me. I realized that was my wish. I had done away with a lot of what Mama taught me. Sometimes I pawed through her old books and journals, looking at the spells we once said together. All the rest of her stores had been burned, and I could not gather more at the risk of someone taking notice of me.

But if I went north, and if all the things Mama had told me of Brannland were true, I could gather lavender by the armful, I could sing songs of sprites and trolls. Being called a

Spriggan would not be out of spite but of admiration.

But a common Playadan vessel would not take me north. We did not associate with the northerners and all our fleets were commanded by Aldina. I was sure some traveled that far north, but it would have to be a private ship, sailing under its own flags and business to that remote place.

There was only one kind of ship that conducted private trade away from the gaze of the Aldinian king.

I knew exactly what I was to do when I looked out at the horizon. The sun was setting and within its light I saw the silhouette of the familiar ship that ported each fall. A ship with three tall masts and mer-people on its flags.

The *Wind Raider.*

II. Call of the Siren

When I was thirteen, I waited on the docks every day for two weeks, hoping to see the *Wind Raider* come to port. Without fail, the ship came every fall to dock in Villaviciosa and spent three days within the town. It was part of the contractual agreement between the pirates and los Dons. Everyone acted like such things weren't so, fearing the Aldinians would see us as traitors to the Crown. I didn't even know the specifics of it, but I knew Captain Malin of the *Wind Raider* had some agreement with my father and the other Dons, and that was why we turned a blind eye when they came to town. If they upheld their end and didn't shed blood, touch our women, or steal anything on our shores, we were at peace with the pirate ship.

Some speculated the captain had a mistress here. If she were to be found out, I feared her fate would be the same as my mother's.

Even at thirteen, I knew being a lady of an estate was not the life I wanted to live. The silly girls of my town may have delighted at the thought of marrying rich and sitting idly while their husband made money and deals with other Dons. But I could not stomach being compliant to a man like that. I wanted to make something of myself, and I knew there was no way to do that so long as I lived in Villaviciosa.

I sat on the docks, watching the ship glide over the waters. The pirates did not so much as glance at me as they disembarked. However, if Lupe or anyone else knew I was down there, I could have been whipped, even as el Don Hidalgo's daughter. I stayed scarce, waiting for the pirates to exit the ship. I walked along the docks as if I was looking for something that was not a way onto the ship.

Mama had died the previous spring. The whole town avoided me. Mateo was the only one who showed me any form of friendship, but we continued to meet in secret. His father might not have looked at me so cruelly, but Doña Ries would have caused an uproar if she knew. It was just another way that I was the villain in my homeland.

Why I sat on the dock, letting my feet touch the water's surface while I watched each pirate leave the ship, was nothing more than a childish desire. I did not plan to join the pirate crew at thirteen, but I still wished to touch the ship. I wanted to look in its holds, and to touch the mer-lady that sat on the front. In my mind, doing so would give me some form of clarity and assurance that someday I would be free of this place and its rule.

There were no women amongst the crew. I had expected as much. Anything I dreamed of doing for myself was blocked by my sex. But it did not deter me from watching the final pirate leave the ship. This was my opportunity to go aboard.

I crept down the dock and watched my back to assure I wasn't being followed. It was late at night, and I could see the lights of the tavern that housed the pirates. There were no city watchmen on duty, all joining the pirates for a drink up the hill. I thought I had made it, but I did not see the layer of algae on the ramp of the ship. My foot slipped and my head hit the deck before I could make it aboard. The next thing I knew, I was in the water.

I didn't fight as my body sank. It was foolish to think I could make it aboard without trouble. Here was the punishment for my naïveté. I was not frightened to drown. In a way, it fascinated me, to see the limits of my own fragile mortality. However, in the months that followed my mother's execution I still was awoken from nightmares of Mama burning. When I passed by shops, I tried not to look at the windchimes and ornaments that hung from the beams. They all swayed in the same way she had.

I did not wish to die, but I did not particularly enjoy life as it remained. At least death meant going to the other side. Where I would no longer be so frightened to live.

The water was peaceful. It soaked into me and grazed my skin like a hug. I waited for the water to fill my lungs so I could go to the next part. I wondered if Mama was right about where we went after. To the starlit fields where the noble fallen go to feast with the gods. My mother was noble enough to sit at their table. I hoped I was too.

Before I could find out, two arms gripped me and fished me out, laying me down on the deck of the *Wind Raider*. The world was still fuzzy, and I could feel the throbbing at the back of my head. All I saw were shapes and I could feel his hands rubbing balm on the wound on my head. Then he wrapped my head in cloth. Slowly, the world came into focus and I gazed upon the face of my savior. A pirate.

He had propped me up against one of the ship masts, unrestrained, but I was still frightened. Even still, I wouldn't scream. Screaming would bring men from the village down and see that I had thought it was a good idea to board the ship to begin with. If the daughter of the burned Spriggan was caught amongst pirates, no one would think twice about putting an end to me.

The pirate in front of me wore a headscarf and a blue shirt, ripped at the sleeves. His skin was leathered, and his remaining hair was white. The crown of his head was littered in splotches and freckles.

Behind him was a boy a few years younger than me. He had a round face and gray eyes.

His hair was like straw. He peered out behind the pirate, but did not get too close to us. He wore the same raggedy attire as the older man. He had to be someone's son or perhaps a crewmate himself. I was jealous of him, if I am to be honest. No one had issues with hiring young boys to work on a ship, but had I expressed my interest as a girl of thirteen, no one would have taken me seriously.

"Briggs, fetch me some water." The boy scurried off to do as he was told.

"Almost lost ye, little lady," the pirate winked. "Gotta be more careful if ye be wishin' to steal this ship."

"I wasn't—"

"Ah, I'm just playin'," the pirate said, chuckling. Briggs returned with the cup of water and the pirate offered it to me. I sipped it cautiously and was pleased to find the pirates didn't drink sea water. I watched the pirate and Briggs for a moment while I sipped. They were familiar with one another and perhaps if the pirate had hair their resemblance would be more apparent. Briggs was certainly his son, free to sail alongside his father.

The pirate regarded the boy with friendliness. He thanked him for completing the task, clapping him on the back and the boy seemed less shy now that I had been tended to.

Once my cup was empty, the pirate helped me to my feet. "Best be gettin' back home."

But even though I'd found my footing, I didn't move.

"Somethin' the matter?" he asked. "Ye hit yer head, but ye should be well in a couple o' days. Though, I would have someone wake you every two hours or so tonight. Don't want ye to catch the Grim Sleep."

"I—" I didn't know what to say. I looked at him and the boy. A large part of me wanted to stay, but I knew that was not possible. I was not lucky enough to be born to a pirate to sail the world alongside him. What else was there to say to a man who was part of the crew that was told to be undead, ruthless, murderous, and blood thirty? "I wanted to touch the siren on the front of the ship."

The man burst into hoots of laughter. His boy mimicked him, calling me a silly girl under his breath.

My cheeks flushed and I wanted very much to crawl back into the water. This whole adventure was a mistake, led by my foolishness.

But the pirate still led me to the front, lifting me up so I could touch the greened bronze of the siren's tail. The siren held an oyster in her hands, and her hair covered her breasts. Below her, in blocked writing said: "Loyal 'til Death."

The pirate set me back down on the deck.

"Thank you, Mr...."

"Starky," he said, shaking my hand.

"Where is this ship going?" I asked, finding more of my voice the longer I was with the pirate.

"All abouts," he replied. "Heading northward now. Into the depths of winter."

"Brannland?" I asked, unable to conceal my eagerness.

"Yeah, we stop there often. See Chief Bjorn. Always got some meat and spirits for us."

I tucked that name away. Perhaps I would meet him one day. And the *Raider* could be my ticket. Away from the traditions of the south and my impending damnation.

"Now, run on home," he urged me.

As friendly as he was and obviously of no threat to me, if he were to be seen with me, a girl and also a Don's daughter, his punishment would be dire.

When I waved goodbye, Mr. Starky and the boy waved back.

While I walked home, I smiled to myself. Despite nearly drowning. Despite my bandaged head. And despite my run in with a pirate.

There were many things I refused to believe because of the different upbringing I had had compared to the other children of Villaviciosa. The Spriggan, if there really were witches and faeries that walked in this world, were not evil. They were as Mama spoke of them in her stories: tricky creatures who would aid if given an offering.

Because of that one belief, I questioned all the things that Villviciosa believed to be true, including that pirates were monstrous people who could not be trusted. It was, after all, a pirate who had saved me from death. Already, I had known that I wished to be amongst them, as a way to get away from a town I didn't belong in. Knowing that at least one of them would show me kindness solidified that dream.

Of course, each year, they came and they went, and I watched them do so, never having the courage to make that final descent. Something always stopped me from ever trying to board again. Much of it was womanhood. The captain of the ship would laugh if some Don's daughter asked for passage as a crewmate. It didn't take long for me to reason that the only way aboard was to conceal my gender and board under an alias.

I saw glimpses of Starky over the years, though I did not know if he remembered me. We had crossed paths briefly when I was sixteen, walking the same path of the open-air market. I hoped he would have said something, acknowledging our meeting three years before, but he did not. I was a woman of Villaviciosa, and he was just following the terms of the treaty by acting as if we had never met.

Some of it was a small pull to be home even if I was not welcome in the village. There was Lupe and he needed me to help run his estate. But now he had Carla.

In my twentieth year, with the knowledge that I was never meant to be in Villaviciosa at all, there was nothing left to hold me back from leaving.

There was only one matter to resolve.

It was evening and a woman was not to wander town without an escort, but I still went to la Casa de Ries. I had never gone to their estate on my own. I had been to formal dinners and gatherings there, alongside my father, playing my careful part as the heiress Hidalgo. Mateo and I spoke politely to each other, but absent of all familiarity.

"Lovely weather today, madame," he said.

"Indeed," I replied, fanning myself against the heat. "I'm sure the weather will bring a bounty of fish to your family."

"Certainly," the corner of his mouth perked. He knew I resented small talk and was dying on the inside. We would laugh about our act the next day when we met at the beach.

"I need to speak with Mateo, please," I told their doorman, Bautista. He gave me an inquisitive look. But he returned with Mateo moments later.

"Mayra?" he asked. He quickly shut the door and we walked to a bench in the garden. "What's wrong?"

"Lupe is not my father." The words tumbled out. Better to just say it than to walk around the subject.

"What?"

I recounted the series of events between our morning boat ride up to the moment I came to his door. I told him of Carla's outburst and of Lupe's confirmation. "So... I think I'm leaving."

"To where?"

"The *Wind Raider* is docking as we speak. I'll offer to work for them in exchange for passage. It will get me away from here. I could sail to Brannland and try and find my mother's family, if she has any left. But I'm not safe here anymore." My hands were shaking, and my voice was going dry. I needed to get a grip of myself if I hoped for my plan to work.

His arms slipped around me, bringing my head to his chest.

"I just needed to tell you. You're the only one here who has never made me feel like an outcast. I think—" I sighed. What was it I wished to tell him? A part of me wanted him to go with me. To be as free as I would be from the village and being the children of lords. But Mateo needed to have his own life and adventures, undetermined by me and my wishes for his comfort. "I think you should go with your father."

Mateo furrowed his brow. "Why?"

"I think we both need an opportunity to get away from here. This town is poison. And I know you have a better chance of making a life here than I do, but I can't help but think both of us would be better off if we left. And I think going with your father to the southern lands is your ticket out."

"I've thought about it a lot," he admitted. "Tomas has agreed to stay here, because he wishes to maintain Pa's estate so he can become the next el Don Ries. It's his birthright and I knew I never had a chance or even a desire to become a lord. But I need to ask you something."

Mateo hesitated. But he removed his arm from around me and placed a hand on my knee. The touch caught me off guard. As familiar as he and I were, we were not affectionate.

"Would you consider marrying me?" he asked me.

"What?" I pulled away from him, furrowing my brow at the boy I'd known since before I could speak.

Mateo was handsome. He had a head full of brown curls and soft tan cheeks. He stood six inches taller than me, and I was not the shortest girl in the village. Other girls watched him as he walked, hiding their flushed cheeks. I would always laugh at their girlish behavior. I had never gawked at a man like that. I had never seen Mateo as anything other than my friend. Our time spent in the fishing boat, while I was dressed in boy clothes, always felt familiar. It couldn't possibly be anything more. But his question made me wonder if I had been naïve all this time.

"I would make a good husband," Mateo said, taking my hand and giving it a squeeze. "We could live on my father's lands, soon to be Tomas's. I know I am only a second son and that you were once a Don's daughter, but we could still have a good life. I would not harbor you like property like another man would. And as my wife, you would be safe from the scrutiny of the town."

I didn't know what to say. Mateo was right in what he said. If I had to pick a husband,

Mateo was my best option. He could offer safety. He could be a friend as well as a lover.

But it wasn't enough. I would still be his wife, locked in the town that burned my mother's body after they hung her. Lupe was still lord of these lands with Carla as his lady. I used marrying Mateo as a threat to Carla's claim on Rancho de Hidalgo, but if I went through with it, nothing would stop Carla from telling the whole town that I was a bastard. While Mateo's proposal would save my life, I would still be under scrutiny for the rest of my life.

Not only that, but it would darken Mateo's name as well, despite also coming from a well-regarded family. I could not bear to bring Mateo down with me. And the bottom line was, I could never love him. I had never loved anyone. Marriage would not change that.

"I can't," I whispered. "I am not fit to be a wife. I know that to be true. I could be your friend and companion, but everything else that you deserve in a wife, I can't offer you."

"I expect nothing from you, Mayra," Mateo said, returning his hand to my knee. "Just to live beside me and brighten each day with your smile."

"What if I never smile again?" I asked. I imagined my mother with Lupe. How hollow her eyes were when they were beside each other. She may have smiled with her mouth, but anyone could see she was never happy. I didn't want a life like that. "I live in a town that views me as a witch, and even as your wife, I wouldn't outlive that."

"Then we leave together," Mateo offered. "Perhaps Pa would bring you along if I declare you my betrothed."

Mateo was trying his hardest to make me happy. He would offer anything in his power to do that. It broke me to refuse. "I don't want to go south. I want to go north, learn of my heritage, find out who I really am. And you are my closest friend, and I love you for that, but I would always resent not being able to go out on my own."

Silence formed between us. I was too scared to say anything more. I knew I was losing him, but in a way, it was simpler. If he resented me for declining his proposal, it might make leaving easier. It was better than leaving with him thinking I would come back for him some day.

"I understand," he finally said. "I don't wish to hold you back and I know you will find your way. You are so strong and so smart. I want to help you any way I can."

I hugged him, relieved by his understanding, and then told him of my plan.

He snuck me to his room, and I dressed in the boy clothes I always borrowed when we went out on the dinghy. I laced up Mateo's old boots, then I put on a large white shirt and an old coat. To hide my curves, I wrapped cloth tight around my chest and several times around my waist. Under the shirt and coat, you couldn't tell how padded I was.

Looking in the mirror that leaned in the corner, I tucked my long black hair up in Mateo's tricorn hat. I still didn't look like a man. My lips were too full, my jaw line too soft. I looked around and saw the dusty shelf, then the dirt on the ground, and used both to soil my cheeks and eyes. It would have to do.

I presented myself to Mateo, who had kept his back turned all while I dressed.

"You look like a fair young lad, looking for adventure," Mateo said, obviously searching for something nice to say.

"But do I look like a man?" I asked, discouraged.

"Enough. Could pass for fifteen."

I sighed. It would have to be enough. I remembered the boy, no older than twelve, who stood near Mr. Starky. Surely a boy of fifteen was more than capable. And I knew how to fish, and a little about rigging up sails, at least on Mateo's fishing boat. I would ask for a position as something I could learn quickly, like a cook's hand, who could join even younger than fifteen, and didn't need any knowledge of sailing. If I could keep up the act for a few months, I could make it to Brannland and go back to being Mayra. But not Hidalgo. I would take my mother's name, Ogden, and find our family there.

Mateo pulled me close to him, wrapping me tight in his arms. "I hope to see you again. I'll be with my father in the south for a while, but I'll be back here eventually."

"I may never come back," I admitted. "I'm looking for passage to Brannland. Not to stay aboard the *Wind Raider* in time to return next year."

Mateo nodded. "I know. And that would be safer. But you know where to find me."

We gazed at each other for a while, his arms still around me. It felt oddly comfortable, despite never having been in them before. Our faces were only inches apart. I had never kissed anyone, nor had I thought of ever kissing Mateo, but here and now, it seemed like it could be right. To have my first kiss with the boy that helped me escape. I leaned in to close the space, but Mateo released me before our lips could touch.

"I can't," he said.

I nodded. I knew it was not a good idea to kiss him after refusing his proposal. But I had hope that it might stir something. Help determine if I could want Mateo the way the other village girls did. But I would never know.

Mateo must have seen my regret. "It's not that I don't want to. It would just make it more painful to watch you leave."

"I will miss you." And I certainly meant it.

"I'll see you at sea," he winked.

Perhaps we would cross paths again while he aided his father and I was amongst the Raiders. That is, if I ever actually got to sea. There were still many trials to endure before I could hope to call myself a part of the *Wind Raider*'s crew.

Going straight to the captain did not seem to be the logical course of action. There were countless daunting stories told about Captain Malin. He was a warning mothers spoke of to keep their little ones from straying too far.

"Stay near the house or the vengeful Captain Malin will snatch ye."

Of course, there was still the truce that was maintained between the captain and the three lords. And a child had never gone missing while the pirates were at our port. But before the *Wind Raider* was tied to our docks, the church bells rang six times, and the children all went straight to their houses, where they would remain until the pirates had gone.

In the evenings, after work had been completed, people gathered near the fountain. Some had guitars or violins, filling the courtyard with music. Some families earned their livelihood selling pastries and fish. But on that night, no one was out playing music, but some of the more stubborn food cart vendors remained. They hoped to get some extra coins from the pirates, but even they were not seen on the streets. Music flowed from the tavern I had found Lupe at earlier that day, though it was more lively than when the dons were within its bounds.

I adjusted my hat and tucked my cloak within the small bag of things I packed for myself. It had an extra shirt, a canteen, a vial of ash and now the cloak. Wearing it was too risky while I still remained in Villaviciosa. Many wore wool cloaks, but mine was made special. I would be easily spotted in the vibrant green cloak lined with gold. I had to remain inconspicuous until I was aboard. My chances were already slim without the pirates knowing I was Don Hidalgo's daughter. Or bastard. Or whatever I was to him now.

My breath caught as I got closer to the tavern door. I could hear the whoops and laughs from within, both from the pirates and the waitresses. My father was in this tavern every week. There wasn't a single person who lived here who did not know me as Mayra Hidalgo. I prayed that my disguise would hold up well enough. I pulled on the pewter door handle.

There were pirates scattered along the tavern. Many joked with the bartender, Rafe, while they were perched up on the stools along the bar counter. Rafe slid them ale and seemed in good spirits. It was safe to say he had the most to gain from their presence. They threw coins for him and his pretty waitresses to keep their tankards full. The more they drank, the better their spirits.

I looked for the captain amongst the men. Every year, I saw him strut from his ship with his long white hair and young face. The only flaw upon him was a scar that ran from the bottom of his eye across his mouth to the corner of his bottom lip. No one knew how he had received the deformity. Likely in battle. Many of his crew had evidence of run-ins with swords, from striking scars to lost limbs. I wondered if I would be aboard long enough to witness a battle, both with curiosity and with apprehension.

But I couldn't get ahead of myself. I still had to gain passage.

"Something I can get for you, m'lady?" one of the waitresses asked.

My stomach churned. "Keep your voice down," I snapped. I didn't know the waitress by name, but I knew every face in Villaviciosa. The barmaid was wearing a wench's dress, cut low to her chest, and bunched at the sleeves. She wore red and orange skirts that flared out.

Her lips were covered in red, and I could see the cheeks of some of the pirates who had met these lips. Her hair was pinned up without a veil, showing her smooth neck. She smelled of whisky and rose buds.

"Sorry, Señorita Hidalgo, I didn't—"

I grabbed the girl, and took her out the door and around the corner, pinning her to the wall.

"What the hell are you doing?" she whimpered.

"You mustn't call me Hidalgo," I seethed. "I'm sorry for being so rough, it's just..." I was not known to be violent, though I was actually quite pleased with myself for being able to hold up the girl and slip from the tavern unnoticed. But if the girl started talking to the tavern owner or the other waitresses about her encounter with me, my plans would be foiled.

"I'm sorry, Señorita, I didn't know, but please don't tell your father—"

My heart lightened. I did have some power left in my belt. "I promise this misstep will not reach my father. However, I need you to act as if you've never seen me tonight. If anyone comes asking, my father included, you will tell them nothing. Is that understood?" I met her eyes with blazing intensity.

Words weren't enough, so I also pressed a small satchel of coins into her hand. The waitress nodded.

"It's just..." Her eyes fluttered down to the ground.

"What?" I asked.

"You still look like el Don Hidalgo's daughter."

My heart sank. "What should I do?"

The girl's eyes brightened. "Take my arm."

I complied. Together, we walked back into the tavern, but the waitress had flung her arms around me, pressing her chest against mine and giggling all the while. Her lips found my cheeks and she marked me with her red lipstick. Some of the men turned their heads. The waitress was nibbling on my ear, making a good show of it. I was utterly embarrassed and unsure how this would help me, but the girl guided me to the bar.

"Rafe, get the handsome lad an ale would you," she fluttered her eyelashes.

He cocked his head when he saw me and I held my breath, but he nodded slowly, passing me the drink.

"If you need anything else, you ask me, okay?" she whispered in my ear. And then she kissed me, long and lingering on my lips, coating me in her lipstick. She winked at me before going about to tend to the other men.

She gave the crew the illusion that I could attract a girl like her, even with my soft features. And she had covered me with her lust. She had done exactly what she needed to do to make the men see me as an equal. I was still stunned at the gestures. Her lips on mine. The way they felt. Soft. Warm.

"Ye have her charmed, that one," a nearby pirate said tipping his drink in my direction.

I was brought from my daze.

The man who addressed me could have been in his thirties or in his fifties. It was hard to say. His face was thick and leathery and nearly the color of my own people, despite his obnoxious lowland-Aldinian accent. His brown hair and beard had been left wild. A piece of rust colored cloth was tied around his head, collecting sweat from his forehead. His loose grey pants ballooned out from him, failing to cover the more unsightly parts of him.

"Ah, yes," I spun up a story. "I come to Villaviciosa sometimes, and she warms my bed," shrugging as if it meant nothing.

"Oh, to be young," a second pirate groaned. "I remember when I could get a lass like that." He looked very much like the first, except his hair had been blonde at one point before the sea water had darkened it. And unlike most of the pirates, he had his cut above his shoulders, although it still hung in ringlets full of grime and grease. His teeth were all different shapes, some chipped and blackened in his mouth. It was hard to picture him as any form of handsome, even in his youth.

"I come here now," I told them, raising some confidence in my voice, "to consult with the captain about becoming a Raider."

"Oh, do ye now?" the first one snorted. "Good luck with that."

"Is there a way to win his favor?" I asked.

"Yeah. Mind yer tongue and shuddup," he hooted. "You speak like you grew up amongst proper folk and that won't impress no one."

I looked down to my glass of ale. Again, I felt like a fool, thinking it would be as simple as walking up to the crew and gaining approval. I needed to be craftier than that.

"What's yer name?" the second asked.

"Finn," I outstretched my hand. "Finn Santana." I made sure to lower my voice a bit, thinking of how Mateo and his father spoke. They were sailors, and had some of the growls and words of these men.

He took it with a firm shake. "Name's Everett and over there is Hagley."

Hagley grunted.

"We're boatswain to the *Raider*," Everett said. "Where ye come from, boy?"

I hadn't put a lot of thought into a false backstory, and I only had one shot at this. If I said the wrong things, then I would never make it aboard. But I took a chance at the truth.

"My mother came from Brannland," I told them. "I've never been. Been on my own since she died."

"So yer a bit Brannish?"

I nodded. I hoped these pirates were not at odds with the north. But I remembered Starky years ago telling me that the crew got along well with Chief Bjorn.

Everett looked me over. I stood rigid while I waited for him to speak.

He stood from his stool. "Follow me. I want to introduce ye to someone."

III. The Translator

Everett took me across the tavern, through the crowd of pirates, to a man who was seated alone in the corner, running his finger across the rim of his goblet. He had a chilled presence. Many of the pirates had gotten jolly with their drinks, but he remained stoic. I knew he wasn't the captain, because he did not have Captain Malin's distinctive white curls or the scar on his face, but he still sat with the presence of a captain. He had a brow like marble and a permanent frown on his lips. His gray hair was kept a lot neater than many of the others that ran down their backs. It even looked like it had been combed in the past few days. He wore a ragged navy coat with several tears and missing buttons. He looked up, seemingly bored as we walked towards him.

"Sir," Everett cleared his throat. "I just met this Finn Santana. He told me he speaks Brannish."

He looked me over, and a chill went through me. He did not change his expression, but it was clear now that my Brannish heritage would either be my ticket or my dismissal.

"Does he now?" he said in a low tone. "That could prove useful."

"Exactly what I was thinkin'," Everett said, puffing out his chest.

"Thank you, Jagged, that'll be all."

Everett's mouth turned, but he returned to his seat beside Hagley, leaving me alone with the man.

"You're Finn Santana?" the man asked.

He gestured to the seat across from his own. I sat and nodded.

"Pleasure to meet you, Finn. I'm Jenkins. Captain Malin's first mate."

The first mate. He could be the key to getting aboard which meant everything I told him had to be calculated to win his favor.

"Was Santana your father's name?" he asked.

"No, sir. I'm a bastard. I never knew his name. Santana was just given to me."

"By who?"

I shrugged. "The streets. Been on the road a while."

"Well, when did you learn Brannish? You speak with a Playadan accent." He seemed to be growing impatient with me.

"My mother was Brannish," I replied. I attempted to mimic Mateo's smooth, deep voice, which was an impossible task with my feminine tone. I did not naturally speak with a squeaky tone, but I also did not have the sound of chains through gravel that a man would have. Mateo did say I could pass as fifteen. "She died a few years back, but she taught me when I was young. Everyone's suspicious of the Brannish down here, so I don't often speak it."

"People are suspicious of Brannish everywhere," he replied. "They're cold folk, brooding amongst the ice. Keep to themselves and their clans and stay out of all the squabbles down south."

Mama had once said the same thing. The war of independence happened below them but they did not side with Playada or Aldina. Aldina was meant to conquer all but the Brannish still kept their stronghold. Mama was a healer to both sides and lent her abilities as a neutral observer.

"So you can read?" Jenkins asked.

"Brannish as well as old Playadan and the Common Tongue."

"Three languages, huh," Jenkins said in a way that must have meant he was impressed, though it was still hard to read him. "Malin will want to speak with you."

"Is he looking for a translator?" I asked. I feigned indifference, but was glowing within.

"Ay and a personal errand runner. Think of yourself as an elevated cabin boy. Bringing his breakfast, managing his quarters, and reading whatever scribbles he gives you," Jenkins explained. "But this all depends if Malin thinks you're fit for the job."

It wasn't what I had expected as far as work. In fact, it was better, but I would have taken becoming a swabbie if it meant getting away from Villaviciosa.

"Where's the captain now?"

Jenkins rolled his eyes and hung the back of his head over the edge of his chair. "Ah, boy don't trouble me with your questions. Go enjoy yourself. We haven't been on land in two months. The captain's not going to be happy if you go barge on him now. Just be on Water Street tomorrow at noon."

I left the first mate to brood on his own. He was going to be a hard man to make an ally, but he had already given me enough to make it on the ship. The captain needed a translator and I knew where to find him in the morning. It was more than enough to get out of here.

For the rest of the night, and for the first time in what seemed like forever, I indulged.

Technically speaking, and the reveal of my birth aside, I was a lady. Which meant I was expected to act the part to honor my father's house. Whenever someone important was in town for dinner, I was to sit proper and not speak unless spoken to. But such formalities were not as enforced when it had just been Mama and Lupe and the few servants that tended to the property. I always insisted on the staff calling me Mayra.

When Carla moved in her exact words were, "Thank the heavens I'm here now to save you from your improper tongue."

Suddenly, I was to address my own father as Don, to wear skirts for dinner, and to not be seen giggling with the maid.

And Carla was sure to correct me should I get anything wrong.

"You're chewing with your mouth open."

"Stop mumbling."

"A lady doesn't sit on the floor."

"El Don did not address you."

And of course the never ending battle of being seen unchaperoned with Mateo.

But on that night, despite my efforts to be a mouse in the corner unnoticed, eventually the ale got to my head and I began to speak and to laugh without thought of how my actions could affect my family's name. My family's name was Santana. It was a name I had heard from a visitor once, a nomad who has traveling through Playada. Mateo had told me it wasn't his true last name. He was too dark to be a true Playadan, so he took the name to be ambiguous. It seemed to suit my purposes well.

The pirates began passing me mugs of ale. I had only ever had a single cup at a time for dinner, but that night I consumed five or six glasses. And from there everything was hazy. But I was certain it was the most free I had ever felt on Playadan soil.

My head was pounding and my clothes were damp when I awoke on the ground the next morning. I couldn't even sit up before I was coughing up vomit into the grass. On my uncle's grass. Somehow, I had wandered away from the tavern to the south edge of Rancho de Hidalgo, making myself a little bed out of my cloak and pack.

I tried to recall the night before. It was undeniable that I had gotten drunk. The pirates kept handing me drinks and I thought it rude to deny them. After a while, I forgot that I needed to keep my guard up around them. The waitress, who I recalled being named Banía, came and sat on my lap, wrapping her arms around me. The others in the crew gawked. I would be forever grateful for her help.

There were more flashes of dancing and laughter. I met a few members of the crew, but was too far in the drink to remember names or faces. They all blurred together and were now lost in the archives of my somewhat more sober mind.

How I came to be on Hidalgo land was a little fuzzier. But one thing was certain — I had not been home the night before on a day pirates were in town and that would cause trouble.

With all my might I forced myself to my feet, swaying slightly, then made my way to the house, letting my hair down from the hat and brushing the dirt from my pants. I needed to be seen at home so no questions would be raised until I was safely at sea. If I left now, someone could spin the story that I was kidnapped.

I ran into Lara, the cook, as soon as I went through the back entrance of the house.

"Where's my father?" I asked.

"Left early, Señorita," Lara replied, giving me a look over. I could only imagine how unruly I looked beyond the pants I wore. My skin felt grimy. My hair was wild. I'm sure I didn't smell like gardenias either. "Would you like me to run you a bath, dear?"

"No need," I said quickly. "Is Carla here?"

"No, la Doña went out. Not sure where."

For once, this was disappointing news. I needed Carla to see me home so she would not cause trouble before I had even left the dock.

"Will you tell my parents I was here?" I asked. "I wouldn't want them to worry."

"Have you gone somewhere?" the cook speculated, growing more suspicious of my condition.

"No, I had a headache so I slept long and then went for a walk to try and get some sunlight," I said, grabbing the papaya from the board Lara was cutting on. "Just tell them you saw me and that I'm okay."

The cook nodded slowly, but said nothing more. "You be careful now. Pirates are in town," she called over her shoulder.

I started back towards the square, to Water Street which was the road that ran behind the Council Hall. I wasn't sure why the first mate would have suggested a place so public for me to meet the captain. It was ten minutes before noon so I kept a slow jog until I was off Rancho de Hidalgo once more.

It was strange that Carla was not at home. She was not one to run personal errands or any sort of errands related to the house. And in her late pregnancy the sitting room was her main perch.

The town still remained quiet. The same stubborn carts were selling food which some of the crewmates now ate along the streets to cure their hangovers. I kept my head down as I went for Water Street. My hat cast a shadow over my eyes and I hoped, hungover, groggy, dirt covered, and in my damp clothes I was starting to look more and more like Finn Santana, the soon to be pirate.

I avoided the front of the Council Hall and went immediately for the back, darting into a gap in the wall when I saw two men talking in the alley, one with striking white curls and the other even more familiar: Captain Malin and Don Guadalupe Hidalgo.

My heart leapt out of my chest at the sight of Lupe with the pirate captain. I knew that the pirates did business with the lords of Villaviciosa, but by the look of them, this didn't seem to be a formal political discussion.

"Afternoon, Lupe," the captain greeted, tipping his hat as if he was a gentleman. His silver curls shined with the high sun.

"Malin," Lupe replied. He fished a large black bag from his coat. It jingled as it left his hands and went into Malin's. "Here is this year's taxes."

Malin pawed at the coins with a grin on his face, looking to do so more for enjoyment than to actually count it.

"Do your tenants know they pay a pirate tax?" Malin jested.

"No, it's filed under 'Border Protection Tax.'"

Malin chuckled. "Ah, you political leaders are the biggest pirates of them all."

Lupe rolled his eyes. "Now that business is dealt with, I wanted to know if you were still agreeable to the matter we spoke of last year."

Malin cocked his head, but then his eyes cleared, remembering. "About your daughter?"

I was still in my hiding spot, but I craned my ear further.

"Niece, but yes," Lupe said in a strained voice. "My wife discovered her parentage and told the girl. I was going to wait a few more years to send her away, but matters are pressing. If my wife were to tell the town, they would have more reason to take her away. The matter has only been maintained this long because everyone believed she was my daughter. I can't allow that to happen. No. She needs to be taken this very day."

"I understand," Malin replied, putting his humor aside. "But my ship was not built to accommodate a lady of status."

"I'll pay you extra for the burden. She is not one to complain either. I promise she won't cause you trouble."

"And where should I be taking the lass?"

Lupe hesitated. "I have... I have names of people from my first wife's family in Brannland. A town called Skarn. I don't know if any are still alive. But if they hear she's Vivanka's daughter, maybe they would take her in."

"They might. The Brannish are more hospitable than your people give them credit for."

"Vivanka was banished," Lupe said. "For leaving her post and getting pregnant with my brother's child."

Malin just shrugged. "They also don't hold generational grudges as your people do."

Lupe sighed. He didn't argue with the captain and his attitude towards the Playadans. Had the captain been addressing Don Alvarez, I'm sure the man would have attempted to take Malin up by his collar for his negativity. But my uncle had enough experience, through both my mother and me, that the people he led were not filled with kindness and understanding.

"I promise she will be taken care of," Malin said.

"Just please—" Lupe hesitated, looking rather uncomfortable about the matter he meant to bring up. "Please make sure her virtue is preserved. I don't think she's ever..."

Malin put a hand to his breast. "I will personally saw off the cock of any man who violates her maidenhood."

It wasn't exactly comforting, but Lupe gave him a curt nod.

More coins were exchanged and they shook hands at the bargain for my transport.

I remained in my hiding spot as the men parted. I had meant to approach Malin after, but now, all my courage had been deflated. I had been sold to the pirate. I wouldn't be able to work or make my own way aboard. No. I was still bound to the life of a lady. Lupe had bought my way.

I wanted to earn this for myself. To show I was capable in paving my own way, but Lupe had stolen that from me. All my life I had been under his protection without really knowing who I was. This was my chance at creating my own identity. Maybe it was childish but I really did think I had the potential to be the mysterious lady who became a pirate and whose face would be in children's books someday.

That was the lofty dream. The dream that was nearly unattainable, but that I allowed myself to have for the sake of moving forward. At the very least, I wished to gain my own passage to Brannland, serve on the crew in the meantime, and prepare myself for whatever I found up north. And from Malin and Lupe's exchange, I now was faced with the worry that even Mama's family might not take me in. I had never known she had been banished. Perhaps that was why she never left Playada.

Malin was gone from the alley when I peered behind the wall. I had to make a choice. Was I to allow the world to tell me who I was and who I was to be? Or would I finally take the reins and pave my own way?

I jogged down the alleyway towards the square, up to the tavern. Malin was gathering his men who had fallen asleep in various places after the events of the night before. I was glad that I wasn't the only one.

"Come along, Stratford," Malin barked through the tavern door. "The lasses will forget your name within a week."

"No they shan't!" The pirate belched as he teetered down the tavern steps. I steered clear of him as he went to vomit in the bushes nearby.

The meek part of me thought I could perhaps just follow the pirates aboard, and originally that had been my idea. But now Malin meant to collect Mayra Hidalgo and I wished to leave that lady behind.

"Captain Malin!" I called after him, hastening my steps to catch him as he started towards the docks.

"What do you want, boy?" he asked.

"Uh—" I was pleased he accepted my disguise, but I also reminded myself I was covered in mud and dirt and beer and tavern-maid kisses. "I was hoping to join your crew, sir."

He looked at me once over. "You're a bit small, lad. Couldn't even lift our cannon balls."

"Jenkins said you needed a translator."

"Jenkins can't read. Can't tell the difference in someone who can too."

"If you would just test me, Captain—"

"Look boy, I get a dozen or so of you a year who think you're something special in your nothin' town but you all have never seen the truth of what happens at sea. You're not prepared to take on what's out there."

I tried not to let my pride get the better of me. "My uncle paid you to take me in," I finally said.

He glanced at me again, giving me another sweeping glance. "You're the little lady Hidalgo?"

"Yes, but I do not mean to sit and enjoy the ride while I'm on your ship," I informed him. "I wish to be a part of your crew during the voyage. I used to man a fishing boat, almost became first mate," I added with pride. "I know how to do basic nautical tasks. And I spoke with Jenkins. He said you needed a Brannish translator."

"You know Brannish?"

"My uncle told you I was Brannish, yeah?"

He looked me over again. "Your Playadan blood is strong, lass." He shrugged. "I figured you were never taught. Your people fear the

Brannish like the wee-folk. Speak some for me."

The abruptness of the command caught me off guard. I was already nervous to be around the notorious Captain Malin. Not to mention I had not spoken Brannish to anyone but the curses I said under my breath every now and again. But now wasn't the time to show fear. Not when this simple act of proof could be my ticket aboard the *Wind Raider*.

I cleared my throat. "Ég er barn Brannland og mun ganga til liðs við áhöfnina þína svo ég geti sameinast fjölskyldu minni á ný."

I am the child of Brannland and I will join your crew so I can be reunited with my family.

Malin seemed to be mulling over in his mind his next move.

"Will you take me?" I asked. "To work?"

He rubbed his chin. "You strike a reasonable bargain. I am in need of a translator. But my men won't take nicely to allowing a lady to work. There are superstitions about such things, you know?"

"Allow me to remain as I am," I said, gesturing to my garb. "I had already planned on posing as a boy. I was taught not to trust pirates."

"Ay, of course you were," the captain chuckled. "You must be Brannish. Playadans have no sense of humor. Or adventure for that matter. Well then, Miss Hidalgo, who are you to me now?"

"Finn Santana," I replied. "I introduced myself to some of your crew last night."

"Alright Finn. Having a woman, especially a lord's supposed daughter, aboard my ship would be messy and I don't want my men losing their heads. So, you will remain Finn Santana. I made a vow to your uncle to keep you safe, but if you wish to be a part of the crew, I will also be working you just as hard as any of my men. I will not be lenient because you're a lady."

I nodded, more than satisfied with this.

"My crew abides by a code of honor. If you're to be a part of my crew you need to abide by the ship's code. Do you know it?"

I nodded. "Loyal 'til death."

He nodded curtly. "That means, I—or any of my officers—give an order, and you will follow it. You will also be subject to punishment should you fall out of line. I will keep you safe, but I will not be having you disrupting the order of my ship. Understood?"

I nodded again.

Captain Malin shook my hand. "Mr. Santana, welcome aboard the *Wind Raider*."

We went together through the streets. With Malin beside me, I was only his shadow, no one looking in my direction long enough to identify me. The villagers still remained behind their doors, but I could see them leaning out to get a glimpse of the captain. Even some of their children stared wide eyed as we passed. But el Don Hidalgo's daughter was forgotten whilst she was in the presence of the legend.

The three masted ship was in the dock, some of the crewmates beginning to prepare to take sail. As we stepped onto the ship, I recalled the last time I had been there.

"Captain?"

"Hm?"

"Is there a Mr. Starky on this ship?"

"You knew Starky?" Malin asked. He led me up the steps to the upper deck, where his cabin was.

"Yes, we ran into each other one of the times you visited Villaviciosa. He was a nice fellow." I kept the story brief, being that it was a law for pirates not to touch the ladies and children in our town. Even if he was showing me kindness, I didn't want to risk getting him into trouble, even eight years later.

"That he was. But Starky contracted an illness when we were west. He unfortunately didn't recover."

My heart sank. "Oh. I'm so sorry."

Malin did not say anything more. Despite having only met him once, I had been hoping he'd be here. He was what had convinced me that the ship had good men and I'd be better off with them.

Malin led me up the barque, which I took care to watch my step, up onto the main deck of the *Wind Raider*. Some of the men had trickled from town, but the ship was largely still vacant. Malin motioned me to follow him up to his cabin. Some of the men peered curiously at me. Most didn't look up at all as we climbed the wooden steps.

"I have an assignment for you," he explained, "that will reveal your usefulness, or lack thereof."

Behind a large red door was Malin's cabin, which was much grander than I had anticipated. The whole ship was grand. It had a lower and upper deck, masts that reached up high, flying the flags of mer-people. I assumed there were lower cabins and a brig. Captain Malin's quarters held a writing desk, littered with various papers, maps, and quills, as well as a four-post bed, fit for a very fat king. It may have been excessive for someone with such a lean, yet sturdy frame like Malin. Even living in Casa de Hidalgo which was modest for a Don, but still a far stretch from the common dwellings, I had never seen anything so comfortable.

Malin offered me a seat across from him at the desk. He pawed through the parchment and took out a crumpled piece with parts of a map on it. There was Brannish script in the corners of the page, telling of the mapped land's whereabouts.

"Tell me what that says."

I read it with ease, aside from some squinting at the scribbles in the handwritten script. "In the recorded year of 682, Captain Kjartan Larsen completes his quest."

The recorded years were kept track by Aldina and now held across Playada and even Brannland. It marked the beginning of what was considered a time of intelligence, when most of the world knew how to read and communicate and they began recording important dates of political triumph. Currently we were in the autumn of 853, a hundred and seventy-one years after Kjartan, son of Lars, went on his quest.

"Does it say anything more?" Malin asked.

"It just says 'From Brannland to the West.' But no, nothing more."

Malin furrowed his brow and stroked his chin. "Hmph. Well there is more to the map. I trust that as we gain more pieces you'll be of great use to me."

"I'm allowed to stay?" I asked.

"Yes. I need a good Brannish translator, and better to have someone not from Brannland themselves to do it."

I did not press as to why that might aid him, instead relishing in my success of making it aboard.

"Translating won't be your only duty though," Malin said. "And what you translate will remain strictly confidential. Only my officers and I will know what the documents say. Other than that, ye will serve as my personal cabin boy. Bring me breakfast in the morning, help the cook, assist the swabbies, and be at Jenkins and my whim. Understood?"

"Yes sir."

"And you will keep your identity a secret. I take no pleasure in flogging a man for ogling at something forced in front of his eyes."

I nodded.

"Is there anyone you wish to tell goodbye to before we depart?"

I had already said my goodbyes to Mateo who would be leaving on his father's ship as soon as the pirates left the cove. I did not wish to ever see Carla again. Lupe was not truly my father and had kept secrets from me since I was born. I shook my head. No, there was no one left in Villaviciosa who needed to ever see my face again.

"We depart within the hour."

IV. One Last Goodbye

If I'm being honest with myself, I never did expect to get that far. Joining the *Wind Raider* had always been a dream that I thought of as something that could happen someday. It was something I fell asleep fantasizing about. But I always kept walls in my head to remind myself it was something that might not ever happen. I hid behind these walls for the fear that once I broke them down, my life, as unsatisfactory as it might be, would never be the same.

In the years since I first boarded the Raider, I had forgotten how large the ship truly was. Mateo's father owned some larger ships, but none like this, and I hadn't even been aboard those. Mateo and I had gone out on his cutter, but it could be manned by a crew of three, and he and I got along on our own for the most part. The *Wind Raider* had three large masts and seemed to get by with a generally small crew, but was still manned by at least eight men at all times. I had a basic understanding of how a ship worked and how the sails and rigging interacted, but not on this scale.

At least I had some sea faring knowledge, as slim as it was. I knew I would not need to worry myself about sea sickness. I did well on the water. And I didn't foresee being plighted with fear once we had sailed off from land. I had heard stories of sailors getting struck with intense fear once it settled in that there was no way out and that they were completely surrounded by water.

And even if I was prone to seasickness or to the fear, I would not have cared. It was better than the alternative of living under a roof with Carla, or with some strange man who would take me as his bride.

I helped the men load supplies onto the ship, which included crates upon crates of potatoes, water, and ale. This seemed to be most of the fare for the crew. There was a pen of goats kept below in the kitchen. Some bread and cheese had been given by shopkeepers looking to make some extra coin, but I imagined that it would spoil long before we ported again.

No one addressed me while I worked, which was just as well. Our close quarters over the coming weeks would give us plenty of time and opportunity to talk. I tried to recall faces I had seen in the tavern while I was drunk, but the men all blurred together in a crowd of strangers.

If I were friendlier, maybe I would have introduced myself, but the way the men worked around me, I did not think they cared who the new Playadan boy was as long as I helped them load.

It was autumn, so it was not terribly hot, but I had still worked up a sweat. I certainly was not incapable even though I was raised as a noble. I was not one to ring a bell to disturb the housekeepers with tasks I could perform myself, like dressing and washing. Mateo and I rarely brought servants with us when we fished. We cleaned and gutted the fish all on our own. We hauled up the nets. We brought the boat in and out of the bay, enduring the splinters in the process. Getting my hands dirty was not as repulsive to me as it was to some ladies in my station. Carla loved her little bell to call upon the housekeeper.

Once all was loaded, I leaned over the railing, waiting for the anchor to finally be lifted. I scanned the cobbled streets, taking my last look at the only home I had ever known. I knew I wouldn't miss it, nor would anyone miss me. Not the townspeople who wished I were hanging in gallows. Not Mateo who would be sailing away to start his own life. Not even my uncle who had lied to me all this time. And especially not Carla who was now staring up at me from the dock.

I ducked behind the railing, hoping there was doubt in her mind that she had just seen her stepdaughter aboard the ship. I could not risk her announcing to everyone in the crew that I was actually a girl and the daughter of a don. Between the rails, I could see her storming off to gather dock officers to accompany her as she stomped up the ramp.

"Not a step further," Jenkins said, him and other larger men standing at the entrance to the ship.

"We need to inspect the ship," one of the guards said. "We suspect you have a stowaway."

"A stowaway?" Jenkins asked. "You mad? Everyone on this ship is accounted for. But you ain't."

"It's my stepdaughter," Carla said, her hands on her hips. "The little wench has run away."

So Lupe had not told his wife of the arrangement with Captain Malin.

"You think I've allowed not only a stowaway, but a woman to board?" Jenkins asked. "You doubt my hold on this ship."

"She's here. I saw her," Carla hissed.

I eyed the door across the ship that led down to the crew's cabins. I could hide there if they were to board the ship. But that would be the first place they'd look.

"I demand to speak to your captain," Carla spat. "Tell him la Doña Hidalgo requires it."

Jenkins looked her in the eyes, leaning in scandalously close to her face. "On this ship, you are no lady."

I could have kissed Jenkins, but instead I ran across the ship to where the dinghy hung, and crawled into it, throwing a torn sail over myself. The guards charged up the ramp, their boots rattling the deck, Carla trailing after them.

"Search above and below," she commanded.

"What is the meaning of this?" it was Malin's voice.

"You have a stowaway, Captain," Carla told him.

"I most certainly do not."

"My stepdaughter was seen leering over the side of your ship."

"Jenkins, do you not have sense to keep a woman off my ship?" Malin demanded.

"Cap'n, on my life I swear, there is no stowaway."

"No, but there is some bitch attempting to command my men. Get her off."

"I am la Doña Hidalgo, Captain," Carla nearly screeched. "You are in my husband's territory and you will show me respect."

"Actually, I am on the ship I command, and I am on the water, so therefore no longer on your husband's land, and I indeed know your husband. Very well, in fact. And I really wouldn't give a damn if he was the king of Playada. You will not come on my ship and command anyone." Malin's voice rang across the ship.

I wished I could have seen Carla's face. No one had ever stood up to her like that as far as I knew. On countless occasions, I had fantasized about telling her off, even spitting in her face, but I had always remained submissive to her. It was my greatest regret when I left: that I never got to tell that bitch all that I hated about her.

"Fine," Carla huffed. Her tone went softer, sweeter, trying to persuade the captain. "I still request a search of this ship. I know I saw my stepdaughter aboard. And if I'm not mistaken, there is a very clear line in the treaty that says you must not harm, take, touch, or ruin any of the women within Villaviciosa, or all agreements made between you and the lords will cease."

Malin was quiet for a moment. "Fine," he breathed. "Search the ship. But no touching my quarters. I can assure you. There is no stowaway there."

The men dispersed around the ship, checking all corners for me. Down to the brig and crew's quarters. To the kitchens. They checked the barrels on the deck, yet to be brought below. They checked every inch of the ship. Except for the dinghy that hung off the side, where I lay, holding my breath.

"There's no one here aside from the crew, madam," an officer told Carla.

"Did you interrogate the crew?" she asked.

"Of course. No one has seen a girl aboard."

"Fine," Carla concluded. "But know this Captain Malin, if I go home, and my stepdaughter isn't there, this will be the last time you land in these ports."

"What is the meaning of this?" It was Lupe.

"Where is Mayra, mi Don?"

They were about to expose me. Yes, Lupe would tell his wife I was meant to be here and she would stop harassing Malin, but then the whole crew would know I'm a girl and the lord's daughter, and I could forget being taken seriously.

"Sir," Malin said. "Might we speak in my quarters? Your wife too?"

"Yes, Captain Malin," Lupe agreed, "I think that would be best."

I could hardly breathe by now. Not only from the anxiety of being caught, but also from the cloud of dust that I was inhaling from the old sail that I tossed over myself. Once I heard their footsteps, I swiftly got out of the dinghy and went towards the middle deck, towards Malin's quarters. I couldn't hear anything from the door, and I wasn't about to walk inside, but Malin's window was cracked, allowing me to hear their conversation.

"You're sending her away?" Carla asked.

"I have raised her as my own," Lupe growled. "I will not stand for this town to punish her. She is like my own daughter."

"Here I am about to give you a child, your real and true child, and yet you protect the Spriggan bastard?"

"Silence," Lupe said.

And she was quiet. Lupe was not easily raised to anger. He scolded me at times, but it was only ever in the chilled quiet tone he spoke to Carla in.

"She and I have made an arrangement," Malin said after the couple had stopped quarreling. "She is to be my translator and work aboard the ship so long as I don't expose who she really is. She worries for her safety should anyone find out she is a Hidalgo."

"But she's not—"

"Hush," Lupe spat. "I think that's wise. So, she took well to leaving?"

"She actually came to me, Don Hidalgo, to ask for passage. I think she meant to before she knew you had arranged it for her."

"Oh. I see." Lupe sighed. "I couldn't keep her safe forever."

There was a pause.

"Carla, you are to go home."

"But mi Don—"

"Now."

She huffed and stamped out the captain's quarters. I turned my back to her and looked over the railing. She was much too irate to take notice of me. I watched as she stomped down the docks back towards Casa de Hidalgo, and then I felt a hand on my back.

"Pa—Lupe," I turned to face him. What was I to call him now?

"Can we talk?" he asked.

I turned to look about. The crew was going about their business, but were interested in why el Don Hidalgo was talking to the new recruit.

"Use my quarters," Malin muttered. "Don't touch anything."

He walked down to the main deck and snapped some orders to the men to mind their business.

"Mayra, I am so sorry," he whispered after he shut the door. His shoulders shook and I could see the red in his eyes. Lupe was known for his stoicism and yet I had seen his each of his layers peel back all in a day. "I should have sent you long before. I should have told you the truth when your mother was gone. I just... I didn't want to lose you."

I looked at him. "Why? I'm not yours."

"What do you mean?"

"You've said it yourself," I shrugged my shoulders, feigning indifference. "I'm your brother's bastard."

He looked me in the eye. "You are my daughter. You might be my brother's blood, but I held you as a baby. I sang to you when you couldn't sleep. I taught you your first words. I was there for every moment I could be. And it may have been strained between your mother and me but that did not mean I loved you any less than if you had been my own."

I shook my head, clenching my jaw. "But when she died you acted as if I was a curse. You can claim that you were there when I was young and things were easy, but you were not really there once she died."

"I know, it's just..." Lupe wept real tears. I could hardly bear to watch, but I remained where I stood, across the room from him.

"You are so like your mother. You do what's right because you think it's right. You are above the close-mindedness of this town, and I knew as soon as I set you free you would never return. As I am now." He stood up a little straighter, wiping the emotion from his face. "I know I wasn't there for you when I should have been. I should have done more and I—it's my biggest regret. But what I can do now to make this right is send you to good hands."

He pulled a piece of parchment from the pocket of his coat and handed it to me. I unfolded it to see a letter.

"It's from your aunt. She's in Brannland. Your mom's sister. She wrote to your mother when you were young. I wrote back when your mother died, and when she wrote again, she asked about you. I never wrote to her after. I was selfish." He looked away from me. "I didn't want you to go. But now I know it is what is right."

I skimmed the letter. She wrote about the misfortune of her sister's death and offered her condolences. Like Lupe had said, she asked if

I was well and how I was handling my mother's death. There was no mention of the trial. Or the hanging. It was signed by Runa Ogden.

"Did you tell her how mother died?" I asked.

"No. I just said she had passed."

I scoffed. "As if she got the plague or had an accident? And wasn't intentionally hung and burned? You couldn't tell her own sister that?"

"I made a lot of mistakes, Mayra." Lupe pinched the corners of his eyes. "I'm not denying that. But you don't need to endure them any longer. You have gained passage to Brannland and meet the family you never knew." He gave me a nod, as if to close the deal.

I couldn't expect more from him. I wanted more. An apology or acknowledgment that he was just as much part of my mother's death as the rest of the town. But this was as much as I would get. If I ever wanted to be right with him, I would need to accept this. But there was one more matter I needed to address before I could put this behind me.

"Why Carla?" I asked. "You could have married any other woman. Why that awful bitch?"

"The estate was suffering," Lupe replied. "If I lost any more, my land was to be given to another family." He wiped a tired hand across his brow, then to the back of his neck. "I lost a lot when your mother passed. Workers. Resources. Accounts. She did far too much, and I never gave her credit for that." He shook his head. "The other dons said if I married, I could carry on. And Carla's father had a large sum of money. She wasn't from Villaviciosa originally. Her family came from Naves, where her father owns a distillery. He came here often to do business with Rafe. He also was looking for ways to get his daughter to marry. As you can imagine it was difficult to secure a proposal. And I was... I was desperate."

"I wish you would have married for love at least once," I admitted. "Because of you and Mama, I never thought love existed."

"It exists," my father said. "But not in my life. And only briefly for your mother. Frankie and Vivanka had love. I saw the letters. And I regret she did not get him longer."

"Me too," I replied. There was a flash on his face of hurt, but he tried to cover it. "But," I continued, "I'm grateful for you as my father. I know you did your best under the circumstances."

He took me in his arms and hugged me tight. Something he had not done since I was small. I felt like that little girl again in his arms. "I wish you well on your journey."

We said our goodbyes, and I was not certain I would ever see Lupe again, but at least I knew I was raised by a man who would do what he could to protect his daughter.

V. Hazed

"Reef the sails!" Jenkins bellowed out over the rail of the main deck. "Weigh anchor! Set course for Port Astreim!"

The *Wind Raider* began to drift away from Villaviciosa. I didn't even bother to look as my childhood home became a speck on the horizon. I had no fond memories.

As we took to the topaz waters, all the men above deck kept their hands busy. Some had climbed the masts to roll or, as Jenkins had said, reef up the sails. Others fussed with the many ropes that hung from the masts. If someone wasn't contributing to the function of the ship, they were shining the shields that bore the mer-women, the crest of the Raiders.

These mystical depictions were proudly shown. The main set of colors that whipped with the sea breeze carried the traditional mer-woman, her breasts covered by clam shells, her dark hair flowing behind her and her mouth opened in an "o" meant to be singing her siren song. Her tail was thick and scaled, extending down the length of the flag. I did not know if she was based on a particular legend or if she was meant to be representative of the sea dwelling fae-folk. Perhaps the Raiders were trying to tell the sea they were Spriggan sympathizers.

Not wanting to appear useless, I assisted the crewmen carrying cargo. Grabbing a decently heavy sack, I followed them down the steps that led to the combined gun room and crew's quarters. A dozen cannons were lined up, shined and ready to see action, should any occur. I was sorely unprepared for the thought of war, and this gleaming evidence it could occur. Behind the cannons and between the stacks of cargo were hammocks looped into the beams above. A few men were occupying them already, still nursing their hangovers and avoiding the work on deck. Each footstep was like thunder from above and I was grateful my headache subsided. Strange to think that just hours before we were in the tavern drinking. Strange to think that it took a mere twenty-four hours to unchain me from a life I'd lived for twenty years.

From what I could tell, there must have been close to thirty men in the ship's crew. I saw familiar faces, but only vaguely. Most were still strangers to me, their names as foggy as my drunken memories of the night before. I knew Jenkins and Malin, and I recalled Hagley and Everett from earlier in the evening. I had spotted Everett pulling up one of the main sails above deck and Hagley was one of the men in a hammock, situated between two cannons, looking as though he had a terrible headache. He moaned as I threw the sack aside the cannon nearest to him. Something clunked against the metal letting out a sharp ring, resulting in more groans.

"Ah, ye whale," one pirate snorted. He had eyes that seemed too small beneath his steep forehead and a wide mouth in a permanent sneer. His dark hair was almost as long as mine and was left loose on his shoulders. He stood a head taller than I, and he had large square shoulders. An earring, the shape of a dagger, hung from his right ear lobe. "We aren't a day into our trek and you're already complaining."

"Shuddup," Hagley muttered, "you know the first day is the worst."

The pirate with the dagger earring nudged me. "The ol' bugger get's seasick. A sailorman who gets seasick?" He repeated with more emphasis to dig into the irony. He looked me over more carefully, seeming to realize he had not seen me on this ship before today.

"Who're you?" he asked, humor being replaced by speculation.

"Finn Santana, sir," I replied, outstretching my hand.

He took it, but slowly, as if wondering why I would be shaking his hand at our introduction. "I'm Stratford, the ship's master o' arms." He puffed his chest out ever so slightly as he declared his title. "You been here long?"

"No, I was recruited in Villaviciosa."

"Really?" he considered, raising an eyebrow. "Strange. Captain don't take boys from here. Some law or somethin'."

I shrugged, running out of things to say to the master of arms. "Guess he made an exception."

"He does know you're here, right?" Stratford asked. "Some bitch was claiming there was a stowaway."

"Go ask him yourself," I suggested. I knew it was only natural that I would be looked at with suspicion. Didn't mean I enjoyed the continuous scrutiny.

He shook his head abruptly, startled at the very suggestion to take up his concerns with Malin. "No, I will not be troubling the captain this early into a voyage."

"Then I guess you better take my word for it," I shrugged.

He raised an eyebrow over his teeny blue eye. "I'll be watchin' you, Santana."

I was not troubled that the master of arms was suspicious of me. Malin and Jenkins both knew I was supposed to be here and from observation, Stratford was already several drinks into his day. I recalled then that he had been the pirate bothering the tavern-maids before noontime. I doubted that he'd even remember our conversation once he reached the top of the steps.

We crossed the threshold of the Playadan bay by sunset, venturing into open water. The sliver of land behind us receded into the horizon until it was swallowed by the sea. As the boat sailed onward and the work diminished, my bones grew weary. Most of the crew stayed on the main deck once the ship glided along, drinking and playing games. All I could think of was sleep. I hadn't received sufficient rest the night before in the wet grass, and my mouth was still parched from liquor. While the men were above, I thought perhaps I could catch up on sleep and prepare myself for the journey ahead. Gods knew I would make an even poorer pirate if I was delirious.

I scanned the room of bunks beyond Hagley's. At the far end there was a door leading to a private cabin. It didn't seem to be occupied, but I knew I wasn't special enough to move into it. All of the hammocks in the crew's quarters had a hat or belt, or something else atop them to make claim. I sighed. I accepted the fact that as the cabin boy and the newest recruit, I was the bottom man. I had planned to take whatever was left, but I didn't realize that would be nothing at all.

"Oy! Need a bed?" one of the men asked in a hammock closer to that door. He had kicked off his boots, revealing his diseased feet.

I nodded, gracious that someone had decided to show me some hospitality.

"New recruits usually get the sacks in the corner." He gestured to a pile of potato sacks, all with holes and frayed edges, splattered with dried mud and whatever else pooled at the floor.

I eyed the bags that had been filled with some unknown fluff that were tossed in the corner upon the damp floor. I had not expected to get a bed as nice as Malin's whilst aboard, though I thought I would at least be accommodated as well as the servants at la Casa de Hidalgo. They shared quarters, the farmhands in one wing and the house staff in the other, all with their own small beds or at least a cot. They did not seem unhappy by the arrangement, and had I been a servant, as I was now, I definitely would not have seen anything wrong with those arrangements. But aboard the ship, where they were unprepared for me, my options were the bare floor that had not been swabbed in years, or the pile of rubbish in the corner. At least I had my cloak.

It still smelled like damp, grass covered earth, like the hills of home, which was welcome when surrounded by the piss smell of the belly of the ship.

A boy watched me as I fluffed up the sack and laid down my cloak to claim it. His face was much younger than the other men. Perhaps around my own age. I wouldn't have thought he could be more than an inch taller than me, standing at five foot, eight inches. I was a giant amongst the petite women of Villaviciosa. He had the beginnings of blonde whiskers and his hair had been cut recently, not hanging in greasy ringlets like many of the men, but in neat spikes. His cheeks were round like a mole and his chin had a large dimple in the center. His blue eyes were close together and looked at me critically.

I tried not to keep eye contact but the way he stared at me while I was stooped over made me uneasy. There were no mirrors aboard, so I wasn't sure how my disguise was holding up. Eventually my feminine features were sure to seep through. I could only hope my ruse was enough to convince the crew of my boyhood in the early days aboard. Soon, they wouldn't look at me so closely and I could become a ghost aboard their ship, making my way peacefully to the north. That was the hope at least.

When I turned back around, the boy was gone. Strange. Perhaps this was something I needed to get used to. Every man would need to get a chance to speak with me, make sure I wasn't a Playadan brat sent to disturb the order of their ship. It only made sense. I knew that many of these men had been on this crew for decades. It was only natural to be apprehensive when a new face showed itself. And Stratford was right—Malin did not take on Playadan men. I had not seen any of my countrymen aboard the Raider. It seemed only logical that all of the crew would wonder why I would be the exception.

Climbing the steps back up to the main deck, I didn't notice the wire that had been tied between two posts, just low enough that my ankle caught it.

I was sent skidding across the splintering wood, my chin scuffed as well as both my knees. There was a pause in the chatter from the pirates on the deck, holding their dice cups and ale mugs in a one second silent pause that seemed to stretch beyond the lengths of time itself. But that moment collapsed under their hoots of laughter.

The scrapes stung and my face grew hot with the attention. I looked at the group of men, trying to identify which one did this. The blonde boy laughed the loudest of them all, and the glint in his eye told me exactly who had laid down the wire. How could I have made an enemy on the first day? And with someone I hadn't yet spoken a word to?

I picked myself up, brushed myself off, and tried to maintain some composure. He would not get a rise out of me. Perhaps it was only a simple prank. I was new and pirates certainly partook in the immature practice of hazing. Or it could have been a test to see my limits. If I burst out in anger too quickly, I would not be fit to serve the ship. Remaining calm was all I could do.

"New recruit's a clumsy one, huh?" the boy bumped elbows with the men. "Hasn't quite got his sea legs."

He made enough comments that the men grew bored with him quickly, taking the spotlight off me as quickly as it had appeared.

I wasn't going to confront him. Not over this. I needed to remain inconspicuous while I familiarized myself with the ship and its crew. To be known early on as anything in extremity, like anger or clumsiness, would follow me as I gained the trust of the men. I'd likely be pinned with one of their awful nicknames too. I tried to find myself to distract myself with and to lower the bit of anger that I kept at a simmer.

All the supplies had been brought below, and now that the boat had taken to the water, the only man on alert was the one who stood at the wheel. He was amongst the younger of the crew, in the same age range as the boy with the tripwire, except he was much more handsome and looked to be more respected. Occasionally, he'd bark an order to a man who would let down the sail or change a knot. Many of these men were Aldinian, with the lofty accents of the kingdom to our north. That was not to say that these men were well spoken. But the accent of the Aldinians was much higher than that of the Playadans. The helmsman had a version of the Aldinian accent, except his voice was not so lofty. Instead, he spoke in fractional pieces of words, his vowels lost in the depths of his throat and consonants rattling against his tongue.

He had gleaming teeth, much cleaner than any pirate I'd ever seen, and his curls were a dark blonde. He stood tall and slender, his body obviously sharpened from the labor of the ship. He wore a simple white shirt, laces undone, and dark-brown trousers with a belt tied tight at his waist, holding a pistol and a dagger at his side.

He caught me looking at him, then smiled at me with his brilliant teeth. I found myself flushed but couldn't explain why. I decided it would be best to avoid his gaze.

Not even a full day into the journey, I realized this was the furthest I had ever been from home, being that Mateo and I had never left the bay during our fishing trips. It was sad to think that this actually meant something to me when the rest of the men had been all around the world. A few leagues was hardly a dent in their repertoire of travel. I did not long for Playada as we grew more distant from it. I clutched the vial that hung around my neck and thought of my mother.

"Ah Cutthroat, if I find out you've been cheatin', I'll make sure you wake up strung to the main sail."

"I'd like to see your string bean arms try and lift me."

A group of men had settled at a small table on the main deck. They shook their hands over their cups, rolling out dice across the surface, hollering profanities at their opponents. My plan was to be aloof, but I was already feeling an outcast amongst men bonded with their crew. The only people who had shown me any attention were the officers who gave me orders, and that damned boy who had humiliated me. Besides, the game looked fun. Perhaps having allies would be to my advantage.

I approached them as a shadow, observing with no intention of taking part. I did not know if it was wiser to stay scarce these first few days or to find ways to build trust with them by joining their social circles. Being a rogue wasn't always a good thing, especially as men who worked alongside each other every day.

They didn't acknowledge me when I sat down at the only empty spot along the table, beside a man two heads taller than me, with strikingly large shoulders. His brow was heavy, giving him an intense serious expression, but when he smiled, his face also brightened dramatically. With his rich dark skin and tight curly hair cut close to his scalp, he had to be from the far southlands.

The men rolled their dice, shielding them with rusty cups.

The master of arms smirked, revealing his silver canine tooth. "Three fives."

The pirate to his right eyed him, cocking his head to the side. He had a brimmed hat covering his shaggy tawny-brown hair. His teeth were yellow as corn kernels in his mouth. "Fine Silver, but I know without a doubt in my mind that there be five sixes."

"Bull shit, Perry," the pirate to his left snapped. He had a skeletal face, his skin drooping beneath his gray eyes. He had greased his mustache to curl beside his mouth. "Show 'em."

Perry bared his stained teeth, revealing three of the five sixes. The others eyed each pile of dice, finding another six under Stratford's cup and another under the third member of the table's cup, whom everyone called the Monk.

The men groaned in unison and Perry beamed as he took the few gold coins that had been placed in the center pot. I was able to gather the basic rules of the game. All it took was bluffing until someone was bold enough called you out on it. A game most suitable for pirates. Having no money to offer to the pot, I continued to sit out. But not wanting to appear unfriendly, I engaged with them.

"So how do you know who wins?" I asked the crewmate I sat beside.

"Whoever wins the most hands if you're keeping track," he replied, his voice full of depth and bass. "But mostly it's about how heavy your pockets are when you walk away."

"We play this a lot, boy," Perry said, leaning in close to my face. His breath stank of ale and rot. "There will be plenty of chances to earn your riches."

The others chuckled, as if the thought of my winning was absurd. Granted, I had never played, and I didn't know the precise rules, but surely it was something I could pick up just by watching. Perry had won even though there were not five sixes under his own cup, but five sixes across the whole table. And that was all based on luck. There wasn't a viable way to force a pair to appear beneath the cup. But if one was good at probability, there was a one in six chance that what you wanted was under your opponent's cup.

I tried to store the names of everyone I met in my mind, but thirty men were hard to keep track of. The man from the far south was Kamau. There were others amongst the crew from lands close to his. Approximately a third of the men looked as though they had lived in the lands of eternal sunshine. And then there was Perry, the Monk—I'm sure he had a first name, but no one used it. I could pick out other faces that I had met at the tavern, but their names were lost to me. Dinner was called as the sun set and I took it upon myself to pass out the bowls so I could get a chance to speak to each man.

I met Peel, the cook, while I fetched bowls and spoons for his goat stew. He had even bought some bread rolls from the baker when they were on land. He had a shiny bald head and constantly wiped his sweating brow with the top of his shirt. He was a head shorter than I, but moved in quick darting movements like a rodent on alert. He was the most fair amongst the crew, Aldinian, but did not have the baked leather skin of the crew who stayed above deck all day.

Peel had his hands busy, preparing the captain's supper and irritably directed me to find utensils and bowls. His kitchen was kept in utter chaos, but he knew where everything was.

"Bowls are in that crate. No, the one next to it. Spoons are over there. And mugs are over there."

The three crates were in opposing corners of the kitchen, amongst many other boxes and crates of ingredients, kitchen tools, and what seemed to just be junk. But somehow the layout made sense to Peel.

Aside from coming back to fetch more bowls, I tried to stay out of his way as he muttered over the roasted chicken and vegetables he plated for the captain.

The stew was not as visually appealing, but the men were overjoyed at the bread. Baked goods were a rarity only able to be eaten the first few days aboard, before they went stale and moldy. I never thought something as simple as bread could be a delicacy. Then again I had never been at sea for days let alone weeks and months.

I helped serve dinner and got to know some of my mates.

From what I had gathered, there were a few men of superiority other than Malin, like the first mate, Jenkins and the master of arms, Stratford. And then there were the boatswain, the gunners, and the deckhands—all ranks above mine I realized as I introduced myself as the new cabin boy. They also viewed me as a child, even though I had to be as old as the boy with the tripwire and the boy at the helm. But that didn't matter, because I was seen as a boy with no hair on my face or chest. If I stayed a decade on this ship, I wondered if they would ever see me as an equal. Likely not, and I doubted I could fake my gender for so long.

I realized I was being pompous. I came from an estate where everyone knew me and engaged with me respectfully. The servants that is. Not my stepmother. But when I walked the grounds, the stable boys waved at me and greeted me. The cook and her staff asked if I needed anything. Yes, the town had a disdain for me, but I was still respected to a certain degree in my own home. I needed to adjust to being small and disregarded and unimportant.

And it was not all so bad. Some of the crew mates seemed to enjoy the presence of someone who had not yet grown tired of their stories.

"Did you know I met the queen?" Stratford asked me, accepting the bowl while he straddled the bench at the dice table.

I shook my head. I didn't know anything about him aside from his title, but Stratford wasn't looking for my input.

"She gave me this rose of honor." He pointed to the little pin on his breast pocket, which was in fact a red rose with what appeared to be the initials of the former queen of Aldina before her son rose to power after her suspicious death.

"She was a rose herself, Lilliana was. Kissed my cheek as if I was a gentleman. Felt bad when I carried out the ruby of justice. But that filled my pockets longer than you've been alive. Until I helped Malin buy this ship of course."

My lips parted ever so slightly. The ruby of justice had been held by the royal family for centuries and the day it went missing, there was fear that a far-off kingdom had stolen it to wage war. A prince from the east had arrived and left swiftly. Some still believed he guarded it in his golden palace. I wasn't sure if I believed Stratford, but what if it all was just a pirate looking for his next meal.

I gave a bowl to Kamau.

"They call him Cutthroat," Stratford piped up when we were formally introduced. "Wanna know why?" he said with a mischievous glint in his eye.

"Oh bugger off, Silver," Kamau snapped back, with absolutely no humor within his strong jaw.

Stratford drew a line across his throat, sticking his tongue out.

Kamau asked for more salt please and said thank you when I fetched it.

Was Stratford wishing to warn me? Would Kamau cut my throat in my sleep? He seemed kind and had shown me a sliver more respect than any of his crewmates. And I would have liked to think Malin wouldn't allow a man who killed crewmates to stay on his ship. But they were pirates. Perhaps it was another unfortunate nickname due to some backstory I didn't know about yet.

I passed bowls to Hagley, Everett, Perry, the yellow-toothed man, and Grover, whose face was skeletal. The four of them were sailors, though I recalled Everett saying they were boatswain.

"Jenkins told them they were promoted to get them to stay in line," Kamau whispered to me when I asked about their ranks. "If a man thinks he has the littlest bit of authority he tends to stay on task easier. And that lot is known to be a little..." he paused but twirled his finger in a circle near the front of his forehead. I caught his meaning.

I found Watson, the ship's sailing master up, in the Crow's Nest where he'd been since the ship docked in Playada. He looked over his maps and checked his spyglass often, taking his post very seriously. It seemed from the pile of frayed blankets that he also slept up there, despite the wind and the cold.

He had a permanent quizzical expression, one brow always above the other. His chestnut whiskers covered most of his mouth, but his bottom lip stuck out as he squinted at his papers. His skin was worn and weathered, like old leather, but still pale considering all the sun he had gotten by remaining in the lookout point. His hair went down to his shoulders, but he wore a brimmed hat to keep it contained. His limbs were knobby, but he still had a bit of a gut that hung over his belt.

Everyone called him the Professor because he often went on lengthy ramblings about the history of political power and the conspiracies of the crown. He also spoke more articulately than most of the men, having a formal Aldinian accent and not the broken ones the other sailors had.

"Slop's on," I greeted after a dreadful climb up the mast, balancing his bowl in the crook of my arm. I was sure the stew had gone cold from the persistent wind chill.

"And who is serving me tonight?" he asked, a bushy eyebrow raised.

"Finn Santana," I introduced myself. I had stopped offering handshakes, being that most of the men looked at me funny when I did and I had stopped trusting the cleanliness of their hands. "I'm the new cabin boy."

"You mean to say that you're Malin's translator?" he asked.

I wasn't sure how transparent I should be about my title. I felt tangled in my lies. But I nodded. There wasn't any sense in denying it to an officer.

"Did you know they think faeries created the Brannish language?"

I wasn't prepared for the accusation. The fact that I spoke Brannish made me untrustable in the eyes of anyone compliant to Aldinian rule. I guess even pirates didn't trust the faerie's tongue.

"I came from the Wastes, you know," he went on.

"Hm?" No one was from the Wastes. The Wastes was a no man's territory.

Being from Playada, I had only heard about the Wastes in the faerie tales my mother told me. The Wastes was rumored to be in the eastern lands of Aldina, but not many lived out there. Besides, there weren't many reliable accounts of happenings beyond the border of what was considered *civilized* land. But many believed that Spriggan creatures lived there, like dragons, unicorns, and faeries. There were stories of faeries stealing from the villages nearby and tormenting their children, even replacing them with changelings. They would take the children back to their mountain caves, fatten them up, and use them as offerings to satisfy their pagan gods.

The Wastes was surrounded by thick mists, and no one could see through the veils. In the night, under a full moon, shadows and golden light would flicker across the fogs. It was speculated what lived beyond the mists. It could have been faeries or wee-folk. But it was also said to be ghosts and spirits of the murdered Spriggan.

But if anyone went missing, whether it be man, woman, or child, they looked to the Wastes. Everyone knew the faeries thirsted for human blood and flesh.

"I mean, I didn't live quite in the Wastes," he admitted. "I come from the village at the very edge of them, as close to that place as you can get. I've certainly seen some things though. Seen whispers of faeries."

"You've seen faeries?" I matched his skeptical expression. No one reliable had ever seen a faerie. Perhaps those who drank too much, or ate red-capped mushrooms, or a person who was mad to begin with. Mama had told me plenty of stories, but she never expressed first-hand accounts of seeing the wee-folk or other mystical beings. The Spriggan of Brannland, to my understanding, were limited to pagans and wise women.

"No, just whispers. The villages that border the Wastes tend to be a bit more superstitious than most. My mum would line our sills with salt and put lavender over our door frames, just to ensure I wouldn't be stolen," Watson said. It seemed like there was more he would have liked to say, but he went quiet, and dug his spoon into the chilled stew.

Despite my apprehension, I was curious about the Wastes. How did it appear in Aldina? The land of no magic? If such a place was contained in Brannland, perhaps, it would not cause such curiosity.

"Did you know any kids who were stolen?" I asked him, not ready to put my curiosity aside just yet.

He shook his head. "No. Not children. I think—erm—I think I better go check on the captain." He took his leave down the ladder of the Crow's Nest, leaving me on my own up there. He didn't even take the stew that I brought up for him.

I climbed back down from the Crow's Nest, thinking about how odd the man was. But also about how I could not judge each person's true character based on these brief interactions.

The rest of the men had eaten, except for the boy with the tripwire and the boy at the helm. Both were at the wheel, whispering about something. I reluctantly passed a bowl to the boy who tripped me.

"Thank you immensely, Finn," he said with glowing enthusiasm.

I wanted to ignore him entirely, but I knew he was just trying to get under my skin.

"Don't mind Briggs," the helmsman said. "He just likes the attention."

"Do not," Briggs shot back.

"I'm Grey," the boy introduced himself, sticking his hand out for me. I took it and was surprised to find his palms near sparkling clean.

"Finn," I replied, taking extra care to deepen my voice. He was even more beautiful up close. His eyes were both brown and blue. They reflected differently based on where he looked. His hair was almost brown, but had hints of gold along the curls. He still had boyishness in his face, but not like Briggs, whose face was too round and too smooth. He had formed definition in his jaw and brow so he held a permanent smolder. Shadow covered that jawline of recently shaved facial hair.

"What brings you aboard, Finn?" The "r" in aboard rang against his teeth and down his throat.

I swallowed, unsure what to say at this point. Would I be putting a target on my back and tell everyone I aimed for Brannland? I glanced sideways at Briggs who sat on a stool beside the wheel, ready to utilize whatever information I told of my personal life. Grey followed my line of sight when I didn't answer him.

"Briggs," Grey said. "Go furl up the aft sail."

"Why?" he scoffed. "The winds hitting the sails just fine."

"Because I told you to," Grey replied, his tone very older brother-like. The same manner that Tomas had with Mateo when he thought he was being a pest.

Briggs looked to his half-eaten bowl and then to me, but then did as he was told.

"There, now that he's gone," Grey smirked, "what brings you aboard?"

"I'm looking for my family in Brannland," I replied. "What is his problem by the way?"

"Who, Briggs?" Grey asked. "Ah, he's the youngest of us, and no longer has his da to look out for him." He eyed me. "But I'm guessing not as young as you? How old are you?"

I was about to say twenty when I remembered I looked like a boy. "Seventeen," I said, which may have still been a bit generous. "Was his pa a crew member?"

"Yeah, and my uncle Starky."

"Starky was Brigg's dad?" I asked, aghast, but my memories fell into place. The small boy had fetched me water and been there to witness my hands upon the siren's breasts all those years ago.

"You knew him?" Grey asked, eyebrows raised.

"I—" Lying had become such a tedious business. "I came on the ship when I was thirteen," I told him. "I had always dreamed of being aboard and I met Starky when I slipped and fell into the bay. I hit my head and he bandaged me up."

I told him the truth before I could hold it back, making the connections that Grey was Briggs's cousin a little late.

"Don't tell Briggs though," I added. "The last thing I need is for him to know I almost drowned in the bay."

"He'd definitely find a way to torment you with it," Grey chuckled. "Your secret, it is safe with me."

"How did Starky die?"

"Cannonball to the stomach," Grey said grimly. "We were against an eastern ship that got the better of us. That's the risk of this life though, and we're all prepared for it."

My relationship to Starky had been brief, compared to Grey and Briggs who had been his family. Even though I didn't want to, I felt sympathy for the boy who lost his father. Perhaps we had just gotten off on the wrong foot.

"Were you on the ship as a child too?"

He shook his head. "No, I stayed in *Monadh Ruadh* until I was sixteen."

I didn't recognize the place he said, and he spoke in his accent where the syllables seemed disconnected.

"It's the hills of Cairn," he elaborated. "Small country between Aldina and the open sea to Brannland."

"Oh," I said, feeling a bit dense. My worldview was so small that I thought everything north of Playada was Aldina until you reached the most north you could go, which was Brannland. Of course there were other countries. Aldina's reach seemed to swallow most of them.

"I furled your sail, Lover Boy, even though we got a perfectly good wind," Briggs said, climbing down the mast.

Did Grey fancy me? I couldn't help worrying. *Is that why Briggs is teasing him? But no, it can't be. They think me a lad.*

"I left *Monadh Ruadh* because of a girl," Grey admitted, relieving me of worry. It wasn't about me at all.

"Not just a girl," Briggs added, "a lady—a girl of noble birth while Grey was nuthin' more than a stableboy."

Grey rolled his eyes. Stratford came over, hearing Briggs's obnoxious voice from across the ship.

"Oh, we're telling Lover Boy's story now?" he hooted.

Between Briggs and Stratford talking over one another and Grey piping in with corrections, I learned that he had fallen in love with a woman in the royal line. She was not to be queen or even princess. But if four or five people were to die, her family would be the next to reign. It was an inappropriate match for her to be seen with Grey, but he truly thought she was the one for him.

"She was beautiful," he recounted, softness in his pale eyes. "A skilled painter and knew of all the birds in Cairn. Her room was covered in their likeness."

He would sing love songs beneath her window. She would find him in the stables and have her way with him, but never acknowledged him otherwise.

"I was a fool. A fool in love. I thought maybe she would eventually come to her senses and run away with me, but who would turn down riches for a boy who shovels shite?"

"Surely it can't be so foolish to do things out of love," I replied. His face held such awe when he spoke of her. It was more than I had ever seen in the marriages I had been subject to. Surely, Lupe did not feel this way about Carla and the Rieses did not look at each other with such sparkle.

Grey looked at me curiously. "Did you leave a lass behind? The tavern wench?"

I nearly flushed at the memory of Banía and her lips all over my cheek. "She's a fine chica," I muttered, indifferently, "but my life's purpose is not to remain in some small coastal town." I urged him to continue his tale, to get the focus off of me.

Her father had arranged for her to marry a lord in the east. The night before her wedding, Grey came to her window and asked her to run away with him, to which she denied there ever being anything between them, and that he best throw himself in the sea if he wished to not be imprisoned for his advances.

"I thought she was bluffing. I meant to go to the wedding," he admitted. "I had it in my mind that I would object and swoop in and rescue her from the snot-faced lord. But they were ready for me. They grabbed me when I only meant to watch the wedding from a window. They had me tied and whipped and were going to lock me away. They were probably thinking of hanging me too.

"I managed to escape but they were on my trail, and I didn't mean to die by the noose. So, I jumped off the sea cliff and swam to the nearest island. For weeks I hid there, eating fish and roots, until I saw a passing ship. I boarded the *Queen's Bidding* where I stayed a while as a cabin boy and ended up on the *Wind Raider* during a battle between the ships. Starky grabbed me and hauled me aboard and attested my value to Malin. I've been here ever since."

I finally sat down and ate my own dinner. The stew was surprisingly good. Peel had incorporated interesting herbs and the meat must have had some kind of soak before it got thrown in the pot.

It had been a good day. I had met most of the men, and some of them remembered me now. I felt a childish sense of pride that first night aboard the *Raider*. In just a day, I had gone from el Don's daughter to a runaway pirate. From detesting my life, to being open to the idea of adventure. I knew it wouldn't be an easy journey and this was only the beginning.

It was only then, in my solitude, reflecting on all I had learned of my crew, that I realized Grey must have misspoken. Malin had told me Starky died from illness, yet Grey said he died from a cannonball.

VI. The Raid

Eventually, after days of sailing toward the horizon, there comes a point when one is at sea in which it is hard to tell where the water begins and the sky ends. It occurs once all glimpses of land have faded and the ocean has settled. The ship had not gathered much wind and we seemed to not be moving at all. There was a haze surrounding us, blurring any impression of a horizon. The sun sat behind the clouds and everything felt flat and still. It was as if the ship was surrounded by nothing and was the only object in existence, floating around in a never-ending abyss.

"You're going to make yourself sick if you keep staring," Grey called from the helm.

I pushed myself from the railing and followed his advice, avoiding the view of the infinite sea.

"Do you ever get used to it?" I asked. "The feeling of being trapped in a place so open?"

"No," he replied. "But you learn not to think about it."

I nodded. I tried not to let on that I was fearful, though I'm sure anyone could have guessed that I was uneasy those first few weeks aboard. I did not fear for my life— mostly—but I was pushed to endure things I did not anticipate when I decided to come aboard.

First, there was the daunting nature of the sea. I didn't know what lay beneath us or around us. As vast as the sea was around us, it was also equally endless beneath the belly of the ship. Who was to say that there weren't sea monsters beneath us, baring their teeth and waiting to strike? I had seen paintings of giant eel-like creatures swallowing ships whole and thought it faerie tales. But I also believed in many of the faerie tales I was told.

Second, the noises of the ship against the sea made me uneasy. One would never expect a ship to groan or to hear howls and screeches in the middle of the ocean. Yet they happened throughout the night. The sea was disorienting. Without the stars and the navigator's compass, I could not tell which was north or south or east or west. And I could not tell from where such noises occurred. Perhaps it was from the screaming beasts below.

The silence was equally as unsettling. I would lie awake on my sack while the rest of the men snored, spinning all kinds of dark tales as to what created such a noise. But when the noises stopped, and even the waves quieted, the silence also drilled into me while I waited for some unseen beast to disturb it.

"I used to get seasick," Grey admitted, leaning his back against the wheel. "I would hide below with a bucket. This was on the *Queen's Bidding*, my first ship. We stopped on an island, and I thought about staying. But a lady there gave me a root that made my head stop spinning. Now I don't even need it."

"Did the crew give you a hard time?"

"'Course," he replied. "They'll find anything. You've seen how they treat Hagley. They brought down eels and oysters while I wretched so I couldn't be free of the smell. If you let them see any weakness in you, they're gonna attack it."

I thought of Briggs and the trip wire.

"And they still mock you," I reminded him, "by calling you Lover Boy."

Grey shrugged. "That's just what they call me. Everyone gets a name. It's a symbol that you're part of the crew."

I hadn't gotten a name yet. Everyone called me Santana, if they chose to address me at all. Jenkins barked orders at me. Sometimes Malin would thank me when I brought him meals. Only some of the men, like Grey, would bother to speak with me as an equal.

"When did you start working at the helm?" I asked Grey.

"A year ago. The old helmsman became terribly sick. Rashes and boils all over and a headache that made him feel like his skull was splitting. He ended up jumping off the ship and drowning himself. I got the job the next day. That's usually how promotions go—someone dies and the ship can't go on without someone filling the station."

It wasn't a comforting notion, but I suppose it was the reality of being on a vessel with limited resources and surrounded by ocean for hundreds of miles. My stomach lurched. I couldn't allow myself to think about it.

The feeling of being an outcast lingered for those first few weeks. Most of these men had been banded together for a decade. Some as long as two. Grey was five years older than me, and was found by Starky when he was my age. He must have understood what it was like being so new.

I made the best of it. Anything they asked me to do, I did it without question. Jenkins relayed information to me from Malin. There wasn't any translating to be done at first. Instead, I fetched the captain's breakfast. I helped swab the deck. I peeled potatoes in the kitchen. I shined the bronze on the siren. I sewed the sails. I refused to complain, keeping my head down as I completed every task asked of me.

Eventually, the orders were less frequent. I would be down in the kitchen long before I was asked to go there. Malin would get his breakfast before he called for it. Things were mended and shined before they reached the point beyond repair. No one said thank you or gave me praise, but I found that I was allowed more leisure time aboard the ship.

I often used this time to talk to Grey or Kamau or Watson. They would tell me of their positions, and I memorized the information. I didn't know how long I would be aboard the *Raider* and it seemed like a good use of my time to learn everything I could. Grey could give me insight on someone who had only been here a few years. Kamau told me of his experience in joining the crew after being captured.

We had been told to shine every cannon. While we were alone, Kamau told me more about where he came from.

"It's a small village, called Dogo, a few miles from the coast. I had a mom and a sister. I never knew my father though. He was taken when I was young. I was taken at eight years old. There was a castle on the coast of my country. It was known as *Ngome ya Kifo*." His voice was like velvet and each syllable danced off the tip of his tongue, free of the throatiness of more northern languages.

"The Death Castle. Because so many were brought there before they lost their homeland forever. They wanted me to go to the Westlands, to work the land. I was put aboard a ship and made to serve a brute of a man. I was there for at least eight years. Maybe closer to ten."

He reached up and rubbed his head. The air below deck grew stale and hot. Kamau peeled off his shirt and I envied his ability to get some relief from the lack of linen. I felt suffocated in all the layers I donned. I still had a piece of cloth tied tight against my chest beneath the thick shirt and vest I wore. I cursed my Playadan heritage that sculpted the mountains of my breasts.

"A lot of us were tied up because they thought we would fight back. I was shoved in the bottom of the ship with a hundred other men, all with our wrists bound and hidden away from the sun. I thought we would die before ever making it across.

"Many of the crew members fell ill and died. And they needed people to man the ship. So, some of us were unbound and learned how to sail. I watched a lot of those men get whipped for taking extra food down to the others who were still tied. Some were even thrown overboard. I wanted to do more, but I knew they would kill me.

"I feel like a coward now, but when we stopped at a city in Aldina, I ran. I wished I would have freed some of those men, but I wanted to live. After my escape, I lived on the streets. I found work at the docks. Rich merchants pay well to have their ships shined before their next voyage.

"The captain of the ship I once served arrived in the city a few years later. He had a woman with him, with dark skin like mine. But aside from his crew, there were no other people aboard. She was dressed in a ballgown, and she looked lost and frightened. I followed them to a tavern where he took her to his room. He left a while on business I assumed.

"She was on the bed, her dress torn and welts on her body. I tried to get her to leave, but she was scared. I lost my language because I was taken so young. I didn't know what she was saying.

"He came back and saw me with her, and thought I—"

He gave me a look, and I nodded at him to go on. I hadn't realized I had stopped shining the cannon, my fingers clenched around the cloth.

"Well, he came for me with a knife. He was very drunk and he missed. Now, at that point I had never killed anyone, but he went to grab the lady. I got the knife from his hands and took it to his neck without another thought. I spilled his blood all over that floor.

"I looked at the lady, thinking she would be happy that I had freed her. But no. She came after me then. Trying to scratch me and hit me and she was so loud. She called the attention of everyone in that tavern. I recognized a word she said repeatedly. Husband. They would have had me arrested and killed. I fled to the docks. Malin was just about to leave. I begged him to let me aboard. I didn't tell anyone what I did for a while, but after a year or so, I got drunk and the story came out. I thought Malin would turn me away, being that I was a murderer. I murdered my captain and someone's husband. But he didn't say anything about it. Just asked me to remain loyal to him."

The ship's motto rang in my ears. "Loyal 'til Death." If Kamau, who had seen just how cruel men could be, still served Malin, I knew I could too.

I had heard plenty of stories since I had boarded. In return, they got pieces of my story. Some ambiguity and half-truths. I didn't hide that I was half Brannish or that I aimed to go back. I held back about my mother. I did not know how to speak lightly of her being tried as a Spriggan. I had never been a liar, but I reminded myself it was for my safety. They couldn't know I fled because of her legacy, or that I was a woman, or that I was once a Don's daughter, now bastard. I was growing to trust some of the men, but not enough to reveal myself fully. There was also my promise to keep to Malin to not reveal my womanhood.

I suppose they may have thought me shallow, or perhaps just young and inexperienced in the world. My story, as I told it to both Grey and Kamau was:

My father was a soldier for the Playadan army and had fallen in love with a Brannish woman. When the war ended, he returned home and she followed, hoping to be with her love, but she found him dead. She instead married another Playadan man with some money, and I was their bastard. She never told him of my real father. She got the plague when I was young and he raised me as his own, but he had since remarried, and I felt like a stranger in their house. So, I aimed to go back to Brannland, to find my mother's family.

It didn't have the same level of romance and adventure, but it was safe. It told them enough without revealing too much.

I also could have told them that I was a runaway circus performer with a bounty on my head and they would have nodded along all the same.

I found myself in the Crow's Nest often, which at times was easier. I wasn't sure how Watson thought of me, but I knew he didn't think of me as any different than anyone else. Watson avoided the entire crew up in the Crow's Nest amongst his maps. He scribbled in his notebook and always had a wild look in his eyes. He may have been staring at the invisible horizon a moment too long. The idea that he had lived so close to the Wastes fascinated me and I pestered him about it as much as he would allow me to.

"Did you ever see twinkling lights, or hear bells?" I asked.

"I heard the wind and saw the stars," he replied, not looking up from his notebook.

"What of ghostly women? Women in black or white?"

"I saw women of all shapes and sizes."

"Have you ever had someone ask to be allowed to enter your dwelling?"

"We kept to ourselves."

Despite my curiosity, I knew when to quit. He hadn't meant to tell me of the Wastes and now he would avoid the topic at all costs. But he still entertained me with other topics.

"What started the war between Playada and Aldina?"

That was when he would shut his book and tell me exactly how the damn land-grabbing Aldinians needed to extend their power south and Playada was their key to claiming the more southern countries, even as far as Kamau's.

"It's all about power. They need all the power in the world so everyone thinks they are the most successful empire that has ever stood. But it will be their downfall one day. Mark my words, those damn Aldinians will get what's coming to them."

And then there was Briggs who still made sure to remind me I was still unwanted aboard.

There was the night I found a dead fish in my sack after sleeping on it for two hours. The stench took a while to penetrate, and I realized it was all over me. I'm sure one could imagine how hard it was to get the stink out on a boat surrounded with sea water and limited fresh water. I would not be given a bath until we made our next stop.

He also swapped my ale for piss, burnt the ends of my hair, and put a small squid in my hat. I kept my composure, but he was getting close to my last bit of patience.

"What is his problem?" I huffed at Grey, digging the muck from my cap, my hair carefully wrapped up in cloth.

"He's a bored kid who finally has someone to terrorize," he shrugged. "It's tradition to harass the newest recruit. He'll get bored of you eventually."

It didn't seem like that time would be soon, but I kept my indifference the best I could.

The crew was called down to the main deck at nightfall with three rings of the bell. I was half asleep when I heard the thunder of boots climbing the steps. No one had informed me there would be a midnight meeting on the main deck. I grabbed my cloak to see what was going on.

"Men," Stratford addressed the crew. Briggs and The Monk, shirtless to show the tattoos that ran down his copper back, stood beside him, their faces curved with sly grins. "We're two leagues off the coast from Port Orem. We will be there well before the sun rises. You know the drill. But I will explain for the new recruits," he added, rolling his eyes in my direction.

Briggs also shot me an annoyed glance. Pardon me for not living years aboard the *Raider* and taking part in whatever it was that Stratford was talking about.

"We take the *Lillian* while she's unsuspecting. Her crew is likely in town and we can easily deal with those who remain. If ye get caught, ye get left behind."

That was the entirety of Stratford's informative speech. The men dispersed and went back to their games while they approached land.

"What did any of that mean?" I nudged Grey.

"Port Orem is a major trading post where the castle receives a lot of their imports. The *Lillian* is a small vessel, but known to carry fineries for the king—things that come from the east that could make us a pretty penny in the capital markets."

"What do I do?"

"As cabin boy, you'll remain on the *Raider*. You'll haul up the loot and notify Watson or Jenkins if we've been caught."

I nodded. Should be easy enough. A part of me was unnerved by the thought of being involved in my first pirate raid. The other was absolutely thrilled.

After an hour of drinking rum and prepping cannons, the *Lillian* was spotted. We approached Port Orem quietly, all ship lanterns snuffed. Lights from the other ships glittered along the black waters of the bay. Even though we prepared to attack, there was comfort in seeing another ship with land behind it after weeks of nothing.

It was well into the night and there was no moon in the sky. The other men were prepped for the raid—pistols on their side, daggers in their sheaths. They were dressed in black, and Stratford had removed all the jingling jewels he normally wore. Briggs' chest was puffed out and his head was inflated well past his skull. The Monk had shaved both his and Briggs' heads clean in some ceremonial battle custom of his people. Briggs had received a promotion to Stratford's third, behind Kamau, making him more arrogant than usual. It baffled me that the boy deserved such a title.

Malin remained in his quarters. Stratford would command the raid and answer only to Jenkins. If things went south, then they were permitted to bother Malin.

The *Wind Raider* glided across the waters without a sound, all men on high alert. As they approached the coastline, the waters became rougher. The waves slammed the sides of the boat in a way that caught my breath. Grey stood at the helm and guided us toward the *Lillian*. It was a modest ship, but the lanterns on the boat lit up the gold masts and red sails. They represented the colors of the king's coat of arms. And sitting proud at the helm was a golden lion, caught in a roar.

The two ships were now parallel to one another.

It may have been my nerves surrounding a possible battle so far from land, but as Jagged Everett lowered the anchor, it sounded like someone ringing a gong to announce our arrival.

But the *Lillian* remained still, and the pirates began climbing up the side of the boat. The men slid over the side of the railing and dropped down to the dinghy below. Briggs went down first, followed by Stratford, the Monk, and Grey. Kamau stayed beside Jenkins, ready to jump into action should anything go wrong. And Watson was perched in the Crow's Nest.

The other men were told to stay below with the cannons or to bugger off until the deed was done.

I gripped the railing while the other men were across. I could not see the action that was occurring on the *Lillian*, but I could hear their boots and muffled screams. The men were gone for only minutes. Watson could likely see everything, but his face did not show any concern.

Briggs appeared first, climbing back over the boat. He had a dark wood chest with him, as well as a grin on his face. I let down the chains and helped him haul it up to the *Wind Raider*. I definitely considered dropping him in the sea below, but that would have sabotaged the mission. Now wasn't the time to get revenge. But even though Briggs was not much larger than me, I struggled to help him get back on the ship. Kamau stood behind me and helped me heave both Briggs and the chest to the main deck.

One by one, the men brought their loot back aboard. I waited for a cannon or a gun blast from the *Lillian*, but none came. And before sunrise, we were back on open water.

There was a sense of freedom and getting away with their treasure without being caught, but my mood soured when I saw the coastline disappear behind us.

"We can't stop where we loot," Kamau said, seeing my wandering eyes.

Briggs had laid out their plunder on the deck and looked proudly at his own loot, like a cat proud of his dead rat. I eyed the blood on his shirt.

"Are you alright?" I asked, surprised by my own concern.

Briggs eyed the splatter and laughed. "Must have been the watchman." There was a wicked glint in his eye.

I remembered the brief scream I had heard across on the other ship. Briggs had killed one of them.

When Malin came out of his cabin and walked down the steps to the lower deck, the men grew quiet and waited for his word. Malin looked upon each pile but gave no notion of pride or appreciation for each man who had conquered it. He dipped his pinky in a container from one of the piles and tasted it. I didn't know what the powder was. Drugs or spices. Malin stowed it in his own pocket.

"Good work, Stratford," he finally said to the battle master. "This will be enough to sell in Astreim and fund our voyage this year." Malin promptly went back to his rooms, taking only the strange powder and a roll of parchment, leaving the rest of the men to pack away the treasure and go on with their nights.

It was nearly sunrise, but no one slept. Peel got up and made everyone biscuits and I helped pass out mugs of rum. I even took one myself and the night was spent in drunken bliss. When I had first tried the drink, it made me self-conscious and restricted and utterly sick. Now, it made my head feel like it flew through the clouds, like I could forget myself for a while. The men sang shanties, and I joined in for the chorus, learning the repetition and rhythm of their sea-faring songs.

My head was in the stars, but my belly was full. I climbed up to sit with Watson in Crow's Nest when the pirates began settling down and going off to bed.

"How were we not caught?" I asked.

"This will be your first of many raids, Finn," Watson replied. "And you'll see there's a reason we're called the *Wind Raiders*. We've been pirating a long time. We come in the night and take what we please and are gone before anyone knows better."

"Did Briggs really kill someone?" I asked. I knew that most of these men had killed. There were too many stories of pirate murders to deny it, but I had thought for a little while it could have been legend. Until I saw it with my own eyes.

Watson shrugged. "It's all a part of doing business."

The thought of killing made my stomach churn. Stealing was one thing—I had enough sense to reason that we were stealing from the Crown. Between being southern and now a pirate, thievery from the monarch did not clash with my morals.

But killing was different. The *Lillian's* crew, while employed by the Crown, were not members of it. The traders and peasants of Aldina likely did not want the war any more than the Playadans did. I would never say that out loud though. Watson cursed anyone with a connection to the Crown, despite technically being Aldinian himself.

That watchman's life was taken so the *Wind Raiders* could steal riches from the King of Aldina. But he had a family. He had manned his post and followed orders. He was killed merely for being on the wrong shift, and that seemed a tragic waste of a life. And Briggs shrugged it off like it was nothing.

I took another swig of rum, then took my leave from Watson, ready to fall asleep while my head still spun in circles. I pushed away the thoughts of the lost life for the sake of sleep. But I took a vow that night that I would not kill another in the name of piracy, no matter the circumstance.

VII. Midnight Swim

Malin called upon me the morning after the raid. I had been in the kitchen, helping Peel sort through the spices we had stolen from the *Lillian*. As excited as I was to have some new flavors for our meals, I was also trying not to hurl at the smell of all the pungent herbs.

Peel clapped me on the back with force. "Ah, boy, just need to throw back some *bakis*." He offered me a drink that smelled like even more alcohol. I pushed it away.

"Santana," Jenkins barked at me, swinging open the door so it hit the tin barrel that was behind it.

The ringing ran through me.

"What?" I groaned.

"Cap'n would like to see you."

I sighed, took Peel's whisky drink and followed Jenkins to Malin's quarters.

Malin, Watson, and Stratford all sat around the desk, obviously waiting for me to arrive with Jenkins. Watson stood and offered me his chair. I tried not to think too hard about the fact that all of the officers of the ship were in there waiting for me.

"How are we today, Finn?" Malin asked.

I sipped the whisky and was surprised to find it mixed with honey. "I'm faring well." I wondered if they could see the bags under my eyes.

Malin pulled out a piece of parchment from a stack and placed it in front of me. "We uncovered plenty of goods that we'll sell in Astreim to prepare for our next few months. But this was the most valuable thing we uncovered."

There was no talk of the events of the night before. It was just another day of work, with no regard that lives were lost by our own's hands. It was uncomfortable, but I buried these feelings. I was a pirate now, and my captain would not coddle me as I mourned lost life.

I looked at the top of the page. It was a sheet of notes written by a Brannish officer, Janne Norberg.

"Of course, because the *Lillian* had it, they could also have the secrets it carries. But that's beside the point. Translate this and tell us what it says."

The three men were staring at me as I looked over the notes.

"He says that they've sailed three months west to a place that reminds him of the old country." I furrowed my brow. Translating was not difficult, but reading in my current state proved to be. The words were dripping off the page.

I continued, "Many of their men have taken ill, and the captain wanted to stop on an island in the middle of the Occidental Ocean. But he urged the captain to keep sailing. There was a ship after them, *Föraktad Förmögenhet* which means the *Scorned Fortune*."

"That ship sunk fifty years ago," Watson said. "Used to be manned by a fellow named Savage. There are stories that there were several Savages who all claimed to be the same man."

"Maybe they got the treasure," Malin said, waving his hand as he spoke. His new ruby ring glittered beneath the lantern light. "Keep reading, Finn."

"The chest was safe from them in this place with green hills and jagged cliffs. It was tucked away in a cave and they put an enchantment on it with the Spriggan they held captive. And the key..."

Norberg's writing ran off the page. He had run out of room and yet did not simply grab a new sheet. He smudged the words together in the corner of the page, the letters bleeding together.

"What's the key?" Malin asked, his voice with a sharp edge.

En droppe älva blod.

"Fae blood." A chill went through me.

Malin's lip curled, his eyes sparkling devilishly. "We get to go hunting."

I didn't understand. My mother had always said Brannland was the one place that faerie folk and people lived in peace. Yet, Norberg and the other Brannish sailors had captured one and used their blood to lock away the treasure.

Until that moment, I hadn't been sure if I believed in the faerie folk. I thought Spriggan were just accused witches like my mother and all that she told me were stories of things people had not taken the time to understand.

But as the officers of the *Wind Raider* clinked glasses at my discovery, I was beginning to question what I believed. The way they spoke, it seemed like our travels would lead us to a real fae in order to use its blood. They pushed the bottle of rum in my direction, clapping me on the back. I merely shook my head, holding up my half full mug of whisky. If Peel's concoction was meant to fix my splitting head, it wasn't working. The pirates took no notice, though, of my squinting eyes or my refusal to celebrate. Stratford followed me out of Malin's quarters, rambling on about the task ahead.

"Ah, Finn, you've just found us the ticket! And we get to spear one of those buggers in the process." He clapped me on the back, his rum falling on my boot, but he didn't seem to notice. He even broke out in song.

"And we'll rant and we'll roar like true brutish sailors,

oh we'll rant and we'll roar on all the salt seas.

Until we strike soundings in the channel of old Brannland.

From Playada to Astreim is thirty-five leagues."

He let the last word ring off his lips, directly into my head.

He finally let me be and I wiped the rum from my pants and boot. When I looked up, Briggs was giving me a rather sour look. I rolled my eyes and went down to the bunks to grab a nap. Let him be jealous that his commanding officer liked me.

I tried to remember more stories that my mother had told me of the fae.

"Are they small?" I had once asked while she let me braid her hair.

"Not all. Some are bigger than you are."

"But why do we call them wee folk?"

"Presumptions mostly," she replied. "And there is a famous tale of a wee folk playing a trick on the king. He gained an awful reputation because of it."

The story was told of a king who was pompous and proud and thought all of his ability to rule was sourced in the jewels he wore and the robes he bore. He was quite flashy with his style, attracting a small fae to take up a job at the castle as a jester. For many months, he simply made the king and his court laugh, but slowly, each time the jester performed, a jewel went missing. The king did not notice at first, being that he was adorned in hundreds of jewels but this went on for a year, and the jester fled the palace with more than half of what the king once wore, taking his belongings to the land of the faeries where they sang songs of the foolish king. This was just one of the tales that painted fae to be thieves and tricksters.

"And are they?" I asked Mama.

"Well, yes," she admitted, "from everything I have come to understand of fae, having never met one personally, I do believe they can be a tricky group of beings. But wouldn't you be too if someone kept trying to take your land and pushing you to remote corners of the world?"

When the captain did not require my services and Peel was ahead on his cooking, I spent my time reading or asking questions. I did not want to be seen as daft. I was determined to become just as capable as any man aboard the ship in my time there. That meant pestering the two most knowledgeable men aboard the ship: Watson and Peel.

Both men were good at their jobs but could also tell you the jobs of every man aboard, and while they may not be in any primary position of command, they were respected. Throughout the afternoon, I watched as Grey, Hagley, or even Briggs would come up the Crow's Nest to ask Watson a question specific to their station. Watson had climbed the ranks since he was a young man and had done every single job on the boat at one time or another.

Peel may have always been the cook, but he filled his head with knowledge so even he knew a lot about how the ship was operated. I knew if I ever wanted to climb rank, or even just gain a shred of respect, I needed to know what I was talking about. I did not have the advantage of spending my childhood on a ship like Briggs. I may still be the age many of these men were when they started, but I still felt pathetically behind despite my time with Mateo on the fishing boat. I had come to accept that his cutter was a children's toy compared to the *Raider*.

Malin had a decent sized library in his cabin and did not mind when I borrowed the books, requiring that I only return them and to try not to spill anything on the pages. Some read like manuals which could have bored me to death, but I learned how the rigging was the system of ropes, wires and chains used to support and operate the masts, sails, booms and yards of a ship. I learned that a boom is a spar along the foot of a fore and aft rigged sail, that greatly improves control of the angle and shape of the sail. The primary action of the boom is to keep the foot flatter when the sail angle is away from the centerline of the boat.

At first, knowing all the functions of the ship seemed arbitrary and needless, but when a single sail got caught in the mast, or there was a rip, I could see how the piece of fabric affected the *Raider*'s trajectory and caused it to veer off until it could be mended.

I read about the greatest captains in history. Those books talked of those who worked for the Crown and established trade routes that brought riches to the king. While that wasn't the goal for a pirate lord, it was those trade routes that provided the pirate ships opportunity to loot and to conquer. Knowing the footprints of the naval captains paved the pirates' way to success. As I read, I jotted these thoughts down on a leather-bound notebook that Malin had allowed me to have.

"Are you sure?" I asked. It seemed like quite the gift for his cabin boy.

"Think nothing of it. You did fine work over those Brannish notes. Least I can do."

I began filling it with all the nautical knowledge I could. I thought that if I knew enough, I would stop appearing as the daftest on the ship.

I was reading about northern sea channels and passageways within the frozen lands when Jenkins barked at me, "Santana! Go tighten the ratline on the foreyard."

I didn't know why he chose me and not one of the other crewmates, but I realized I knew what he was talking about. I had gathered that information from one of the dull manuals I had borrowed from Malin. The other men were playing dice and I proudly marched to the loose rope on the front mast of the ship and pulled it tight with a hitch knot.

I looked up at Jenkins who gave no notion of approval or disapproval. He didn't give me any further commands so I figured I did it right.

To my dismay, none of the crew had noticed, or even looked up to see me perform the task. Because knowledge didn't impress them. Especially knowledge they had when they were lads of twelve. Only raw strength and bravery can impress men who grew up on the sea.

We were still several days from Astreim. I had fallen asleep on the main deck at some point in the evening with a mug in my hand and a book on my chest. Some of the other men were nearby drinking ale, and I had paid no mind to them. I went along reading until my eyes grew heavy. I had fallen asleep on deck before and woken to the complete darkness that took over the sea when our lanterns had all been blown out.

Often, I'd wake up to solitude. With no one on deck, and all the men below, there is an eerie loneliness that takes over. For a moment, one forgets that there's anyone left in the world. In those moments, it's hard not to remember, that even when I was amongst people, or when the crew was nearby on the main deck, I was still alone in this world. I had no living family, aside from the man who I once believed was my father.

I tried to not feel empty, but sometimes it was hard to reason with myself why I continued to push. I had dreams of going to Brannland, but I didn't know what I expected to find if I ever made it there. My mother had left to follow a Playadan soldier more than two decades before. And I was sailing after ghosts with nothing more than the hope that there were still people in the north who would know who my mother was. They probably didn't even know I exist.

The list Lupe had given me was safe in my pocket, but also committed to my memory:

Vivanka's family:
Runa - sister
Alma - mother
Nils - brother
Goran - father

It had been twenty-one years since she had left. Lupe had shown me a letter written by her sister, but even that was nearly a decade before. Who was to say that any of these people were still there, or that I would be warmly received. If she was willing to follow my father, maybe there was nothing left for her in her home. Perhaps she was once as empty as I felt.

I was not depressed. Nor was I hopeless. I just had a twisted sense of purpose. My purpose up until I left was to be the dutiful daughter. And now it was whatever task that Malin gave me. I could not foresee how living in Brannland might give me a new purpose. I knew little of their customs, especially those surrounding women. What if I was told again that I must marry and birth children? I prayed my mother was not of noble birth so that perhaps I would be free of such pressures.

Idealistically, I hoped there was a family there for me, but one that may inspire me and encourage me to find myself within my mother's culture. I could learn more of her *Spriggan* ways. I'd make a good herbalist. Or apothecary. I could cure their sick and tend to their wounded. I had enough knowledge based on my mother's teachings.

I just could not stomach the idea that what waited for me on the other side of the world was more patriarchy. More talk of my role as a woman. There was a bit of regret in my gender. I could not help but think how much simpler the world would be if I had been born a man. I would not be binding my breasts and condemned to a never-ending sore throat from my forced pitch change. I wondered if I was permanently ruining my voice in speaking this way.

Perhaps the men and I would take to each other more quickly. I had made friends and counted myself lucky on that front. But it seemed I was constantly calculating what to say or not say so as to conceal my lies and deception. Sooner or later I was sure to say the wrong thing, and they would see me for what I was. Then I would find myself left behind. Or dead.

But Malin let me aboard, I reminded myself. He knew what I was. It was just his men I needed to deceive, all while he knew my true identity. This offered enough comfort to quiet my mind, and I drifted into a brief sleep, my book on my chest beneath the stars.

When I awoke that night, it was not to reflect on my solitude. No. I awoke to hands on each of my limbs, lifting me off the deck.

Briggs and Grover, hoisted me up and I was thrown over Briggs' shoulder. Grey and Kamau were nearby, drinking from their mugs, not bothering to come to my aid.

"What the hell?" I screamed. I did not speak in the voice I had molded to fit Finn Santana. I didn't give a damn in that moment, knowing whatever reason Briggs had for handling me was sinister.

Briggs reeked of rum and cackled as he carried me closer to the edge of the ship. "You're lighter than I expected."

"Put me down!" I shrieked.

"I shall," he promised.

But that was when we were at the edge of the boat, and he set me on the railing where I teetered back, using all the balance I had to not fall. I leveled myself and glared down at him. I tried to climb down, but Briggs blocked my way.

"I'm going to give you a choice," he told me, his rancid breath inches from my face. "You can jump. Then I'll let a rope down and help you up. You have my word," he said, putting his hand to his heart, as if that made him more sincere. "Or I push you and we can pick up your corpse on the way back from the Astreim."

I couldn't believe him. I knew he had the maturity of a boy, but I did not think Briggs was dangerous. I underestimated him. It was my mistake to think that pranks could be innocent. I only wish I could have gotten back at him before it came to this.

I looked down at the black waters. My fears of unseen sea beasts resurfaced. I could be eaten before a rope ever hit my hands. I wanted to believe that Briggs's cruelness was not so dire that he would leave me to drown in the ocean. But that wouldn't be something worth betting my life on. My crewmates watched as I thought through my choices. I could not live with myself if I allowed them to continue to see me as a coward.

Grover cackled like a porpoise. I never trusted that he had anything but gunk between his ears.

I looked in Kamau's eyes, and he seemed indifferent. Likely too drunk to rationalize how cruel they were being.

Finally to Grey, who gave me a single nod. Out of them all, I trusted Grey to stick to his word and hoist me back up once I accomplished Briggs's sick form of initiation. This could be settled once and for all.

I looked at Briggs right in his toad-like face. He grinned as he waited for me to make my move.

"See you in hell," I spat right in his eyes and plunged into the waters below.

The anxiety of being alone aboard the ship was nothing compared to the anxiety of sinking amidst miles and miles of vast ocean. Terror swept over me as soon as my body made contact with the waves. All around me was dark and cold and empty. Though it dawned on me that I wasn't alone.

I was surrounded with the great sea beasts, the ones who moaned and howled throughout the night while we feigned deaf ears. Though shivers traveled our spines, even the bravest of men did not want to acknowledge the mysterious creatures swimming in the miles of water beneath us. On the ship, we could pretend the weathered wood and open air included a barrier of protection from the savage beasts of the ocean. But as I sank in the dark waters, I was vulnerable to anything with teeth that wished to rip me to shreds.

But I couldn't succumb to that fear, or I'd surely die. I thanked any god who would listen that I could swim. When I broke the surface, as promised, a thick rope was thrown a few yards out. I kicked furiously until it found my hand, then swam with leaden legs as the bastards pulled me in.

I wriggled over the railing, then collapsed on the deck, taking large breaths of air. My shirt clung to my breasts and my long hair fell over my shoulders. Mateo's hat was lost to the waves. The list Lupe had given me was in a soaked wad, illegible. My hand flew to my neck, and I was relieved to find my vial of ash, unharmed. I hadn't thought to toss it aside before jumping, but she was still there.

The men gawked at me as I stood and rung out my clothes and hair. I didn't think this would be the night my crew discovered I was a woman. But I had passed Briggs's test. Hopefully they would no longer see me as a coward.

I met their gazes. Kamau and Grey averted their eyes after taking a prolonged glance at me. Grover looked even more dumb than usual. And Briggs could only stare.

"I bid thee goodnight," I curtsied low in front of Briggs, whose mouth was still open. The men watched as I retreated to the bunks where I shivered the entire night in my damp clothes.

When I awoke, it was to a new pair of pants and a shirt, set on the floor beside my bed. Briggs, I presumed, even left me my hat, smeared with the salt of sea water.

The sun rose, and there was no mention of the night before. Briggs stayed out of my way in the days leading to our arrival in Astreim. Kamau, Grey, and Grover seemed to acknowledge me differently, with a scant more respect. But they said nothing. I continued as if nothing happened, though I could not deny my pleasure that I had finally proven myself to Briggs.

VIII. Part of the Crew

"You're going to want to hold the dagger tight, like this," Grey said, placing the hilt in my hand, and arranging my fingers to secure it properly. "And aim low. You go flailing it too high and your attacker will easily swipe it from you."

Grey had been giving me lessons in combat when there was time to spare. Thus far, he had taught me how to load a pistol, and about the delay in firing it. But that day, we practiced more close-range combat, should I be jumped in an alley or taken unsuspectingly amidst a raid. He showed me where to stab should I ever become grappled with someone and I only had my dagger. I was instructed to always have my dagger strapped to my side, concealed so that even if I was told to drop my weapons, it was still within reach.

It had been four days since I had jumped off the ship, and all four boys who were present remained quiet about it. But they all adjusted their behavior toward me in their own way.

Grey insisted on teaching me to defend myself, claiming any good sailor should know what to do in case of attack. He chose his words carefully, appearing to take extra care because he knew me to be a woman, as if this meant I couldn't defend myself. It was in sharp contrast to his lack of defense when he thought me a seventeen-year-old boy, when I was ordered to jump twenty feet into the bottomless sea.

Kamau and I still did small jobs together, and he would politely engage me in small talk.

"Fair winds today," he commented one day as we untangled old ropes.

"Not as hot either," I agreed, nodding.

"No, it's been quite pleasant."

I smirked. He had never said anything like "quite pleasant" before, but now he spoke to me in a much more Aldinian way, cutting off the bits of pirate-speak from his vocabulary.

Grover avoided me. He and I had never gotten along, and I rarely spoke to him. My opinion of him being a baffoon had not changed and he did not feel the need to prove me wrong.

And Briggs... Well Briggs kept being Briggs.

He watched Grey and I practice knife movements, leaning against the railing and snorting when I made a misstep or wasn't able to make contact with the dummy Grey had crafted out of burlap sacks and straw.

"Wanna fill in?" Grey asked, holding out the dummy towards him.

He scoffed. "No, I just don't think that *Finn* will ever be the swordsman she thinks she will be."

I rolled my eyes. It was a pain with him knowing I was a girl, but he still never said anything when anyone was in earshot. Only when we were in private to try and get a rise out of me. Instead of giving him the satisfaction, I continued to close in on my target and focus on stabbing its weak points.

Briggs grew bored with me soon enough and left Grey and I to focus on our lesson.

"Wanna learn about cannons?" he asked me.

I nodded, both eager and intimidated.

He took me down below, where the twelve cannons sat all in a row awaiting their chance at battle. They were intimidating, but when he started to show me the mechanics, I realized it wasn't much different than a handgun.

Grey had me use the jammer to force down the black powder, and then several wads of cloth, followed by the cannon ball that was an impressive mass for only being the size of an orange. Then I poured the powder in the touch hole.

"Now," Grey said, while he held the unlit piece of string, "you musn't be afraid of it. It's a lot of power, and there will be a kick back, but there's no room for hesitation, especially if we're amidst battle. Understood?"

I nodded. I tried not to show on my face as I calculated the potential kickback in something the size of the cannon when the small pistols were enough to jolt me back a half step.

"Once I light it, there will be a three second delay. But I want you to hold your aim. Those three seconds are gonna feel like an eternity."

I went behind the cannon and tried not to make it obvious that the metal barrel was nearly all I could manage to lift. Grey gave me a look to let me know he was about to light the wick.

I braced myself, waiting for the explosion to come. Those three seconds truly did feel like forever. I was so tempted to drop the cannon and give my shaking muscles a break, but I remained fixed on the cloud that Grey had instructed me to aim at. Finally, there was a boom and I watched as my cannonball did a perfect arc through the air.

"Well done," Grey said. "A lot of fellows aim too low which means the ball falls short and never makes contact. That ball would have made a nice hole in the belly of a ship from a few hundred yards out or so."

"What the hell is going on down here?" Jenkins came storming down the steps.

"Just showing Finn some basic battle practices," Grey said casually.

I looked at Jenkins, whose face was aghast. I hadn't thought we were doing anything wrong, but the first mate's expression said differently.

"You're wasting good cannonballs on the lad," he shot back.

"He's a good shot," Grey countered. "Taught him to use that pistol and he gets his target within inches every time."

"Is that so?" Jenkins put his hands on his hips. He called above, "Briggs!"

The Kid appeared within a moment. He'd likely come to eavesdrop when he saw the first mate on his way to scold me.

Jenkins brought us above and set up targets on the side of the ship, giving both of us a pistol. It was clear what he wanted: me, the novice sailor, who had never engaged in combat to face off against the Sailing Master's apprentice. It was a chance to put both of us in our place which was why I needed to beat Briggs.

"You get three shots," Jenkins told us. "Try and get the shots as close to each other as possible. We're looking for accuracy. Got it?"

I nodded. Grey and I had only fired the pistol together three or so times, the first time being the previous day. He had always been there to instruct me through it, but this time I had to go off of my memory and hope I was as good of a shot as Grey insisted I was. I'd never hear the end of it if I wasn't.

Many of the men gathered on the main deck, watching as Briggs and I prepared. Jenkins had brought targets from below, both with a new piece of canvas across them. He had drawn a quick target in red paint with a clear bullseye in the center.

Our weapons were readied, the flint rotated to half-cock and three rounds loaded.

"Don't let the gun scare you, Santana," Briggs spat.

I rolled my eyes. "It's pretty sad that Stratford's apprentice is all talk."

Some of the men chuckled and Briggs's fleshy cheeks went scarlet.

"I've been on this ship since before you grew breasts."

I nearly faltered, but kept my face neutral at his attempt to unnerve me by revealing my secret. As far as I could tell, no one noticed, only chuckling at what they thought was an apparent dig. I knew not to let his remarks get to me, though I burned from anger. I had thought jumping in the ocean was enough to get him off my back, but I suppose I had Jenkins to blame this time for our rivalry.

"Ready!" he called. "Aim! Fire!"

Expecting the delay, I held the pistol steady even as it kicked in my hand a second later. My bullet aimed true, missing the very center only by a half inch to the left. I couldn't suppress my smile. I looked to Briggs's target and his bullet had landed quite near the same distance as mine.

"Ready!" Jenkins called again without pause. "Aim! Fire!"

Again my bullet went sailing, this time a little to the right, leaving the center wide open for that third shot.

"Ready! Aim—"

BOOM!

I nearly jumped back, but stayed steady, the bullet landing directing in the center of the target.

There was a roar of cheers but Jenkins shook his head. "You were early."

"So?" Grey asked, standing beside me now that the round had gone off. "Finn hit it dead center."

"But he didn't follow protocol," Jenkins said. "If Briggs makes his mark he wins."

Jenkins called Briggs off to fire. His bullet almost hit the mark, except it was a good two inches from the center. I whipped my head to the first mate, ready to accept my victory.

"Briggs wins," Jenkins said, looking me in the eyes, "for following directions."

There was more than just Grey and I who were unhappy with these results. "You have gotta be kiddin' me," Grey scoffed. "This was a friendly wager. Not an official match."

"And she didn't follow protocol," Jenkins shrugged. "So, naturally, Briggs wins."

This time, the mention of my sex didn't go unnoticed.

"She?"

"Finn's a lass?"

I could feel the heat rising to my cheeks as murmurings and side glances came from all directions. Jenkins may not have witnessed my jump off of the ship, but he was Malin's first mate, so it didn't come as a surprise to me that he knew. It did, however, bruise my pride.

"Fine," I said in a level voice, whipping my gaze from the first mate to the Kid as I held my head high. "Briggs wins by default. I hope you're happy with your win based on technicality." I nodded to the targets which clearly showed who the better shot was.

I couldn't say for sure if the first mate had meant to expose me. But I felt damn near naked up on that quarterdeck.

Nothing more was said—about my superior shot or about my being a woman. I think many thought perhaps the first mate made a mistake, though I got more careful looks. The men walked slowly around me, their eyes peering me up and down. My efforts to appear as a male were not strong to begin with and things were quickly falling apart. Perhaps it was time to release myself from the falsities. But I had made a vow to Malin to keep my secret and I did not want to cross the captain's wishes.

I stormed to the crew's quarters to read my book by the gun holes, with the men leering at my backside as I stomped away.

It was as if I had never left Playada. The men looked at me like I was a curse. Everyone knew a woman was bad luck on a ship. I would bring storms, doldrums, and sea beasts. The gods would ensure we didn't arrive at our destination. But just like at home, no one told me this directly, but their sideways glances let me know what they truly thought.

"Who are you really, Finn?" Grey asked me while he stood at the helm and I sat on the step behind him reading about naval combat. I had read the line "Many conflicts between passing ships resulted in underwater archaeological sites such as the *Rhodarian Boneyard* in the Sepsarian Sea" at least seven times. My mind could not stay with the words on the page.

"Hm?" I closed my book and pushed the brim up on my hat to meet his eyes. The sun beamed down on the ship. There weren't many places that offered shade unless you opted to roast with the stink and damp below deck. My skin had darkened considerably that month from light honey tones to rich bronze.

"You told me a bit about where you're from, but I'm guessing it all wasn't exactly true."

I looked around. Grey and I were the only ones on the quarterdeck. Some men lounged about the main deck, the closest being Pierce, the doctor, and Jagged Everett. They were far enough away that I couldn't make out their conversation.

Watson was above us, but I was indifferent as to whether he heard us or not. The captain and Jenkins knew. As did Grey, Kamau,

Grover, and Briggs. The rest of the crew may not have known for certain, but after the shooting match, there was enough speculation in the air. It was only a matter of time before questions became answers and my lies were uncovered. I had been on the ship over a month and felt as though I were holding the veil of Finn Santana by a splitting thread.

"I haven't told anyone," Grey said, as if reading my mind. "I don't know about the others, but there's enough old timers aboard to still think it's bad luck for a woman to be on a ship."

"Where does that superstition come from?"

He shrugged. "Where do any sailor superstitions come from? All ships have them. Someone can say something—anything really—and it will become a superstition. On the *Queen Anne*, we had to carry salt in our pockets on the full moon to ward off angry sea demons."

Superstition was another way of saying permissible witchcraft. I knew plenty of people who performed rituals to ward off supposedly magical occurrences. A pocket full of salt would ward off sea demons, but tossing salt over your shoulders as offering to faeries was unacceptable. I was reminded of the upside-down broom Señora Ries kept by her door.

I had reached for it, but Mateo stopped me.

"What?"

"Mama keeps it there like that," he'd replied.

"Why?"

He looked away, embarrassed by the custom. "It deters unwelcome visitors from knocking."

"Yet here I am," I'd jested, "so it must not work."

A common superstition is almost always rooted from pagan traditions and many who follow these rules of life seem to overlook that.

"So, who are you?" Grey repeated now.

"Promise not to tell? Especially Briggs?"

"You have my word."

If it were anyone else on the ship, their word would have little to no value to me. But Grey had proven to have my back. He listened to every word I said without judgment. He taught me to fight. He spoke to me like a comrade rather than a woman to look after. I was growing to trust him more than the others.

"My name is Mayra Hidalgo and I was raised by el Don Guadalupe Hidalgo, one of the lords of Villaviciosa." I told him what I knew of my birth, then of my mother's hanging and why it had occurred. I told him of my life after, in the town that cursed my heritage. I told him of Carla and her plot to get me out of the picture, which could have ended in a fate like Vivanka's. And I told him about how the *Raider* was my only chance to finally get out and start over.

Grey didn't interrupt me as I spoke but took in each of my words, considering each element of my story with care.

"Malin hired me as a cabin boy, but also as a translator," I concluded. "He's after Brannish treasure and I've aided him in gathering clues as to where it may be."

"The dwarf's treasure?"

I nodded. "You know of it?"

"It's one of those old sailor's tales. Most ships know of it, but think if it did once exist, that its contents are lost amongst the sand at the bottom of the ocean."

He shook his head, putting aside that matter for the time being. "You're a lord's daughter? You don't seem like the other noblemen's daughters I've met."

I nodded. "Well, technically I'm the lord's niece."

Grey rubbed his chin considering all that I had told him. I felt the shift in his view of me. It was what I feared of people knowing who I was. Suddenly, I was incapable and meant to be protected rather than trained.

"Why pirates?" Grey asked. "You could have gotten a ride on a merchant ship, couldn't you?"

I shrugged. "I don't have endless options. My stepmother wishes me hung. I took the first opportunity I saw to get out. My father even asked Malin to take me. But I chose to work. My life was always a lie. Had my parents lived, I still would have been well-off as the daughter of a soldier. But I am not the typical lady, existing under the power of a husband. Had my mother lived, maybe we could have partnered in a business. I am not delicate, and I don't wish to be idle. This is why I learned to fish and sail, and why I came aboard this ship to learn to fight." I pause, considering the ways my life had changed in such a short amount of time. "I suppose I must learn to pillage and murder now, too."

Grey smirked at this, but the look of approval on his face reassured me. "You're more than capable as a member of this crew, Mayra," he said. "I don't ask because I think you're not. I ask because none of us necessarily chose this life. It came at a time when we were out of options and faced punishment for our crimes."

"We have that in common."

The light of understanding finally crossed his face. "I guess—I guess you're right."

"I'm not ready to let go of Finn Santana," I told him. "If you see me differently as a woman, so will everyone else, eventually. They all follow your lead. I'm finally proving to them I'm not useless and all that will be for nothing should they learn I'm a lord's daughter."

Grey nodded. "For the record, I don't see you as different."

"You weren't teaching me to defend myself before you saw my breasts," I shot back.

He turned back to the helm, guiding the wheel while we were out on vast open waters, but not before I saw the flash of scarlet flow to his cheeks. "Everyone should know how to defend themselves," he said simply, as if anyone with a working brain should know it.

IX. The Hanged

Port Astreim was less impressive than I had imagined. Growing up in a small village in the south, I heard many stories of the triumphant ruling country and had pictured a dazzling capital city. Clean streets and everyone fat in the belly from wealth. Even the animals seemed to prance in this land where everyone thrived. But those were the musings of a child that had never seen the world. In fact, I would daresay I was lucky to have grown up in Villaviciosa rather than in Astreim.

The palace loomed ahead of us, perched on a monstrous hill of decaying pasture. The colossal castle was made up of white pillars and gold towers, though it appeared dull and bedraggled under the slow-moving gray clouds overhead. The palace was surely a grossly overstated home for the spoiled king. It seemed this garish monstrosity served no other purpose than to remind the king's subjects of his wealth.

Driving this point home were the people of this land. The nobility walked the streets seemingly with blinders on, their noses in the air as they passed the hallowed and worn common folk. I dared a glance at the less fortunate of this town, my heart bleeding as I noticed the calamity of these people. So many were nursing a deformity or the long-term effects of illness. Several hobbled the streets with missing limbs, or hid their pock-marked faces behind shrouds. But it was the sight of the children that affected me most as I took in their missing fingers and welts along their arms and legs. Villaviciosa may have not been perfect, but children were fed and cared for, even if scrutinized. Here I saw a boy, no older than six, on a corner selling goat's milk and jam while his mother nursed a wailing baby. His eyes and cheeks were hollow from malnourishment.

The *Raider's* flags had been hidden below and we all wore merchant scarves, posing as a ship transporting goods from Playada. The crew walked along the roads while the commoners looked at us with suspicion for sure, but not malice.

We navigated the streets towards somewhere called the Sly Tavern.

"Max Sly knows Malin well," Grey explained. "We get him foreign wine and spirits when we're nearby and he lets us sleep there during our visits."

A bed sounded wonderful. And if it was a quality tavern there might be a bath in my future. I had not bathed since days before I boarded. Whiffs of myself drove me mad those first few weeks, but like all the others, I slowly dismissed the smell and the dirt I was caked with. I had dunked myself in the ocean just a few days prior so at least not all the dirt from Playada to Aldina still clung to me.

We'd gotten through the rougher area of the city and I thought we had seen the worst of it. Grey, Kamau, Briggs, and I ventured from the group a moment to fetch meat pies, dripping with butter and gravy, at a stand in the square. It was the most delectable thing I'd had in more than a month.

"Ugh, I don't think I could go back to fish stew after this," I said, my mouth full of pie crust. My fingers were greasy with oil, but I licked them clean.

"You're gonna hurt Peel's feelings if he hears you," Kamau joked, his lips also shining with grease.

We washed it down with swigs of rum from our flasks. I had become accustomed to keeping one on my belt like the others. To think, a month before I had never tasted rum. Now, my mind was in a constant state of fuzziness, and my limbs free of aches as long as I kept up the steady stream of spirits.

After we had our fill, we made our way back towards where the lads said the tavern was. Every turn led to a maze of alleyways, and it was hard to tell if we were lost or on the right path, or if we were just plain drunk.

"You just make a left up here, I think," Briggs muttered.

"You think?" I groaned.

"I know where I'm going," he shot back.

I rolled my eyes. Briggs, of course, had to pose as the leader, taking us down more dead-end paths and winding roads that seemed to go away from the inner city.

"Do you know where we're going?" I asked Kamau and Grey behind Briggs.

Kamau shrugged. "I've been here twice. Not enough to know my way."

Grey squinted at the passing street markers. "None of this looks familiar, Cousin."

We ended up in another square, likely in another section of town. There was a crowd gathered by a stage, a few hundred people at least. They cheered and shouted, but not in a joyous way, as one would do during a festival or musical performance. Their shouts were filled with rage and apprehension. They were filled with eager anticipation. Full of loathing. Full of deceit. And I had heard them before.

The boys were curious and craned their necks towards the excitement.

When I finally spied the reason for the commotion, I immediately recoiled. A woman stood at the gallows, her hair covering her face in greasy, dark ringlets. Her eyes were closed, but I knew they could have been icy blue. The crowd shouted all around us, but I was back in Playada, eight years ago, trembling as my mother appeared to me for a few moments more. Her hands were clasped in front of her. The noose hung from her neck.

I couldn't look away. The executioner waited for the priest to give his verdict. Two bodies were discarded off to the side, hung like animals, the word "Spriggan" in painted red letters on a sign around their necks. My breath became shallow as the past became the present.

"Mayra," Grey murmured, and I swayed as I looked at him, my limbs feeling detached and tingling. He hung back as Kamau and Briggs kept walking through the crowd, and his face held a look of curiosity, and then concern.

"Ég elska þig, lambið mitt." *I love you, my lamb.*

"I —" I couldn't speak. My throat ached and everything around me blurred. "My ma—"

He nodded, realizing the terror my body felt. I had gone cold, as if my blood stilled and nothing was left to pulse within me. So much burying, only to be forced to feel it all again with the smell of death so close. I could have wretched if I could have moved.

Grey was the only one who knew of my mother. I couldn't let the others see me, to know my greatest weakness. Even if I had proven myself to them, shown them my strength untied to gender or title, I still could never trust them to know of my darkest day.

The only person I had grown to trust on the ship cradled my head in his hand so that it would not hit the stone street.

He brought me up to my feet and whispered in my ear, "I'll get you out of here."

We left without collecting Briggs and Kamau, as they mindlessly gravitated towards the crowd witnessing the execution.

Grey found me a bench far enough away where we couldn't hear the crowd any longer. He left me for only a moment. That poor woman had to be swinging by now, hanged for crimes for which she likely held no guilt. A neighbor hearing her sing a fairy song, or touching herbs known for magical spells. Witchcraft was the likely charge, but I would have bet my life that no magic had ever left her hands. Perhaps she had children who were sick, and she knew the properties of the roots she ground to allow them some relief. She might have sung silly Brannish folk songs to them about sprites and wee-folk. But I knew in my heart that she had not committed any crime worth death.

Grey returned with a cup of water. I couldn't bring myself to drink. The last thing I wanted was for him to see me cry, but I couldn't help it.

"I'm so sorry," he said. "We should have never been there. I should have never let you see that."

I shook my head. "It's not your responsibility to care for me."

"Isn't it?" Grey asked. "I seem to have assumed that role. Willingly of course. And not to say you couldn't handle yourself. It's just, I enjoy helping you."

I raised an eyebrow at him. "You enjoy helping me?"

He shrugged. "Even before I knew you were a lady—I just—Oh," his face flushed. "Never tell Briggs I said that."

Even while my hands still shook and tears clung to my eyes, I laughed. "Never tell him I nearly fainted. Can't give the bastard more reasons to torment me."

"I'll strap him to the siren for a week if he says anything," Grey said sharply. "Don't hold back for the Kid's sake. He's not worth that."

I still couldn't find it in me to cry. I had only needed that moment to let go. "Her ghost will never leave me." I thumbed the vial of ash on my neck.

"You keep her with you?" he asked, taking notice of it for the first time.

I nodded. "I want to take her to Brannland and lay her to rest there. Most of her body is in the trash of Playada, but maybe this little bit is the important bit."

He nodded.

"You're the only one who has faith in me," I told him.

"What do you mean?"

"You saw it in me to fight, to learn, to be a better pirate. Everyone else never had faith in me, even before they knew I was a lady."

"Well, you're a hell of a pirate, Mayra," Grey said, clapping me on the back. Sensing the doubt on my face, he added, "And I mean it. You came aboard knowing next to nothing –"

"I had been on fishing boats before," I interjected defensively.

Grey rolled his eyes. "That's not the same and you know it."

I didn't argue.

"But in remarkable time you've managed to learn combat and rigging and had a whole crew convinced you were a lad."

I hoped he couldn't see my flushed cheeks. "I just learned what I needed to survive."

"Still. Some lord's daughter could have come aboard and demanded passage. You didn't take the easy way."

"There you two are," Briggs called from the end of the alley. "C'mon, I found the way to Sly's."

Grey stopped me once more before I turned to follow.

"I want you to take my pistol."

I stared down at it. "Why?"

"The city isn't kind to young women," he replied.

I stared up at him, thinking he was being a little rash.

"Ay, I know you look a lad, but we're in the city and anyone will come after you if they think you have something worth taking."

"Like a pistol?" I said, hesitating to tuck it in my belt.

"Just do it," he insisted. "It'll make me feel better about you walking about."

I sighed, but stuck the pistol beside my knife, which I thought would have sufficed if anyone tried to jump me. But I knew it gave him comfort to know I was protected. And as much as I wanted to deny it, it gave me comfort too.

X. The Tavern

We finally found the tavern after wandering the town for another hour. Sly's was unlike the tavern in Villaviciosa. This was the kind of place built for a common man. I doubted anyone of noble birth had ever walked through the swinging door. In a large city like Astreim, there were so many options that even the bars were separated by class. Villaviciosa only had the one—Rafe's—that was shared by both los Dons and common folk. Years before, los Dons had proposed the idea of a gentleman's club, but the church deemed it improper, so it never happened.

Despite its common status, Sly's was a well-kept establishment and the kind of place one could find solace in taking their boots off and sipping a cool drink. Max Sly was the kind of man who drew people near him with stories and laughter. He was round in the face, in the gut, and in the shoulders. He also had a smile that went from ear to ear. His beard was jet black and curly, with silver strands threaded through it. He wore a piece of green cloth tied around the top of his head to collect the sweat that dripped from him as he moved about behind the bar. He had an apron tied beneath his robust belly and trotted about the bar in boots too large for his feet. All the men clapped him on the back as they entered and spoke to him as though he was one of the crew. He was only a stranger a moment before I felt perfectly at ease being near him.

"Ay lads, good to see ye," he greeted us. He spoke in a low growl in the same lower Aldinian accent many of the crew had.

The four of us had chosen a table in the corner of the dimly lit room. The rest of the crew had been there a while and were deep in their ale and conversation with the waitresses. The tavern was about the same size as Rafe's, being enough to seat thirty men comfortably and fifty less comfortably, but it could still be done.

Max was assisted by two barmaids, who flowed through the tavern like water bugs, gliding between tables, untroubled by the abrupt and direct nature of the sailors.

The barmaids were opposites in a lot of ways. The taller, and seemingly older of the two, was like autumn. Her eyes were hazel and she had long dark hair and thick eyebrows that she used to lure men. Her skirts were burgundy and her bare shoulders were pale white. She rarely smiled with her teeth, but a smirk remained fixed upon her darkened lips.

The other was like spring, with a head of bouncing red curls and glimmering clover eyes. Freckles dotted her freckled honey skin. She smiled wide and often, revealing perfect white teeth. She was perhaps my age, if not a few years younger. That did not deter my crewmates from telling her bold lines to try and make her blush. The girl took them in stride and offered her beaming smile to them, but I knew she did not actually fancy any of the men.

Well, maybe she liked Grey. She leaned her elbow on the table and allowed him to tell her all about his run in with the monarch. His stories were the only ones that she seemed fully invested in. I rolled my eyes. I knew Grey was handsome and charming, but did not understand why girls became simpletons around him.

"Another ale, Miss," I said, turning my empty mug over to her.

"Right away, Mr. Santana," she said, and brushed her fingers across Grey's back when she went to the bar to retrieve it.

"She's new," Briggs noted. "Was a different girl with Ruby last time we were here."

"She's hardly off her leading strings," Grey replied. He had seemed hesitant to her touch. "Can't be older than seventeen."

"She fancies you," I said flatly. "Is it not obvious?"

Grey eyed back at her over his shoulder. "Ah, she's just trying to get a few extra coins out of me."

Surely Grey knew the impression he had upon all women he met, but he always played his part. He never engaged with them, but allowed his charm to lead them along only to politely refuse them when they seemed to lose all sense of chastity. He was forever faithful to his first love.

"Everyone knows Grey doesn't want the girl," Briggs shook his head. "And I respect you for it, mate. So, maybe allow me to have this one."

I snorted.

"What's so funny, Santana?" he spat.

"Oh nothing," I said into my empty cup. "I'd love to see you try your hand at the young lady."

The gal returned with a full mug for me and another for Grey. "Thought you looked a little dry," she winked at him.

"I'm in need of some more too, Lass," Briggs said, showing his own empty cup. "And it would warm my heart if a pretty lass like you would fill my glass, Miss—."

"Laina," she replied, smiling out of the corner of her mouth, but did not offer a view of her white teeth. When she returned, Briggs tried to keep her attention.

"Good to be back on dry land, Miss Laina," he said, swirling his cup. "Seen many terrors out on the open ocean."

"I bet," she replied, not even bothering to feign interest, her eyes darting to Grey beside me. "But it must make life exciting."

"Oh yes," Briggs puffed out his chest. "But I was bred for the sea, just like my pap was before me."

"Oh, I'm sure," she replied. I could almost hear her eyes roll when she turned her back to us to set the dirty glasses on the counter.

"He was bred from the banshee's chamber pot," I said under my breath, mostly for Grey's benefit, who smothered his laughter.

Briggs shot me a glare. "Mind yer tongue."

The barmaid's turned shoulders shook in her own effort to hide her amusement.

I shrugged, innocently.

"Anything else I can get you, boys?" she asked, turning back to us.

"You mean boys and *Mistress* Finnigan?" Briggs quipped, taking my remark as a challenge.

Laina raised an eyebrow at him, no hint of a smile upon her lips.

"Sorry, 'bout him, madame," I replied. "Apparently he wasn't stewed long enough to know how to address a lady."

She gave me a smirk and without looking away from my eyes said, "Well, aren't I lucky some of you were bred properly. I'll be right over there, should you need anything."

She went back to the bar where Ruby and Max were talking.

"Now, why'd you have to steal that from me?" Briggs seethed. "You obviously can't have her, so why take my chance?"

I chuckled. "If you think I'm stealing your chances with her, you really do have a fat head." Though my pulse beat a little quicker, her sweet voice, light and charming, still in my ears.

The others laughed, but the conversation glided into the normal banter we shared. Even though Briggs and I had reached some form of truce, it was clear we were never going to quit taking shots when we could. It had become part of the natural order of things.

"If you think that's funny, you should have seen him last year," Kamau nudged me. "There was this other girl, Allison—"

"Don't say it," Briggs tried to interject.

"Briggs's voice hadn't quite ripened and he cracked as he asked to get her a drink," Kamau could hardly contain his laughter.

"The girl was in stitches over it. Let's just say Briggs hadn't been taken upstairs that night either."

Briggs glared at him. "When was the last time you bedded a lady, Cutthroat? I can assure you I have more recently."

"Oh, do you mean Miss Helda in Perth?" Kamau's eyes gleamed. "The homely lady who skinned the pigs."

"Laugh all you want," Briggs sneered, as Grey joined in on the joke, "she was a goddess betwixt the sheets. I'm beginning to think you're a eunuch, Kamau."

Kamau shrugged, drinking from his cup. "Think what you want. My endeavors are not of your concern."

Unlike most, Kamau got the final word often. He knew how to put the Kid in his place.

A few more drinks had been passed around and my head began to lift to the stars. Ruby had taken over our table. She did not hold back as Briggs tried to be sweet on her.

"Surely you need a man to warm your bed tonight. I could tell you all sorts of stories of the savages of the Westlands and the monsters of the depths," Briggs said, his speech getting more and more slurred.

"You are the only monster of the depth haunting me, lad," she smirked. "Come back when your feet touch the floor."

Briggs scoffed while the rest of us were bent over with laughter.

My glass seemed to refill each time I was close to the bottom. I soon lost track of how much I drank. All the men were claiming the half-league gaze one gets on a night of good drinks and company. I suppose my eyes were drifting away, sometimes just to the art on the walls. More often to the lovely lady who kept us well-cared for.

We continued to watch Briggs crash and burn in his efforts to get Laina to spend the night with him. He had given up on Ruby, who was like a viper to his advances, but Laina seemed too considerate to tell the boy off as her companion had. She danced around his questions, answering in as few words as possible.

"Where did you grow up?"

"Far from here."

"So, you're well traveled?"

"Not really."

"Do you like dancing?"

"No."

"Do you have many hobbies?"

"Yes."

Even Briggs could sense after twenty attempts at conversation that he was getting nowhere. Growing tired of her passiveness, he went off to sit with Stratford and Watson. Once he had left, she had become a bit more talkative.

"You're new here?" Grey asked.

Laina nodded. "Ruby took me in as a sort of apprentice I suppose."

Grey's eyes widened, but he didn't say anymore, instead taking long sips from his cup.

"Where were you before?" I asked, hoping to keep her engaged enough to remain near. It had been so long since I had conversed with females, especially ones as lovely and charming as Laina.

"All around," she replied vaguely, making me feel much like Briggs pestering her for unattainable information. She busied herself with shining tankards. Ruby had stopped working and was currently rubbing Stratford's shoulders while his eyes rolled back. Laina seemed to want to remain focused on the tavern work. "And yourself?"

"Playada," I replied, remaining as elusive as possible. If she wasn't to divulge details about herself, why should I?

Max began to pass out more drinks, not bothering to mark the tabs. Grey and Kamau slipped away at this opportunity, presumably bored at our small talk. That left me alone with the red-haired waitress.

"Do the rest of them know?" she asked me, without hesitation.

"Do they know what?"

"That you're a woman," she elaborated.

I hardly reacted, knowing my hair was loose and my voice had risen back up to my natural tone. I still bound my breasts though. I didn't have a proper bodice to contain them, and I didn't need to catch anyone staring down my shirt. "Most do. Everyone else either suspects or doesn't care."

"That's brave of you to board a ship as one woman amongst men." She took a seat beside me, still shining her glass on the hem of her apron.

"It hasn't been without its challenges," I chuckled. "The irritating one, Briggs, has given me hell since before he knew. And my womanhood has not stopped him."

"The rest of them respect you though?"

I shrugged. "I suppose. I'm seen as a member of the crew, just like anyone else."

"What's your real name?" she asked.

"Mayra." I didn't offer my last name. I doubted any young Aldinian lady could possibly know of some Don in a small Playadan town, but I still liked the idea of her just knowing me unattached to the titles and the labels—as the woman who joined the pirate ship.

Without the others around, I grew more at ease with Laina. She coaxed bits of myself from me. I sat the way Mayra sat. I spoke the way Mayra spoke. I let my body relax from all the things I thought would be qualities of Finn and what was left was the parts of Mayra that would once only come out as I was on the fishing boat off the land of Villaviciosa.

I still knew nothing of her, aside from her name and that she had been working for Max the last six months. We were two strangers who had spoken for two hours at that point, but still had learned little of the other's core self.

"So, Grey?" she asked with a glint in her clover eyes.

"Grey," I repeated back, not grasping her question regarding my crewmate.

"Do you?" Her eyebrows raised and wiggled.

I blinked, unsure why she couldn't manage to formulate a complete thought.

She sighed. "Have you bedded him?"

I scoffed. "Oh—no, absolutely not."

"Hm." She did not seem displeased, but she contemplated my answer. "Have you bedded any of the men?"

I shook my head. "No—I..."

I did not wish to divulge my entire history to this girl. Nor did I wish to tell her that I had never bedded anyone at all. Her questions led me to believe she had. Many times. I also did not trust her enough to reveal such a sensitive matter. Despite my resistance to my status as a lady, I did have to live with the fact that there was a high price on my maidenhead.

For once, Briggs's timing could not have been better, as he slumped into the chair beside us, with a sour look on his face.

"What's your problem?" I asked.

"Ruby stole Stratford," Briggs grumbled.

"Stratford?" Laina asked, surprised. "Odd choice."

"They go at it every year."

Stratford was not the ugliest man aboard the ship. Objectively speaking, he may have been one of the more attractive ones, with soft brown eyes, a chiseled jaw, mostly unmaimed from the scars of battle, and a light stubble across his chin. But like Laina, I could not imagine touching the man a bit. I had seen him drunk far too much to wish for such things. He was also well into his forties, or maybe his fifties. He could have been either of our fathers. But I had seen that look of longing in Ruby's eyes before they disappeared upstairs.

Briggs's arm stretched out across the bench, reaching for where Laina sat.

Laina popped up from her seat in haste, standing in front of me. She had that same look. "Mr. Santana," she said, loud enough for the whole tavern to hear, "would you care to continue this conversation *upstairs*?"

All eyes shifted to me, the ones who knew who I really was, as well as the ones who didn't. I probably should have put all the pieces together prior, but it wasn't until that moment that I realized that the barmaids did not only make their living filling beer glasses. Ruby had taken on Laina as an apprentice, in all angles of the trade. Meaning she wished to bed me.

"I—" my eyes searched for Grey's but he was nowhere to be found. If he were to give me a nod, or a shake of the head, maybe I would have known what to do.

"But she's—" Briggs started.

"Doesn't matter," Laina cut him off. "So, Mr. Santana, shall we?"

My stomach twisted at the thought. Perhaps she only meant to bring me to her room to talk. Surely two women could talk in private, definitely more often than a man and a woman could. I couldn't refuse—not for the sake of maintaining Finn's reputation. And especially to remain ahead of Briggs, whose face was satisfyingly baffled.

"It would be my pleasure, m'lady," I finally managed to say, in a voice that was sultry and didn't seem to be my own. A whole room of men glared at me as I followed the red-haired lass up the steps. Thank goodness for the ale that gave me the courage to climb up to her room without my knees turning to jelly.

Laina's room was on the third floor right at the top of the stairs above the tavern. There were a few rooms on the floor, including Ruby's across the hall.

"There's a good lass," Stratford's low growl seeped through the walls.

My cheeks burned and Laina shut her door. Her room was quaint, but her bed was larger than Lupe's or Malin's, covered in rich scarlet sheets. With the knowledge of how Laina and Ruby made extra money, I wondered how many men had occupied that space Laina sat beside. She motioned for me to sit beside her, on the indent in her mattress.

We sat apart, a solid foot between us, and even then, I noticed how close she was.

"Finally free of the annoying one," Laina sighed, giving me a smile, leaning in slightly. "I'm not sure how you could stand being in such close quarters with him."

I shrugged. "I don't know either."

She placed her hand on my thigh and leaned close to my face. I felt her breath on my cheek. My heart fluttered and my stomach hurt so much I thought I would keel over. Not to mention that I was very aware of the dirt and filth that was still plastered on me. I had not yet found my way to a bath.

"I don't have any money," I admitted. It wasn't necessarily a lie. I did not think my five drabs would be enough for an evening with her.

She laughed, fully and lovely. "I did not mean to charge you. This is just for fun." She leaned in again and my chest quaked.

"I've also never done this before," I blurted out when her lips brushed my skin.

She leaned back a bit, but still stayed very close. Her voice was full of breath. "Been with a woman?"

"Been with anyone," I clarified. "I was kissed once, I suppose." I recalled the girl in the tavern who helped me escape. It was nice, and I thought of her lips often, but it did not seem like a proper first kiss. Everyone talked of their first times as less of a favor and more of a mutual effort.

"I didn't mean to be so bold," Laina said, sitting back, appearing to reconsider her offer. "I thought perhaps..." She shook her head. "Never mind. It was my mistake."

"What?"

She twisted her fingers in her lap. "I just thought if you didn't want Grey, or anyone else in the crew, perhaps you are just not comforted by the company of men."

"I'm not comforted by the company of anyone," I said, foolishly. I knew the company she meant. I knew she smelled like rose oil. I knew I wanted her hand to go back to my leg. I knew I wanted Laina's company more than I had ever wanted anyone else's. But I also knew I needed a bath.

Laina led me up to their attic where there was a bathing room. She drew the water and allowed me to bathe while we continued to speak to each other.

I shied at the idea of baring my naked skin to her, knowing where it could lead. Yet, as soon as I was in the tub and ran a rag over my body, the conversation carried on as normal.

We still did not reveal any identifying details about ourselves. I was careful to not divulge anything about my mother or el Don Hidalgo. She didn't know the real reason I left home, but I did tell her about Mateo's proposal and of Grey's lessons, and how I felt broken because love seemed to evade my affections.

"My best friend promised to care for me if I became his wife, but I know I'd never love him that way. He would have loved me more than anyone ever has, but I could not find it in me to return the sentiment," I reflected. "I have only ever seen unhappy marriages, so I never wished to marry at all."

I ran a damp rag over my arms and neck again. Laina sat on a bench, sipping a glass of wine. She gave me sips in between my scrubbing.

"Perhaps it is only because they are men," Laina suggested, twirling the wine in her glass.

I was thoroughly clean now, but I remained in the tub, even as it started to grow cold. "Are you fond of women?" I found myself asking. All hesitancy to ask questions had disappeared amidst the previous glass of wine.

"I am fond of many," Laina said. "I work to entertain men much richer than me, and I wouldn't say I'm fond of them, but I can find enjoyment with them. But I'm like you—I remain adrift because it terrifies me to give myself fully to someone. Perhaps someday I'll find someone who cherishes all that I am, but I don't think that's possible in these lands."

While I spoke to Laina, I was aware of how my body moved and how it pulsed. I ached in a way I had never ached before. My awareness of my own movements were enhanced by

Laina's. Her tongue moved behind her lips. I could see her perfect teeth, except for one slightly turned tooth on the bottom row. Was it chipped? Somehow this slight imperfection made me want her more.

My examples of longing had been rare, but I had read books of women who desired the touch of a man. They were stories though. I could not imagine any of the ladies in Villaviciosa desiring their husbands like this. Certainly not my mother with Lupe. Mateo and I had almost shared a kiss, but unlike with Laina, I did not feel like I was on fire, gulping for air, and still wishing to be burned even more.

"How does one find enjoyment with another?" My boldness was still drowning in wine.

Her green eyes met mine. "You truly have never laid with anyone?"

I shook my head. I was not entirely naïve. No one back home had told me what happens between a man and a woman, of course, but I spent my life amongst fishermen, and then pirates, so I knew enough. Pirates spoke of such acts so extensively that I could picture every movement between lovers. I had also unfortunately seen the nakedness of many of my crew mates while aboard the *Raider*. I knew what a man's parts looked like and where they went in a woman. I shuddered at the thought.

But the possible acts between two women were still somewhat elusive. I could go on imagining, but as Laina's eyes went heavy, and her hands reached into the tub I was submerged in, I hoped I would soon find out.

XI. After

I woke up to the clatter of plates below as the staff prepared breakfast. The air felt stuffy, telling me that it was well into morning, perhaps even afternoon. It was a wonder no one had woken me, or that Carla hadn't crashed into my room to remind me what a lazy *puta* I was.

Rolling onto my side, I felt a warm lump in the blankets. Sometimes, one of the barn cats that I fed scraps to would sneak in through my window and sleep on the end of my bed. It had been in a few fights with the other cats and was missing an ear and its tail hung crooked. She would purr and rub her rust-stained body against me when I scratched between her eyes. I reached my fingers to brush her fur, but was met instead with the softest, smoothest skin.

I recoiled even though it was the loveliest skin I had ever felt. My mind spun in circles as I blinked my crusty eyes open, remembering where I was and why I was naked in the lovely barmaid's bed.

There had been more wine, but that did not mean I had lost the details of the night before. They rolled back into my mind as I became aware of my surroundings. In fact, I had felt the effects of the alcohol release from me as soon as Laina brought me back from the attic down into her room. It was late into the night by then, even Ruby's room had grown quiet. All between us was quiet, except for the small gasps and moans that neither of us could contain.

I had been wearing only a robe to cover me from the short trip to her room, but Laina was still in her corset, skirts, and apron. I watched as she began to undo her laces and strings. She let her red hair fall to her bare shoulders, hanging in loose copper curls while giving me sultry looks with those bright clover eyes. She was dusted with freckles, like delicate kisses across her collarbone, over her shoulders, and down her creamy white back. The skin at her navel was soft and white, untouched by the sun, but glowed with the tones of the moon. She did not look like other Aldinians, resistant to the sun. They were pasty and sickly. Her skin glowed and called to me.

Her body was small but robust, with her tiny waist, plump backside, and luscious thick thighs that sloped down like a vase. Her shoulders were narrow but appeared well-muscled. I imagined she must have worked on a farm at one point, or maybe tended mountain land, carrying things up and down hills. I still knew nothing of where she came from, but I pushed that far from my mind. It didn't seem important then.

She didn't speak as we settled into bed, but there was nothing more that needed to be said. I allowed her to take the lead, being that she knew what to do and how to do it. I was just grateful it was being done to me.

"Just tell me if you want to stop," she whispered, her lips against my bare thigh. I knew I would do no such thing.

At first, I wasn't sure where to put my hands or where to look or if I should mask the way my face scrunched at her touches. She laughed seeing my efforts to remain desirable and soothed me.

"Just breathe, Mayra," she said, hushing me as she continued to touch every part of my body. Her fingers ran circles over my stomach, up my chest, to my breasts. She kissed my nipples and climbed on top of me, taking my mouth often. Everything about her was soft and smooth. That was one of the things that always made me grimace at the thought of being with a man: they seemed too rough, hairy, and unkept. But Laina's body hair was much softer than a man's would be. However, even if Laina had body hair or imperfections, I would not want her any less. I just wanted her—that I was sure of.

I began to let my hands wander, gripping her hips as she rocked on me. I reached up for more kisses or to brush my thumb against her nipples.

As if things couldn't get any better, she ran her hands between my legs, cautiously at first, making sure this was still something I wanted. I tilted my head back, urging her to continue.

To think I had never known this kind of pleasure before. I had been robbed of the knowledge that my body could feel like this. Like my body was submerged in the cold sea, dazed by each pulsing wave. Breath burst from my lips, but I dove back down, desiring to be hit by those delicious waves.

Laina built me up and struck me down again and again. I clung to her, unafraid that I could drown in the pool of our love making. My first was always meant to be with Laina. I wouldn't have wanted anything different.

Laina began to stir beside me. I could feel her waking, and the memory of last night gave way to the reality of the woman beside me.

"Sleep well?" she murmured. She had turned to face me, pressing her face into my chest.

"The best I ever have," I replied, taking her into my arms.

"I have to be up," she yawned. "Likely there's clean-up to be done from your crewmates."

"I have duties too," I replied regretfully. The rest of the crew may have risen. I could still hear the rustle of activity below us in the tavern. I knew no one really needed me during our time of recess from ship duty, but I had not seen Malin since I had left the ship. What if he still needed me to be close by to run errands for him or bring up his breakfast? And yet this woman made me want to throw my duties and responsibilities aside forever.

"I had a really great night," she told me.

Great didn't seem a good enough word. Extraordinary. Astonishing. Metamorphic. But I didn't say as much. Perhaps Laina, being a tavern maid who gave pleasure to others often, had forgotten how transformative the first time was. I didn't want to reveal my greenness to this way of life, even though she was aware of my former virginity.

I simply replied, "I did too," tipping her head back to take her lips one more time before we dressed and went downstairs together.

It was not quite so late in the morning, the sun not yet reaching its peak. Some of the men were downstairs chatting with Max. Ruby and Stratford were still amiss, but I saw Grey, a cup of coffee in his hand. I took a seat beside him, and Max brought me my own cup. I looked over my shoulder to watch Laina work. She cleaned up glasses from the night before. She wiped down the sticky tables and looked cautiously at what looked like someone's forgotten breeches.

My mind drifted to earlier. To what she looked like before she put her skirts back on.

"Good night?" Grey asked, sipping his coffee.

"It was," I replied, containing the smile that tugged on my lips. The thoughts of her were intoxicating. I had grown sober since last night but could have been mistaken for drunk all over again. "Where did you disappear to?"

"We only get beds about seven days a year. I figured I'd go enjoy mine."

"Was it all that you dreamed of?" I asked. I sipped the coffee Max brought me, with cream and sugar. It was delicious. I hadn't had coffee since I had left home.

"Well, I didn't get to bed the tavern maid, but I guess all things considered it was pretty good," he chuckled.

Grey seemed good natured enough, but I still could not help but feel self-conscious about my night. It was wonderful, and I could not find it in me to regret it, but I began to wonder if it was not the wisest thing to do as my femininity became revealed amongst the crew. I had not considered the implications of what might happen should they find that I was a woman, and now that I had bedded a woman. Such things were a hangable offense in Villaviciosa. Surely in Astreim as well. Laina seemed unbothered, but she lived the life of a pleasure maid. I did not know if pirates dwelled on such things.

"You alright?"

I hadn't realized that I wasn't until he asked. That I was holding onto my emotions all at once. Some were lingering from the night before. Others were still settling from the moment I boarded the *Raider*.

I spotted Briggs stomping down the stairs. I knew he would pester me about the night before and I wasn't ready to face him just yet.

"I need some air," I said, grabbing Grey's hand to follow.

Late morning Astreim air was not as refreshing as I'd become accustomed to out on the water. The sky was gray and damp. It smelled of all the bodies who resided in the city. People hurried around us, unbothered by the two pirates in the alley, paying us little mind. Maybe our inconspicuousness was due to us both finally bathed.

"You look like you're going to be sick."

"I might," I swallowed. "Am I to be condemned should anyone find out what I did?"

"Condemned?"

"Imprisoned? Hung? Executed?" I clarified.

"For spending the night with the tavern maid?" he asked me, an edge of humor rising in his voice.

"For being a woman who lay with another woman," I stressed, hoping he would grasp how delicate this really was.

"Mayra, we do things every day that could get us hung. I doubt your beddings are at the top of the list."

"Would Malin release me for it?"

Grey shrugged. "I wouldn't think so—who a man chooses to bed is hardly a worry of the captain."

"But I'm not a man."

"You are still a man of this ship."

I considered this sentiment. I was a part of the crew. I was no less loyal to the ship and the captain than I was before. Stratford bedded Ruby and he was one of Malin's officers. Surely my bedding wouldn't be seen as any worse.

The matter of my being a woman still clung to my mind. That was the one thing that would always set me apart. My maidenhead was always my value, and I had lost it to a tavern maid. If I was still back home, it would have been added to the many claims against me, building up the mountain of shame as they had with Vivanka. It was instinctual for me to fear for my sins even when I no longer followed their god or their code. The pirates did not seem to worry about one's maidenhead, or their purity, or if they followed every damn rule in the holy book. I had to keep reminding myself that I was no longer being threatened to be roasted on the pyre.

"So, did you enjoy her?" Grey asked, meeting my eyes.

I wasn't sure how much he wished to hear, or how much I wanted to say. I knew the crew did not shy away from discussing their escapades, but it had never been about me. And what Laina and I had done seemed to be something secret between us.

"It was a pleasurable night," I answered.

He nodded, bobbing his head a few extra times. He tilted his head, opened his mouth, but then shut it again, shaking his head.

"What is it?" I asked.

"I need to ask you something."

I nodded, urging him to continue. There was an uncomfortable layer of formality that hadn't once been there.

"Was there ever a chance for us?" Grey asked, adding, "Is there still a chance for us? I mean, she is just a tavern maid. Perhaps she is a bed you take in this port. But that doesn't mean we couldn't work around that and... just... would you have ever had me?"

I knew this conversation was coming. We had grown as friends, but it was hard for a man and woman to grow as friends and be simply that, even amongst pirates. Maybe especially between pirates, with the long days at sea and a cold bed at night.

"Laina made me realize a lot of things about myself," I replied, softly. "I don't think I could have ever felt the things I feel for her with you."

He nodded, understanding my meaning. I had sworn to never take a man to wed, implying the bedding part, before I even knew women were an option. I was ready to live a life without this pleasure. I admired Grey very much. I did not want him far away and I did not want him to see me as any less than I was.

But I knew I could never be his wife, or his partner, or whatever it was that pirates took.

"I pray for your happiness," he told me. "I just needed to know."

"Will you stop teaching me combat?" I asked.

"Of course not," he smirked. "But I do expect you to rub in Briggs's face that she chose you over him."

We went back into the tavern and enjoyed breakfast with the mates. Eggs and bacon and toast and jam and coffee and biscuits and sausage. I wasn't sure I could contain that much food, but I still managed.

Laina gave me fluttering glances as she cleared our plates and Briggs watched our interactions. I pinched her waist. She leaned over across me, breathing on my neck. Her lips nearly touched my cheek. All the while the Kid muttered into his coffee about all the curses he wished upon me.

"Santana," Malin called behind me.

I looked around Laina's frame at the captain in the door, immediately standing to meet him.

"Have you enjoyed your recess?" he asked, eyeing me and Laina.

I remembered Grey's words. The captain did not care who I bedded. "I have, sir."

"Good. We still have business to discuss," he said, motioning me to follow.

Malin stayed in the largest room, of course. His bed was as large as Laina's but he had his own place to bathe and many sofas and areas to sit away from the bed. Perhaps the captain paid no mind to my nighttime dwelling, but perhaps he also resented holding this much space alone.

And that's when I noticed the white handkerchief lined with lace, peeking from the corner of the bed. An awfully feminine slip of cloth. I averted my eyes, straining to keep from peeking again. Who the captain bedded was certainly not my concern.

We did not speak until Jenkins fetched Stratford and joined us. His neck was covered in bright red bruises and I shied at the thought of what he and Ruby had occupied their time with.

"Wonderful," Malin replied. "I spoke with a medicine woman down the street. She operates as a spice seller, but she had some information worth noting. She has heard of a

Spriggan working at one of the taverns in this part of town."

"Wouldn't the medicine woman be a Spriggan?" I asked. They all looked at me incredulously. "Most medicine women are at least presumed Spriggan."

"She said fae," Malin clarified.

"One of the tavern maids?" Jenkins asked.

"Let's ask these two," he said pointing to Stratford and myself. "Do you believe either woman to be fae?"

Stratford shrugged. "I've known Ruby for years. She is a temptress in bed o'course, but I wouldn't say magical or fae-like."

Malin looked at me.

"Same experience," I said. Her touch had been magic, but I couldn't say for certain that it was caused by the powers of the wee-folk.

Malin shrugged. "There are plenty of taverns in the area. I would like to find the fae before we leave. It would be a hell of a lot easier than convincing a Brannish-folk to join us."

I knew then that I had been overthinking my bedding to Laina. Grey was right: pirates do things every day that could warrant execution. I recalled the story of Starky, killed in the line of duty, whether it had been a cannon ball to the gut or an illness. That could be my fate on any given day, as much as I wished to avoid it. But I had bedded a woman, bedded out of wed-lock, fraternized with pirates, stolen from a royal ship, and I'm sure I could think of other hangable offenses if I thought long enough. They would need to bring me back five times more to hang me properly for all my crimes. Might as well enjoy myself in the process.

XII. The Fallen Lord

The captain lined our pockets with coin, paid from the raid on the *Lillian.* Malin required little of me, so I was free to wander Astreim with the others to spend it. But I spent it on my ales and lunch at the tavern, pocketing the rest. Who needed treats and bobbles when I was able to spend my day talking to Laina? I was beginning to understand how easy it was to deny the usual pleasures in the face of infatuation. I couldn't fathom requiring anything that would bring me away from the tavern. I had all I needed: food, water, ale, and Laina.

"My father played the lute," she told me, dreamily, watching that night's performer tune his instrument in the corner of the room while I sipped my ale. "That's how he enchanted my mother: by singing her songs on his lute."

"Did he teach you how to play?" I asked. I rested my head on my chin.

"No," she sighed. She sat across from me, folding napkins to keep her hands busy while she was otherwise idle. Her foot traveled up my pant leg. "I was involved in my studies."

Her toes were smoothing the skin along my calf. I had never imagined such a gesture would make me ache so much. "What did you study?"

Her eyes seemed far away. I tried my best not to stare into them, knowing they would continue to lure me in. How did anyone think of anything other than bedding once they had performed the act?

"Holistics," she finally said after a long pause, removing her foot from my leg. "I'm from a small village and they needed a proper healer."

"In Aldina?" I urged, hoping to hear more. She still felt so closed off to me. I knew her physically. I had seen her body and yet her mind was almost a stranger to me.

"I suppose. It was towards the border and I don't think we cared much for the king's rule, even if we're all bound by it. Even you Playadans."

I nodded.

"What were your ambitions back home?" she asked me.

"To get out," I replied honestly. "My situation in Playada was a bit more... stifling than my present circumstances."

"I imagine. Being that it took joining a pirate crew as a male in order to escape it."

I chuckled. "Indeed." I didn't offer more though. She had her secrets. I had mine.

"I know I'm more fortunate than many of the women in Aldina. They are bred to marry. That was never my upbringing. Even now I enjoy so much more liberty in my life than a lady of noble birth could possibly have."

She spoke of me without even knowing it. I still had not told her of being raised as a lord's daughter. I had this sense that she knew though. She could read me so much better than I could read her. But until I could figure her out, and feel her open to me, I held onto the facts of where I had come from.

I shifted away from the topic, approaching another delicately. "May I ask you about your job pleasuring men?"

Without hesitancy she agreed, adding "I'm not ashamed of my work."

"I didn't mean to imply that you should be."

"I know, but you grew up in a place that refuses to discuss such topics because of shame. I wish for you to know that I speak openly on those matters because I was raised to not feel shame around natural pleasures."

I wanted to know where such a place existed, but I held onto that question for later, allowing her to lead me into her.

"I do it because I'm free to," she explained. "I have always lived freely. All my life, except a brief moment. And that moment was enough for me to weary of ever feeling contained ever again.

"Ruby offered me work. I refused at first, because I was able to freely do so. It was my choice when I began. At first, it was terrifying, because I didn't want to feel controlled. But as I developed relationships with my clients, I realized I was the one leading them. They relied on me to create the fantasy, and with the security I have with Ruby and Max's protection, no one crossed the lines I drew. I have maintained anonymity with many of my clients because I know the dangers of allowing strangers to get too close. Never again will I make that mistake."

I was taken by Laina's boldness. I knew I lived a life of freedom as well, but she had done so without denying her gender or social status. In my mind, full of secrets and shame, it seemed like a more admirable way of life. There might be things she kept hidden, but I would not press her. She might never tell me, but I would respect her decision. I was just happy to be near her, especially as her toes resumed their playful journey along my leg.

The day grew late, and I remained glued to my booth, soon joined by Grey, Kamau, and Briggs when they returned for dinner. They included me in conversation, but I was only half there, the other half completely aware of Laina's every movement. I felt drawn to her, like leaving her side was impossible. Not only had our bodies collided, but slowly, I was beginning to feel as though I understood her to her core. She was like me. She ran from something in her past because moving forward was easier than repairing a shattered past. Facts mattered less and less. I knew Laina. I was sure of it.

The entire night, I longed to be near her. She drifted in and out of our conversations, laughing at our jokes as if she had always been a part of our group.

I imagined staying, but quickly withdrew that notion. Astreim was a larger version of Villaviciosa. Even worse because it lay beneath the king's nose. I was just as much at risk here as I was in Playada. Without my crew to surround me, I felt more exposed to the laws of this country. I knew I couldn't settle just because I met someone who made my heart beat faster.

I imagined Laina joining the crew. Then again, many of the men had made it clear I was the only woman who had ever and would ever join them. I would not want her to feel like an outcast like I had. She would have me though, and I'd be sure to shield her from the pranks and cruelty I had endured.

But maybe she loved her life here. I could never steal her away if this was where she was happy.

"Someday I hope to get to Brannland," she replied to something Grey had said.

I perked up. "Brannland? Why?"

"I have family there. I've never met them, but I always thought someday I would."

"That's where we're headed," Briggs said. "That's where Finn plans to leave us."

"Really?" Laina asked.

I shrugged, wanting to appear indifferent. "Maybe."

Brannland was my planned destination, and like Laina, I wanted to meet my family. But I had grown comfortable around the crew and looked forward to being back out on the water. In that time, I had debated the real benefit of starting over again. Like Laina, I longed to be free. With my womanhood and identity exposed to the captain and most of the crew, I finally was. I had settled into the idea of staying with the crew beyond our mission in Brannland, but when Laina said that was her destination as well, the allure to my mother's homeland resurfaced.

It was the last night before we would set sail to the north. I had hoped that night would be spent in Laina's bed. I sat in the common area, sipping water from my mug so as to not grow too drunk before I went to bed. Max was still there, tending to things beyond the counter. We engaged in some small talk, but for the most part enjoyed our shared solitude.

It grew later and later. The other's had already gone up to bed to enjoy the comfort before returning to our hammocks below deck. I watched as Laina worked. She was occupied, so I did not bother her. I continued to watch her though. As she reached the top shelves. As she poured drinks and flirted with patrons. As she slipped coins into her pockets and boots. As she handed me secret smiles to know that I still had a cozy place in her mind.

The lutist had brought in a small crowd, and she tended to their needs, leaving me to think. I wanted to ask her to come. To give her the opportunity for passage. To come with me. I decided I would wait for us to be nestled in bed together, after we had made love, to suggest the idea to her.

I nodded off in the booth, my head resting on the back of the seat.

I awoke in the dark tavern. Max was still behind the counter. I wondered if he ever stopped working. But Ruby and Laina were no longer there.

"Where's Laina?" I asked, wiping the drool from my mouth.

He shrugged, stirring some kind of liquid in a large kettle.

I went upstairs to her room and saw her door ajar, thankfully, so I felt less invasive cracking it open to see if she was there. She was not.

I went back down to the tavern. I was in utter dread to think that she may have joined one of my other crewmates for the night. I was silly to believe I would have another night for her. My innocence perceived her kindness for affection for me. This was her job. I should have realized our night together was not as special for her as it had been for me. I had been the virgin. She had made it clear that she was not and was beautiful enough to spend her time with anyone she wished.

Surely not Grey, I thought in horror. She had expressed interest in his looks and charms when we first spoke. I understood his appeal. I, myself, had felt it before. But I had thought that when she bedded me it was because I suited her tastes more, as she suited mine more than any man could have. But perhaps I was a last resort while Grey was occupied.

I returned to the tavern feeling hollow. Perhaps I was never anything special to her. I was an evening, that perhaps would not even last in her mind after I sailed away again. It was despicable how much I had allowed myself to fall for her, especially when I could never stay here and she could never go with us. It was better for my emotions if I cut them off here and now, knowing that was nothing to her.

"Oh," Max suddenly said from behind the counter, "she went for a walk."

"What?"

"Laina goes for walks sometimes after busy shifts. She should be back shortly."

"Oh," I breathed, feeling the labyrinth of insecurity I had formed in my mind untwist. I had always thought about how foolish girls became when they fell in love with men. And there I was, the biggest fool of them all. I needed to clear my own head. I was too caught up in her. But I didn't know how else to be now that she had seen all of me.

I went outside the tavern, looking down both ways. I didn't know which way she would have gone. It would have been wiser to wait for her to return, but my head was so twisted with feelings and worry. If I spoke with her, maybe some of this would go away. I could be honest and tell her of my conflictions. Perhaps I'd sound young and naive to things like sex. But I was. A woman like her could have insight.

It was past midnight. I began to question why Max had allowed her to venture out this late on her own. I would have offered to accompany her. There were beggars gnawing on bones in the alleys, shooting me glares as I walked swiftly past. They did not approach me, but I didn't take my eyes or ears off them until I was far enough to run if I needed to.

I was hardly a quarter mile from the tavern when I heard harsh whispers. It probably would have been smart for me to mind my business, but I saw a flash of bright red curls.

Laina was being held against the wall by some man with a lavish coat and a gold chain hanging from his neck. He could have been one of her clients. He had his mouth close to her ear, but from the fear in her eyes I could tell that it wasn't pleasantries he spoke to her.

I backed my way to an alley across from them, tucked behind the wall so I could see. I didn't have the nerve to act on impulse and I feared my interference would do more harm than good. I couldn't just stand there and do nothing though. I had Grey's pistol. I just had to work up the nerve to bring it from my belt.

"Let me go," Laina said. She didn't yell, but there was urgency in her voice.

If I waited too long, she could be harmed by him. I didn't know his intentions. Perhaps she stole from him. Perhaps he was taking advantage of her and would leave her in the alley when he was through. Even if she had harmed him first, there was no reason that man should be placing kisses upon her throat while she tried not to cry.

"Let her go," I tucked the tip of my dagger in his neck. I spoke as Finn Santana, knowing a woman would be no threat to a man of high society. I knew he had to be some kind of lord with how he openly wore jewels and white gloves.

"Mind your business, boy," he grunted, still with his hand on Laina's collar bone. "And lower your weapon or the bitch gets it."

"Let her go," I said again, the tip penetrating his skin, a single line of blood dripped down to his white shirt. I spoke with a steady voice and worked with all my power to keep my hand steady. I didn't know what I was meant to do next. I had never killed a man. In fact, I had distinctly taken a vow swearing I would never kill a man in the name of piracy.

I knew defending a barmaid was a noble act, perhaps honorable of breaking that vow. But was I doing it for honor, or for blind, love-drunk courage?

He swept the knife from my fingers and now held it to Laina's neck.

"Go back to the tavern, boy," he hissed. "This doesn't concern you."

"Mr. Santana, please," Laina whispered, but her voice was clear. Her eyes still held fear, but I read the message clearly in them. *Return to the tavern. Don't make matters worse for either of us.*

I couldn't just walk away though. I would protect any damsel in distress, but for her, I'd burn the world.

I pulled the pistol from my belt. "The lady will be coming with me."

The man cackled. "Put that thing down, boy. You don't even know how to use it."

I had learned how to load the gun, to place the powder, and had proven I was a good shot. But no, I had never fired it at a man. I didn't expect him to know that. I had hoped the threat would be enough.

The wind picked up around us. I caught eyes with Laina. Her emerald irises glowed and she gave a jerk of her head. He released her immediately and he crumpled, clutching his hands in his lap as if they were seared.

"You fucking, Spriggan whore," he groaned, then scrambled at her with my knife.

I took the shot. The bullet seemed so much louder in these quiet streets then it ever had on the open ocean. The boom rang off the walls of the alley. I realized how silly it was to fire at such close range, but it was the only way. The bullet landed in his leg and he was down again. Seething in pain.

He writhed like an animal, my bullet reducing him to a whining beast. His earlier arrogance and confidence was taken by that bullet. By me. Blood flowed from the wound, but not enough to kill.

"Finish him," a voice said behind me. Grey came from the shadows, another knife in hand, placing it in my palm.

"I—"

"You need to know what it feels like, Finn," Grey said.

He meant killing someone. He meant breaking my vow. I was to take this man's life for dishonoring Laina.

A few months ago, I would have walked away. But I knew the look in Laina's eyes, and I knew he had done unspeakable evils to her. I knew I would forever hold myself as a coward if I didn't follow through with this. But it still wasn't my choice.

"Do you want him dead?" I asked Laina who was glaring at the man, still pressed against the wall of the alley by her own will. She looked up at me and nodded.

I approached him. He couldn't fight me off for the pain in his leg. I took him by the hair, sliced across his throat and watched as the blood pooled beneath him. I didn't hesitate when I did it. Laina saying he was worthy of being killed was enough for me at the time. But the realization of what had done, sent me stumbling back.

Grey caught me before I hit the pavement. I felt like I would be sick.

"It's okay," Grey soothed me.

I shook my head, on the verge of tears. "Who was he?"

Laina stood and stepped around the body. "He raped me. He raped me so many times and held me against my will. I was captive to him before I came to the tavern. He is better off dead. His name was Lord Prath. I was a maid in his house. His wife was barren and uninterested in him, so he used his maids in her place. He would give us money for it, but it wasn't worth it. I escaped, but I knew he would find me eventually."

I nodded. Knowing he was a monster helped my morality, but it was not enough to calm my pounding heart. At least I didn't kill someone who could have had a reformed life.

"We have to move the body," Grey told us. "He's too important to leave to rot. Someone will find him."

My limbs were shaky, but I released myself from Grey's grasp and helped move the slacken body. Laina retrieved a burlap sack from the scraps in the alley and we tied the body within it. I tried not to think too hard about what I had done, or what we were doing as we lifted his lifeless carcass in the sack and carried it to the docks. My limbs shook, and I flinched at every noise, but we carried on. As we passed the beggars gnawing on bones, I prayed my limbs would maintain their grip. If we dropped the body, these vacant eyed men would know what I'd done. But they paid us no mind, just continued to grumble and eat their meat.

Laina seemed a lot less fearful than I was. She helped us carry the body, but I could have sworn she smiled the whole walk to the docks. She had said this man violated her and used her. I suppose it was a weight off her shoulders as we went to dump her attacker in the bay.

"Will anyone come after you now?" Grey asked the tavern maid.

"No. Well. Maybe," Laina muttered. "I...I got into trouble at Prath's estate. I've been hiding at Max's the last six months."

"What kind of trouble?"

"I—"

We were nearly in the water when a voice stopped us.

"Grey? Santana?"

I yelped at the sound, but kept a firm grip on the body. Laina slid behind me.

Malin and Jenkins came from the ship, looking at us with the dead body in hand.

"Who do we have here?"

"He was harming the lady," Grey explained for me, seeing that I had gone mute. "Finn was defending her. The bastard meant to slit Miss Laina's throat."

Malin looked behind me to where Laina was.

"I'm sorry I caused the trouble, sir," she whispered. "I didn't mean for your men to be involved."

"Finn killed him?" he asked, looking at me.

I nodded. "Yes sir. He had a knife to Laina's throat."

"Is he of importance?" Malin asked Laina.

She looked down at her feet. "It's Lord Prath, sir."

"One of the King's Counsel?"

She nodded.

"His death could cause an uprising. It's a threat to the crown and would come back to us as if we're trying to start a war." Malin pursed his lips. "Well go on, throw his body in the bay. But if he's found, people will begin to fear the other lords of the crown are next."

Laina removed the bag from his head. His face had gone pale with the lack of blood, and I could see where his skin opened at his throat. She took the chain that hung from his neck, with the king's crest on it and stuck it in her pocket. She placed her hand upon his mouth and eyes and the skin sizzled beneath her touch and he became unrecognizable. It was as if she had placed an iron to his skin and then melted it like dough, reconstructing something ugly and grotesque so no one could ever know who he once was should they ever find him before he was nothing but dust.

Malin watched her with his eyes wide, but he said nothing until the body was sinking to the bottom of the bay.

I knew what Malin suspected. Laina had burned the man only with her hands and those same hands made his face unrecognizable. No common barmaid could have done anything like that unless something more ran through her blood.

But the captain did not immediately seize the Spriggan. He disappeared into the streets, which gave me the time to get more answers from her.

Jenkins was not far away, but also wasn't in earshot. He leaned against a barrel on the dock watching her back where she sat overlooking the bay. Laina hugged my cloak to her shoulders, seeing that she had bare shoulders and goose pimples from the lack of fabric on her shirt. Her brow furrowed and her green eyes had gone glossy.

I sat beside her and didn't break the silence. Laina didn't even look up at me. She clutched the cloak and ran her thumb over the rings on her hands. There was a simple gold band, a twisted knot with an emerald, and a golden leaf.

"Is your captain going to turn me in?" Laina asked, keeping her eyes forward, her voice quivered ever so slightly.

I shook my head. "Grey and I killed the lord. Captain wouldn't risk his crew turning you in."

"Not for murdering Lord Prath," she said sharply.

I waited for her to spell it out.

"He knew," she said instead. "He knew what I was and he used me for it. He knew there was nothing I could do without being trialed and killed. I was like an exotic animal to him."

Tears slid down her cheeks. I did not press her. But I ached for her. Before I knew her truth, I could feel the loss she had endured and the pain and the torture through the lord that I killed. I still wasn't sure how to feel about what I had done, but I hoped it put some of her demons to rest. I also knew Malin wanted a fae and here she was.

"His wife didn't want him and couldn't give him an heir. At first, he slept with the maids purely to have a child. Even a bastard could inherit his title if it was male. But it became a game to him. He hired young girls in desperate places and would give them gifts and charm them, only to treat them worse as soon as they gave in to his advances. And he has influence over the entire court. We couldn't just walk away without risking persecution. Me especially.

"The game got even darker. He would make his wife watch as he touched us. Yelling insults at her while he did it. And we couldn't speak. Not without punishment. And believe it or not, punishments were even worse than what he was already doing to us."

I believed her. And wished I could pull Prath from the water and do it all over again for her, so she knew she didn't need to fear him anymore. My hand laced with hers as she continued.

"He didn't know at first what I was, but he crossed a line. He made my body react to his torture. I had contained myself until then, knowing I would be killed if I was found out. But he didn't turn me over and he didn't kill me. He used my magic for pleasure. He used me as a pet. And he made it clear that if I ran or tried to expose him, I would be pinned to the walls of this city and put on for display for my blasphemous existence.

"I was there for a year. I had nowhere else to go. And then, one night, my door was left open and unlatched and the patrols were all asleep. I looked around for my savior but found no one. There were stories amongst my clan that our ancestors still live within us and fuel our magic. Prath knew the tools to wield to limit my access to my powers, but that night, I had all that I was and made it out. I always thought, perhaps, the wisps helped me escape.

"I was going to board a boat to Brannland but didn't have any money. I didn't want to stay here, but I couldn't find anywhere safer than Max's. They know what I am but vowed to keep me safe. I lay low. Not everyone in this city wants me dead, but the most powerful certainly do. Brannland is the last safe place for Spriggan."

"Come with us," I found myself saying, gripping her hand tighter.

"What?" she asked.

"Come with us. You and I can escape together."

"Your men would never take a fae."

"They took me. My mother was suspected a Spriggan," I revealed.

"Was she actually?" Her eyes widened.

I shook my head. "No, she was a medicine woman. She was Brannish and practiced the old ways, worshipped the old gods. Which is enough to be hung and burned in Playada."

She looked as though she was finally piecing me together, as I had been piecing her. She was a fae. And I wasn't sure if that scared me or not.

Malin returned with Max Sly who took Laina aside. Jenkins and Malin hung back, cornering me when Laina was out of sight.

"What did you learn from her?" Jenkins asked.

It all felt so personal. Everything she told me were the intimate details of her life. But I had a duty to my captain.

"Prath kept her as a pleasure slave," I said. "He knew she was Spriggan and used it to blackmail her. She said she ran away to Sly's for refuge and this was the first she had seen him since." I gave them only the necessary details, trying to preserve some bit of faith that Laina had to tell me any of it.

"Did you learn where she's from?" Malin asked.

I shook my head. "No, but she aims for Brannland."

"Lucky us," Malin smirked.

A chill ran through me at the way the captain looked at the girl like a prize. But I was the one who had told him that he would need a faerie to get his treasure. I had hope that the captain would not be worse for Laina than Lord Prath once was.

I was a fool.

We sailed away from Port Astreim that very night. Malin did not reprimand Grey or me for killing the lord, but it was clear that it was our fault that we were cutting our time on land short. There were too many risks if we stayed any longer. I added enemy to the crown as part of my long list of crimes that I could be hung for. But perhaps the lord's corpse would never be found at the bottom of the bay, and it was unlikely they would connect the killing to some girl gaining passage on a pirate ship. I repeated this to myself a few times to make sure the words sunk in.

I never meant to kill anyone. I never meant to become a pirate. I was merely seeking passage. But I was no longer just a lord's daughter from Villaviciosa.

At least we were headed for Brannland. There was still a possibility of safety for me on the northern shores.

But for Laina...

I had tried to convince myself that by bringing her aboard, we were doing what was in her best interest. She was unsafe in Astreim and needed to flee Aldina entirely to lessen the risk of her being caught as a Spriggan fae. We would bring her to Brannland and once Malin got what he needed, she'd be free to go.

Surely, I had not damned her. Surely, Malin did not mean her any more harm than what awaited her should she be caught.

Grey and I joined the others from the tavern and made our way back to the *Raider*. Malin and Jenkins had escorted Laina to the ship ahead of us. I watched them carefully but did not sense harm. Malin's deep voice rattled through the alleyways and all I could think was how the captain needed to tighten his jaw if we meant to make a clean escape.

I was also still consumed within myself. I was only an hour past my murder. No one else had taken notice of my shaking hands.

"Fearless Finn strikes again," Briggs beamed as he had Grey tell the story once more. "I hope for your sake they put that on the wanted posters."

"Wanted posters?" I asked, my blood sparking.

"The lad's just tryin' to get a rise out of ye," Stratford rolled his eyes.

Wasn't he always?

"Wait until yer third or fourth murder to be special enough for a poster," the battle master growled.

"Do you have a poster?" I asked Stratford.

"I'm not careless enough to kill a lord in the open," he shrugged.

Still, my murder of the lord was a triumph amongst the crew and while I didn't want it to be my legacy, I did not have much say in the matter.

"I wish I could have been the one to stick him," Briggs grumbled. "I would have attached a love note to the king and left him fearing he'd be next."

"Oh, shut yer gab, boy," Stratford snapped, but even he seemed in good enough spirits as a result of my crime. "Bet the king will be watchin' where he pisses fer a while." He then began whistling a shanty tune.

Meanwhile, Jenkins and Malin had already boarded the *Raider* ahead of us. I had lost sight of Laina's vibrant hair. She still wore her barmaid's outfit, unfit for the chill in the air presently. I thought of how I'd be sure to acquire materials to fashion her a proper wool cloak before we were too far north.

"Where's Laina?" I asked Jenkins. He and Malin were speaking quietly on the quarterdeck.

"Gone below to fetch some sleep," Malin replied.

Jenkins entered the captain's quarters without any acknowledgement to me. His brow was furrowed, and his forehead creased.

"It's been a trying day for the lass," Malin continued, unbothered by the first mate's cold shoulder. "Best you let her sleep."

"Oh, in the crew's quarters?"

"No, I arranged for the girl to have her own quarters. She shouldn't have to sleep with you lot," he chuckled and followed Jenkins into his quarters.

It had been a long day and the toll of it brought me to my sack in the corner. My shoulders ached. As did my temples, my eye sockets, and even my chest. I was breathing just fine, but there was still a constant ache.

"No," Briggs called, peering at me from his own resting place. He pointed a finger at the empty hammock beside him. "We found this in some rubbish. Sleep here."

Could it be another trick? The rope wasn't frayed enough to be from the rubbish pile. It was clean and well strung up, so I didn't expect to fall in the middle of the night. My preference was certainly not to be beside Briggs.

I fell asleep, too dazed to question anything further.

XIII: The Dwarf's Treasure

I awoke the next morning unharmed and with heavy eyes. I must have slept twelve hours, yet it still didn't feel like enough.

It took several moments to recall the events of the previous day, or the previous three for that matter. To recall that Laina was real and she had allowed me to explore the deepest parts of her. Those memories were warm and brought life back to my blood.

But there was an uneasiness that would not leave me. I had not seen her since the previous night. Since I killed her attacker and watched as she burned his corpse with her hands. Malin said she had been given her own quarters. That had to be the vacant cabin in the cannon room. The bed in there had to be more comfortable than the hammock I was in, though I was grateful to no longer be on the floor.

The crew was already up and attending to their tasks for the day. The air had become hot and stale below, and with the light that poured in from the hatch above, I could see that I was alone. I slipped on my boots and crept towards the door to the private cabin, thinking of the silkiness of her skin and the taste of her berry lips. I regretted sleeping alone last night, wishing I could have been lost in Laina's touch again.

I was only slightly apprehensive that she was a faerie. I am my mother's daughter, so that did not make me think of her as a true monster. But I had realized how little I knew of her and how much she may have kept from me. For a moment, I lost myself to darker thoughts, resentful that she didn't tell me the truth. But I pushed back against those intrusions. She was just trying to survive in a place that was out to hang the likes of her. I could not blame her, not when I had so many night terrors of the noose around my own neck, and my feet dropping off the end of the platform.

I turned the handle to Laina's cabin and found it locked. That didn't concern me. She was paces away from thirty men. And sure, they hadn't bothered me much these past months, but that was after binding my breasts and hiding my femininity. Many of them still only knew me as Finn. Even after I was revealed as a woman, surely I was seen a bit differently than the tavern wench who sold her body.

I knocked on the door and was met with silence. Perhaps, she was asleep or wandering above. The trials of yesterday were harder on her than they were on me, I was sure. Best to leave her be for now. I would see her soon enough and be able to kiss her flame-colored hair.

I departed from the door and heard footsteps coming down. It was Pax, Jenkin's new errand boy. They had found him looking in the trashes outside of the tavern and decided to save another rat from the streets. I had not yet spoken a word to him, so I went back to the hammock side, avoiding the interaction. We could be introduced when I wasn't so tired and irritable.

He held a tray of soup and bread and held the key to the private cabin. I watched as he turned it in the lock.

"Here's yer slop, lassie." He spoke with the grimy lowlander accent of Aldina. He must have come from outside of the city, settling there only out of desperation. He certainly looked desperate. Sixteen or seventeen years old, but skinny as bones and pock scars across his face. I couldn't help but judge that he wouldn't make it on the ship. I may have grown leaner since I came aboard, but I could also feel the shape of my hardened muscles beneath my shirt.

I stared as he brought in her food. It didn't seem hospitable the way the tray clattered on the bare floor. Something was off.

I grabbed my hat and made my way up the stairs, hoping to catch a glimpse of her before I went above. She didn't see me, but I saw her in the quarters, her wrists and ankles bound and Pax feeding her like a dog with her head in the bowl.

My stomach churned. Laina was not a guest aboard this ship. She was a prisoner. Worst of all, I knew why.

Malin needed her blood.

"I found this in an herbalist's shop of all places," Malin explained after handing me the stack of parchment. "He said it was a bunch of rubbish that didn't mean anything, but it was protected behind glass. I replaced it with some of Peel's cookbook pages on how to make winter stew." He chuckled, but he watched me intensely. Obviously, gathering these pages could be our missing piece to finding the Brannish treasure.

And he would be right. Just skimming them, I knew this was what we needed. I played off my stalling for deciphering the words from the twirly handwritten script, when really, I was trying to decide if I wished to tell Malin anything at all.

Since we had been in Aldina, I had my suspicions of the captain. But now, I knew who he really was. The memory of Laina, bound like an animal, made my stomach churn. But I had been the one that told him the treasure would need magic, so was it my fault the faerie was now our prisoner?

I had agreed to join this crew and work rather than be taken as a passenger. Every day I questioned whether I had made the right choice. I knew they would not have respected me, but they also would not have made a lord's daughter jump off the ship, as they had made me back when they thought I was Finn.

I knew what they thought of women, and I had defied those notions by working as hard as I could. My duty to the *Raider* was more than just being obedient to Captain Malin. It was showing that I could be a worthy pirate regardless of my sex.

With Laina tied down below, the captain I once respected was no longer in front of me. I had thought he had done me a favor by allowing me to be his translator, but I was a tool to him. I made it all too easy to get exactly what he wanted. And the worst part was, I wasn't the one paying the price.

I wanted to confront him and know why Laina was bound and try to bargain my way out of this. If I did what he wanted, perhaps he would set her free. Or perhaps I would prove useless to him, and I'd have nothing left to use as leverage.

I knew Malin could not be trusted, but I had worked hard to be where I was, and I would not accomplish anything further if I lost my position now. I had hidden my identity for months. I could hide that I knew the truth of his plan with Laina. He would gain this knowledge somehow, whether it was with me or not. If I resisted, I could be risking my security upon the ship and lose trust with the captain. And trust was the only thing that could save us in the end.

I took a breath and told him of the story that was printed upon the pages.

Along the Helika Ridge, where fires seep from the cracks in the ground, there was a dwarf from the high mountains that fell in love with a girl from the lower village. He offered her many gifts that he forged with his own hands, but she turned each one of them down.

"All men seek to impress me," she taunted. "You've made me nothing I have not seen before."

And he thought she was right. He looked around his forge and realized all that he had made her was junk.

First, he had crafted her a necklace from dragonstone that glowed bright in the moonlight. But to the eyes of a lady so fair, it was dull as a pewter spoon.

Next, he made her armor that was impenetrable to any weapon—but she was no warrior. She didn't even care to get her hands dirty.

Finally, he made her a seax of the sharpest metals with an engraved handle. He made the steel look as if it were crafted from oak trees so that the lady could touch his beautiful engravings while she slayed her enemies. But again, she was a village girl, and a knife could not impress her.

"Your gifts are plain and ordinary and do not distract me from the ugliness of your face and body. But if you make me something I have never seen before, something that will impress me, I will take your hand," she told him.

The dwarf became determined. She had given him the hope and drive he needed to craft something that would impress her.

He spent fourteen days and nights in the forge, hardly eating or sleeping. His body grew lean and his mind went in spirals. His eyes only focused on the task in front of him. He hardly noticed the sun and moon setting behind him.

On the fifteenth day, he met the girl at the river to show her what he had spent all this time crafting. The dwarf revealed a ring and before he could explain, she cackled.

"You think you can buy me with a simple ring?" she asked. "You foolish dwarf. Go back to your forge."

She snatched the ring from his palm and flung it into the river, and it sank to the bottom.

The dwarf, defeated and exhausted, lay to sleep on the riverbank.

When he awoke, a beautiful woman, even more beautiful than the village girl, for she was the Sjöfru of the river, held his ring in her hand, admiring it.

"This is a special ring," she said in a dreamy voice.

"My beloved does not think so," he sulked.

"She did not take the time to feel its weight, to see your engravings, or look closely enough to know this is no ordinary ring."

"And you have?"

She nodded and allowed the ring to take in the rays of the sun and harness its power. It shined on the ripples of the water and at the bottom of the river, jewels and coins appeared. The Sjöfru took them into her hands and smiled at them.

"You see the gift I made," the dwarf mused. He took the Sjöfru's hand and his heart quickened. The girl was easily forgotten when he saw this beautiful woman in front of him, who acknowledged his talents.

The girl saw it too though, for she watched them whilst hidden behind a birch tree.

The girl was jealous and shrill. She went to the goddess's temple and asked for help to claim back the gifts that were hers. The goddess could see that she possessed a cruel and selfish heart. She told the girl she would help her, but instead turned her into a starling.

At first, the girl thought this was the goddess's blessing, and that she would be able to take the gift more easily, being so small and quick. She found the lovers, still caught in an embrace by the river.

She swooped down and snatched the ring from the Sjöfru's hand. The dwarf quickly drew up his bow and shot down the starling, not knowing it was the jealous girl. She fell into the river and was washed away with the current. Her and the ring. When she hit the water she flailed around, for the arrow had only brushed her, losing sight of the ring. She looked around for it, but it was gone, swept away with the current.

She went to the dwarf and the Sjöfru and stole the other gifts he had offered—the necklace, the armor, the seax, but each time, the dwarf shot her out of the air, and the gifts were lost to the river.

The dwarf's heart broke a little because now he worried he would lose the Sjöfru. He had nothing to offer her. He offered to go back to his forge, to make her things even more impressive than he already had.

But the Sjöfru had a pure heart, and she kissed his brow.

"There is no need to impress me. I see the beauty in your craft, but it is not the gifts themselves that I find beautiful, but the hands that created them."

The Sjöfru lived with the dwarf in a cottage by the river, and they never left each other's side.

I looked up at the captain and the first mate who were mulling over the story I told them. I thought it sounded a lot like one of the bedtime stories Mama used to tell me, but I wondered if there was truth to it. Malin never told me what the treasure he looked for consisted of, but maybe it was this collection of magical items supposedly lost in the river.

"Is it real?" I finally asked, when neither of them said anything.

"I believe it is," Malin said. "There is another story that tells of treasures like these—the necklace that reflects the moon, the impenetrable armor, the enchanted dagger, and the ring. I have known of the ring because it is said to multiply riches. But I believe the rest are real too.

"The story is that a fisherman was out in the ocean and a terrible storm hit. He was destined to die, but a Havsra—an ocean Sjöfru—took pity on him and dug out these items for him to wield. The necklace guided him home, the armor protected him from the blistering winds, the dagger struck a kraken that had its tentacles around his boat. And the ring made his boat larger and faster so he could overcome the elements that blocked him. He was unkillable, but once home, the sea took back the gifts.

"And then there's this," Malin said, pulling out a yellowed piece of paper, scrawled with more notes.

He handed it to me. It was another diary entry from Captain Kjartan Larsen.

"In the Devil's Rock, I found the hoard. The items four, but my pure hands could not touch them. I did not possess the key that would allow me to wield them," I translated. Furrowing my brow at the riddle, I began to link all the stories in front of me, before Malin spoke.

"You've determined that magic is needed to touch the treasure," Malin said. "Dwarves, the Havsra, and the Sjöfru are Spriggan creatures and they were the ones who brought the magic out of the items. I think to mortal men, these treasures would be junk. But if they are touched by something that has magic, their powers come out."

And Malin's need for Laina became that much more apparent. I was giving him more reasons to hold her captive.

"The Devil's Rock," Malin continued, "is an island south of Brannland, on the side of the country the White River flows out. Many Brannish folktales take place along the White River. It would make sense that the treasure would be there. And so that is where our course is set."

Jenkins nodded and went out of the cabin to inform Grey, leaving Malin and me alone.

"Mayra," he addressed me.

It made me uncomfortable when he used my real name. I had gotten used to being Finn and felt respected when the men continued to address me that way, even the ones who now knew I was not a boy from Playada.

"Will you perform a task for me?"

I didn't see as though I had any other option, so I nodded.

"You know the faerie is below," he said. "And I don't wish any harm to come to her."

"I find that ironic since she's in chains and behind a locked door with one key," I retorted.

"It's for all our safety," he said, in a controlled tone. "I wish you to care for her, bring her meals, and make sure she doesn't do anything rash. She is restrained from using magic, but we need her to be healthy to help us acquire the treasure. I believe this is a situation only a woman can handle delicately," he explained.

My pride simmered, as well as my guilt. "You wish for me to comfort her, while I am the very reason she is locked away," I said. "And you couldn't get Briggs or Grey or someone else to do it?"

"She trusts you more than any of us. Perhaps even now. And I need her to complete this mission." Malin swallowed. "I know because of your upbringing, you wish to see her as near human. But I need to warn you of creatures like her. They can penetrate your mind. I gave her things that will limit her power, but don't for a second think she regards you kindly. She will turn on us, should we give her that chance."

"She is a nice girl," I shot back. "She hasn't done us any harm."

"She tried to attack Jenkins and myself. That is why she is bound."

I blinked at him. "When?"

"When we brought her aboard," Malin said. "I did not wish to throw her in a cell, but I had no choice. She was ready to attack us, to take hold of the ship so she could sail to Brannland on her own. I couldn't allow her to cause a mutiny."

I thought about the girl I met in the tavern. The girl I had spent a wonderful night with. The girl who wept when Prath was finally dead. When I discovered she was an orphan like me. And when we just held each other for comfort. I couldn't see that girl attacking Malin when he offered her passage, but then again, maybe I had not known her long enough to see her character. She had neglected to tell me that she was a faerie.

My mother may have been tried as a Spriggan, but there was a difference between a woman who used herbs to heal and those with inherent magic that was not always used with good intentions. It was because of the reputation of malevolent Spriggan that my mother was mistrusted.

Mama told me of the fae creatures. She spoke of them as kindly as she could, but one could not ignore the more sinister tales of agreements gone wrong, of the changelings, and of the Talurc de Ruh—the cult of dark Spriggan.

I did not know Laina well enough to know her allegiance. I didn't trust Malin. But I could not put my trust fully in her either. However, I could continue to absorb as much information as possible before I began to make moves in either direction.

But I knew she would not care for me to tend to her either. She had once allowed me in her bed, but I did not foresee that ever happening again now that she knew I was on the side of those who had locked her away. She wouldn't trust me at all. My act of bravery was nothing while I was working for the man who captured her. But I couldn't tell any of that to Malin.

I had sworn an oath of loyalty.

"Yes, Captain," I replied compliantly. I needed whatever leverage he allowed me to help her get out of this.

XIV. Wild Heart

"Watson?" I approached the sailing master as he fiddled with a net, untangling the infinite mass of knots. It had been two days since our departure from Port Astreim.

"Hm?" His eyes never left the net, but it seemed he was listening.

I leaned against the railing. "When you lived near the Wastes, did you see anyone or anything?" I rubbed at the back of my neck. "I mean, any fae?"

Watson thrust down the pile of ropes, unable to concentrate at the task at hand and talk to me all at once. He rubbed the sweat from his forehead, smearing more dirt in its place. "My town was outside of them. The fae never left. But there was a thick mist around it. And sometimes you could hear the pounding of drums."

"That's it?"

He nodded.

"How do you know it was the Wastes from the stories if you never saw anything?"

"It's the same spot as it has been for a thousand years," Watson replied. "And everyone knows the signs. The mists, the drums, and sometimes men would get too close and come back red in the face, with a deathly headache and claim the buggers got in their heads."

"Got in their heads?"

"They would hear voices, like devils. Speaking of the lies they had once told. It was enough to drive a man insane. If he wasn't taken, he would never speak above a whisper after that."

"Can Laina get in our heads?" I asked before I could stop myself.

"No, boy. Malin has her wickedness contained."

I raised my eyebrows.

"I need to get this net untangled. Leave me be." Watson busied himself, dismissing me.

I had asked one too many questions. Malin used magic to stop Laina. Such things were illegal. Though, so was kidnap. So were the Spriggan. So was piracy.

I was to bring Laina two meals a day—one in the midmorning, and one in the evening. They fed her well, but she didn't have much appetite. I removed the stale bread and cold soup from her cell, replacing it with a fresh bowl. She didn't look up at me as I gave her fresh soup. I didn't blame her. We held her prisoner when she had done nothing wrong.

She was tucked in the corner, hugging her knees. Her fae features were more apparent without her magic to conceal them. Her ears came to a point. Her eyes were not their vibrant green. Her hair was like mud. And her skin nearly showed gray.

"The food gets worse the longer we're at sea. In a few weeks, it'll just be potato water. Maybe rats. I suggest you eat while there's still goat and spices."

She glanced at the soup, but it was clear she wouldn't eat until I left, if at all.

I was under orders to give her food, empty her bucket, and have minimal contact with her. Malin wished for me to gain her trust, but Malin forbade me from sitting beside her for hours, gossiping like silly women.

For several days, I complied, convincing myself it was for the greater good. I knew very little of real magic and its bounds. If we let her roam free, what was to stop her from crawling into our heads and driving us mad? This thought consumed me as I tried to sleep or focus on the words of another book on rigging. I had taken so much time to fill my head with knowledge, and yet I had grown daft to my surroundings.

I had witnessed the church fill the villagers' heads with fear so they would feel no sympathy when people like my mother were condemned. They worked to hide away any goodness they might possess, shielding it with demonic propaganda.

And I had fallen for it just as they once did.

Laina had become shriveled and broken since we left Astreim. I could only imagine what she had been through. From living at Prath's, to hiding at Sly's, and then to becoming a prisoner once more aboard the *Raider*.

I worked for the man who shackled her. There had to be a way to keep my trust with Malin, while also making her feel less alone and hopeless.

I made small gestures.

"There's a good wind today. Grey says it will take a few days off our voyage."

She didn't move. Her back was to me and she sat cross legged, like a patient monk.

I felt like a fool. The things I spoke of made no difference to her. A good wind just meant less time before Malin had his way with her.

I longed for that brief moment where we had felt mated. I had the opportunity to build something with her and threw it all away because of Malin's greed.

My routine continued. Left her food, took her scraps. She nibbled on them, but only enough to keep her alive.

She consumed my thoughts. Watson said she couldn't penetrate my mind and yet she was all I thought about. The memory of before her capture. And the dread of what I had done.

It was all foolish.

I nearly wept as I saw her, so still and silent, awaiting her torment without any fight left in her.

As I stared at her back, I was tempted to tell her of my intentions to make sure Malin did her no harm, but I feared such blatant disloyalty would come back to haunt us. Instead, I just started to speak, and I told her of my truth.

"I joined the *Raider* to gain passage to Brannland. My mother was from Brannland, but she fell in love with a Playadan soldier during the war. I don't know much about that part of the story, but I know that he loved her. Enough to make me at least. Which I know doesn't mean they were in love, but my mother left her homeland to find him. That has to mean something, right?"

Laina kept her back to me, but her ear, long and elegant, twitched.

"She was very beautiful. And tall. Taller than any woman in our village. As if she didn't have enough ways to stand out with her light eyes and fair skin. Her eyes were like frost and starlight. Any man would have loved her if they saw her. Even more if they really knew her."

I swallowed the lump in my throat but continued to speak.

"She went looking for her love after the war, with me in her belly. But when she found his hometown, a thousand miles from her own homeland, my father's brother told her that he was dead. With nowhere else to go, she married him—my uncle that is. It could have been worse I suppose. He was a lord. He was never cruel to me. I didn't even know he wasn't my father until just before I left home. But they made me think love was meaningless. Two people who spent decades together but had no love for each other. If that was to be my fate, I didn't ever want love.

"My only love was my mother. She never let go of her traditions. The Brannish practice religion differently than the Playadans. And that made her, and later me, an outcast. You know about the war on Spriggans, of course. And I know it's different for fae born than for my mother who was called a witch, but the outcome was still the same. I watched her hang for singing a song in Brannish. I was there when they took her. Her last words were my own name. And I thought I was next."

I started to tear up. I hadn't meant to tell her that. I hadn't meant to tell anyone that, but it boiled out of me.

Laina was quiet, but I could tell she listened to me. She turned and watched my face as I spoke and as I tried to get my hands to stop shaking.

"What was her name?" Laina asked, her voice sweet and steady.

"Vivanka," I said, wiping my cheeks with my sleeve.

"What was the song?" Laina asked.

"I—" I hesitated. I hadn't spoken of it since that day.

Laina's hand went through the bars, and she touched my knee.

"*Wild heart*," I said in Brannish.

Laina's eyes brightened at this reveal. Perhaps she recognized the song, but I could only speculate. She maintained a chilled silence for several moments before removing her hand and saying, "You know, it is absolutely despicable that someone who claims they understand my struggles, whose own mother was killed due to the war against the Spriggan, would remain loyal to the side that lit the fire."

Laina crawled back to the corner of her cell.

There was so much I wanted to say. If my voice was not caught in my throat, I would have denied her claims. I was escaping my enemies, not joining them. Malin gave me refuge from the people who would have killed me. And I fought for my freedom and would fight for hers as well.

But it was all lies.

I swore an oath to Malin to gain information from Laina. I practically served her to the captain on a platter.

To Laina, I was just as much the enemy as Malin.

Finally, because there was no use hiding from it any longer, I admitted the truth. "You're right. My mother would be ashamed of me for allowing this to happen. But I will make it right."

Laina did not move towards me and I did not trick myself into thinking she believed me. The only thing I could do was stay true to my word.

I wiped my eyes as I left her cell, ready to lay awake for the night.

Jenkins watched me from the top of the stairs, and my stomach hollowed. There was no way to know what he heard or what he thought.

I lay in my hammock that night, my stomach tight with dread.

XV: The Kraken

What would my mother think of me? My mission to the north was all so that I could be back amongst her people and learn of her culture, and escape the place that condemned her to death. All that sounded noble. But I knew I was fooling myself into thinking everything I did was to preserve my mother's memory.

I knew her mistrust of the wee folk, but there was no disdain towards them. Had she found Laina, so human, so sweet, so bold, she would not have turned her over as easily as I had. No. Despite the pure magic that was in Laina, my mother would have seen very clearly that it was Malin's heart that was cold and wicked, and Laina's that was just trying to survive in a world that would never accept all that she was.

My mother lived by her own moral code even when it went against those in power. She was willing to die for such a cause. She was willing to die for me. I couldn't waste her memory.

The sea grew much colder a few weeks after our departure from Astreim. The Aldinian waters had already been much icier than those to the south, and it was only to get worse as we continued north to the lands of eternal winter.

We only stayed above deck when we were on shift. Otherwise, we shivered below, hoping to spare ourselves from the wind chap and frequent rainstorms. I clung protectively to my cloak. Blankets were scarce amongst the crew, being that they hadn't sailed above Astreim in years. There wasn't a need when you only took ships around the Playadan coast.

I prayed that Laina had been given warm clothes and a blanket. That cell must have been even colder than what we suffered here with the whole crew providing body heat.

Perhaps I could go check on her when night fell.

"Watson's still up in the crow's nest," Briggs chattered from his hammock.

"Won't the old man ever quit?" Grover asked.

I had seldomly seen Watson come down from his post except when food was not brought to him or when he had to meet with the captain.

"Surely he doesn't sleep up there," I speculated, but as I said it, I couldn't recall ever seeing him in the crews' quarters. There were three beds in the officer's quarters, for the first mate, the battle master, and supposedly the sailing master, but I didn't think Watson had ever joined them there.

"He's stubborn as a mule, he is. Da used to say the same thing," Briggs said. "Da and him joined 'round the same season."

"Wasn't your dad the sailing master before him?" I asked.

Briggs nodded. "Watson was the oldest crew mate other than Jenkins when Da died."

"How did he die again?" I asked.

"Sickness. But it was more about loyalty to Cap'n. Malin's always chosen folks based on loyalty. He knows Watson would never go against his wishes."

I couldn't imagine any of the officers working against Malin. Which was why there was a faerie shivering in a metal cell for the sake of legendary treasure.

I had not seen her in several days. Jenkins's boy took my duty of bringing her food and emptying her bucket. Ever since Jenkins had walked in on us, I had felt uneasy, but I was yet to hear from the captain. It was Jenkins who told me I had been relieved of tending to her.

"Malin believes she will never open up to someone who is obviously following our orders. Pax will bring her food. You just work on the larger task at hand. Befriend the fae. Charm her again."

Jenkins had heard us talking and while I had thought it would be enough proof to show I was not loyal to Malin, perhaps it was perceived as efforts to get closer to Laina. If they only knew we had grown worlds apart.

I was meant to befriend her, but she did not want me, so instead I kept my eyes open for anything that could help me help her.

My duties had dissolved down to dinner prep with Peel, swabbing the deck and cleaning the officers' and captain's quarters. There was nothing to translate, giving me too much time to sit around and worry about the schemes I was not seeing. Nothing felt tangible, everything just out of reach. All I had was the translation that promised that he needed her blood.

That wasn't enough. The crew would not save the faerie if it were only her life at stake. And with such little evidence, who was even to say her life was at risk? He just needed faerie blood, which didn't require killing her.

I had a feeling there was more I wasn't seeing. Time was running out for me too. I was the lowest member of the crew and, therefore, not someone who had the right to question his methods. I had gotten lucky with Jenkins, but if anyone thought I was not following orders, or that I had lost my trust in Malin, I could be disposed. I was just a part of his crew, a piece of his ship. But I was also the only one who spoke Brannish. Perhaps that would be enough to buy me more time to find answers.

The captain allowed me to see Laina to gain her trust. I needed it for my own reasons. But

I knew that would be unattainable without some kind of tangible evidence that she would make it out okay at the end of this. I needed more answers before I went to see her again. I left my wool cloak on the ground near her cell, choosing to shiver in my hammock rather than let her go cold alone.

Malin went with Watson and Jenkins for an hour each day to the navigation room to ensure we were on course and address any repairs or other concerns regarding the ship. That was when I was expected to go clean his quarters so he could come back and not be bothered for the remainder of the day. Before, he had not minded my infrequent visits and even seemed to enjoy our small talk. But those days had since passed.

Still, even after everything, I wanted to believe that Malin was not the true villain. He had saved me from Playada after all and allowed me to learn aboard his ship. I couldn't imagine many captains giving liberties to some lord's daughter like learning to fight and sitting amongst the crew as an equal. Yes, life had grown more difficult the last few weeks, but I still was on my way to Brannland and that was all I had hoped for before I had ever joined the *Wind Raider*.

In those weeks, while it bothered me that Laina was locked away, I also still believed it could be for good reason. She could get into our minds. She would rebel against the captain. And at the end of all this, when he got her blood and his damned treasure, he would free her and we'd be on our way. As soon as I found something, like a diary entry or a written statement that said as much, I could go to Laina and promise her safety and assure her passage to Brannland in exchange for her services to the captain. Maybe I could also convince Malin to allow her to walk free in exchange for her compliance.

I cleared his dirty plates and food waste piled from lunch and breakfast. I got the honor of emptying his chamber pot and turning over his bed sheets. There was no way to wash them, so I had to take them out to the main deck and give them a good shake to at least remove any dirt or crumbs that slipped in from the bottom of his feet. I dusted the corners of the room, somehow finding spiders even though it had been weeks since we had been on land.

I may have said curses under my breath while I cleared his room, but I still did not openly complain. To do so would risk my lowly station. I needed to keep my nose clean enough so that I still would make it to Brannland. And not take away the responsibilities that gained me information on Malin's business.

I organized his desk, under strict orders to not read any of the papers unless the captain handed them to me personally. Being able to read three languages made the task more difficult. Most of the time, I only caught glimpses of random coordinates or names of ships or places, which out of context held no meaning.

On that particular day, his log had been tucked away, and maps folded over. I shouldn't have been able to read anything, but when I lifted the map only to wipe down the desk beneath it, a note fluttered to the ground, scrawled in Playadan.

I knelt to pick it up, starting to fold it over again to put it back, but some of the words leapt out at me before I could help it. *Fae. New girl. Sly.*

I looked at the clock before continuing. Malin would be away another twenty minutes with the officers. Unfolding the note, I read the rest of what I now saw was a journal entry.

"Spoke to the apothecary in Astreim about the rumored fae. I am certain she is the new girl working for Sly. The woman also told me more about the Dwarf's Treasure. She confirmed it could be found at Devil's Rock and she confirmed the theory that Spriggan magic is needed to activate the tools. She also revealed that a worthy sacrifice is needed to take the prize. There is a guard there, a legend the Brannish have spoken of. She seemed to believe it to be true."

My heart stuttered. *Sacrifice.* Laina would be used for more than just her blood. Malin meant to kill her.

How had I not seen this? Despite my bitterness toward the captain, I'd clung to hoping Malin's need for Laina's involvement, albeit barbaric in her capture, was for good reason. But this note disproved all of that. There was no longer room to deny the captain's intentions. This wasn't just about using Laina's magic to get the treasure.

He wanted her blood. He was to sacrifice her to fill his pockets. All for a legendary treasure that may not even exist.

I had known Laina was in danger, but I had hoped that once Malin had his hands on the treasure, he would release us both to Brannland. But with this information, Laina may never get to see Brannland, unless I somehow stopped him. But how was I to do that, when my life also depended on making sure he could trust me?

I thrust the note beneath the map. I couldn't risk him knowing I had read it. But if I were to confront him later, he would deny it. And I knew no one would be on my side if I accused him. This was how tightly Malin had a hold on his crew. I would be foolish to try and combat him. But what other choice did I have? He would kill Laina. And what was to stop him from going after me or anyone else that got in his way?

I needed to talk to Grey, but as I moved to the door, the ship shuddered, and I fell back, knocking down the rest of the parchment off the desk. In a bold move, I grabbed the note and stuffed it in my pocket, hoping Malin would blame its disappearance on the quake of the ship.

I fled the cabin and could see the officers and Grey at the helm pointing out at the ocean.

"I swear, I saw it come up from there," Grey said, pointing at the water right in front of us. "It pushed the ship, knocked us off our course."

Malin looked up at the gray clouds swirling above and then at the spot of water. The sea was becoming rougher from the turning weather.

"Well, get us back on course. Must have hit a rock or something."

"It wasn't a rock, Captain," Gray protested, his face grave.

"You've been on shift for ten hours, boy," Jenkins said. "Go below and get some rest. I'll man the wheel." He looked over to me. "Santana, turn the rudder starboard."

I nodded, immediately going towards the stern.

As I turned the rudder pedals, I looked up across the water. There was a bubbling at the surface of the water a hundred feet out. I stared at the water for a moment, still working the pedal, my mind not yet comprehending what I was seeing. The surface of the water broke and I looked into its great big yellow eyes. Its purple head was oblong, curving back so the base was still submerged. I couldn't see anything below its eyes, but I could see one of its bright orange tentacles reaching to swipe at the ship.

I scrambled back to the main deck.

"Jenkins!" I called to the first mate at the helm. "There's—"

I stumbled in front of him, tripping over his boot.

"What the hell is wrong with you?" he asked.

I pointed back. "Just look!"

He turned his head to the back of the ship, but the beast had already resubmerged its head.

"There's nothing there."

I looked around, to the sides and front of the ship. It was swimming around us, playing with our minds, maybe knowing Grey and I sounded crazy to the others. I leaned over the portside when a tentacle came up again, swiping the side of the ship so that it lurched again, spinning the ship back in the direction we came from.

Jenkins had fallen back away from the wheel, but I could see from the horror in his eyes he had finally seen the monster's tentacle. He ran to ring the bell, calling the entire crew to the main deck.

The *Wind Raider*'s crew had raided the king's ships. They had battled the royal navy. They took prisoners and killed them if it was necessary or profitable. I had seen the blood of sailors on Briggs' shirt. There was a faerie being held below deck. I had even shot a man. But nobody amongst the crew had ever battled a sea monster and I could see from their horrified faces that they didn't even know where to begin.

Stratford, the brave battle master, teetered as he watched the monster emerge its face and spit water over the side of the ship. It thrust another tentacle against the side, tilting us starboard. I lost my footing, as did many of the other men.

"Awake ye lazy buffoons!" the battle master called, shaking his head as if to shake all fear from it. "Man your stations! Get below if you don't want to be a kraken's dinner!"

Kamau had no issue following his commander down, as did a few of the other braver men. But Briggs and Grover had frozen. For once, I didn't blame them. I didn't see how this encounter wouldn't end with us at the bottom of the ocean. But there was no room for me to think like that. That wouldn't keep us alive.

The men below had lit the cannons, shooting them at the beast. Many of them couldn't make contact, unable to direct at a moving target when they were used to the slow crawl of merchant ships. A single shot hit right into what I perceived to be the creature's neck. But the beast just glared at the ship, the cannonball sinking into its jelly-like flesh. Another round of shots went off and a few men had gotten a hold of their pistols and were shooting towards the thing's head, but it didn't seem to care.

Another tentacle made a grab for the deck. It snaked its way along to my foot. I scurried back, knocking into Briggs. The tentacle made do with him, wrapping itself around his leg and pulling him towards the railing, where he would dangle over. My eyes whipped around for something, anything that could stop it. An axe had slid across the deck, lodged between two barrels. I grabbed for it and sprinted for Briggs, reeling the axe back above my head. It came down on the tentacle, cutting right through. It bled black and the creature let out a screech.

Briggs was still near frozen, looking to me and to the tentacle. He looked as though he would faint.

"Get up and go for its tentacles!" I told him, gripping his shoulder, hoping to rouse him from his petrified state. "Get an axe or a sword or anything that could cut them off."

He snapped out of it and searched around himself for another axe. The creature tried to grab for others, but now that we knew its tentacles were its weakness, other crew mates worked at trying to cut them off. The squid wasn't stupid. It tried to be quick, going for our masts. It knocked down the main mast, but when the large tentacle hit the deck, I cut it halfway up and the thing screeched again, falling back into the water.

"Stop shooting at it!" I yelled down to Stratford. "The balls don't hurt it!"

In addition to my two, three others had been cut, leaving the creature with only half its limbs. It disappeared beneath the water, and we had a moment to rest, though all of us kept careful eyes around us for any more tentacles.

Looking around, the creature had cut a nasty slice into the side of the ship. I thought, with utter dread, of the water that might be seeping below deck. That needed to be mended. The mast had fallen which meant we were near immobile.

Captain Malin was on the main deck, looking at the damage with the same horror I was. We would sink in hours if the creature didn't come back to finish us off first.

"We need Laina!" I called to him.

He snapped a look at me. I feared he would be foolish and prideful and not utilize the magic that she wielded, but he nodded once. I moved to go below deck, but a shadow fell over me, as one more tentacle lifted from the water, swatting at the crow's nest where Watson still was. I could do nothing but watch as he fell to the main deck, his head and back hitting the wood.

"No!" I screamed in unison with Jenkins and Grey. It was Kamau who cut that sixth and seemingly largest tentacle, but the damage had already been done.

"Go get the faerie," Jenkins said to me, putting the keys in my hand, before rushing to the sailing master's side.

I did not think there was a possibility he survived but I had to hope. I looked at the ocean, the squid resubmerging in the water. Would it be back? We had six of its tentacles, more than half. I waited another minute, but it didn't reappear. Maybe we had done enough to avoid being killed by the sea monster.

"Laina," I whispered to myself, my hands shaking, remembering we needed her to help mend the ship and to save our sailing master. I stumbled down the steps to her cell, gripping the bars. "Laina, we need you."

"What's happening up there?" Laina asked, her eyes giving away her worry. My cloak hung around her shoulders.

"There's a sea monster," I spoke shakily, my whole body fading with fear. "We did what we could and almost nobody was hurt, but it got Watson and there's a hole in the ship. We need your help." I held the keys up to her and her eyes brightened.

"Malin's agreed to release me?"

I nodded, sticking the key into the lock and unlatching it. Laina got up and followed me to the main deck.

Malin stopped us at the top of the stairs. "The kraken seems to have fled. Can you mend the ship?"

She snorted. "Pity about your boat."

Malin glowered. "We'll all drown if you don't help us."

She looked around, taking in the damage the monster had done. There was no denying that we were in a desperate place. "You stripped me of magic and continued to feed me the poison. I can do nothing."

He held a vial up to her. "This will reverse what I have done temporarily, but I need your word that you will use your powers only to mend the ship."

Laina seemed to consider this, but shook her head, smirking at the captain. "You haven't let me see daylight in weeks. You take my powers and only release me now that you're in need. Doesn't seem fair."

I looked around Malin to where Watson's body was. The crowd was still there, many holding their hats, their heads bowed. The top of the mast was draped across the deck, its sail blanketed over half the ship.

"Please, Laina," I whispered.

"Not unless the captain agrees to allow me freedom aboard the ship," Laina glared at him.

He sighed. Even in his pride and rigidness, he was not unreasonable. Water dripped below and that drip would only grow if we did not tend to it fast. "Fine."

I could not determine if the captain was being truthful. I knew there was a large possibility of him taking her below again as soon as she did as he desired. I felt the note burning in my pocket. Malin only saw Laina as a tool. Perhaps that is what we all were to him.

Still, Laina took the vial from his unwilling hand. I was sure she did not trust his word either, but a chance at gaining magic had to have been too tempting to withhold any longer.

She drank the liquid from the vial and her eyes grew vibrant and her skin regained that soft glow.

Her magic was not infinite. She could not repair the ship with anything that wasn't already within our possession. But her powers did assist in raising the mast, locking it in place, and her efforts allowed the men to not do so with the last bit of energy they had.

She lowered them down to the water, so they hovered without ropes or hands. They patched the leaks in the ship before too much water seeped through. Many were apprehensive to allow her magic to touch them. Afterall, a flick of her wrist could be their death. But she lowered Grey and Kamau, and after they made repairs, they returned to the deck safely. The others grew to trust her in minuscule amounts when they saw the colors raised and a dry lower ship.

Laina could not raise the dead. We gave Watson's body to the sea, binding him in cloth and casting him into the ocean with two cannonballs tied to his feet. The crow's nest was back in its place, but empty without the sailing master's presence. Even in my despair, I wondered how he would have felt about a faerie repairing all we had lost when he was amongst the most superstitious of us all towards the wee folk.

With Laina being our lifeline, the men did as she said and spoke to her tactfully. They had all admired her when she was our tavern maid, but upon finding out she was fae, many of them began to speak of her with spite and prejudice. Malin's attitude towards her kind was catching and I had heard the nasty remarks they made about her. Just like the ones made towards my mother back home.

"Laina," I said, catching her hand once the ship had been tended to. She pulled away from me, narrowing her eyes at me.

"Thank you for helping us," I said.

"Better the ship can sail then for us all to drown I suppose," she replied, though I'm sure she was thinking of a few she wished had drowned.

"Laina, I'm so sorry."

"For what?" she sneered. "For locking me away? For taking me from my home? For ruining everything I built for myself all so your captain can get whatever he desires?"

I was. For everything she said, but I was trapped in a corner. I knew of Malin's plan but I couldn't turn on him. I'd be risking our lives. The whole crew would have no problem disposing of two women who turned on their captain.

She was still looking at me as I worked out in my brain what exactly I was to tell her to gain her confidence in me and to assure her that my plan was to protect her. I motioned for her to follow me to the railing. The men were still repairing the ship but had their eyes on us.

In a low voice, I told her, "He's after the dwarf's treasure. He believes you are the key."

"But it's just a legend," she replied, her brow furrowing.

"He thinks he has enough evidence to prove that it's real. He was after a fae to use them to get the tools. He thinks your touch will bring them power."

"I've heard of them."

"I need to find out more. I am still Malin's cabin boy, so I still get to clean his quarters."

Laina nodded slowly. "How can I know you won't let him have me in the end?"

"You will just have to trust me," I said, knowing I still had nothing tangible to prove myself to her. I only had my word. "But I do know, my mother would never tolerate a greedy captain capturing and exploiting anyone for their magic."

She nodded more confidently this time, and she placed a small kiss on my cheek.

I did not tell her of Malin's plan to kill her. I was conflicted and felt as though I owed her that explanation, but I feared she would lash out if I said all I knew of the plan. There were more pieces I needed to collect. I still did not have all the answers and if I told her, she could act too quickly and blow all trust I had with Malin. I kept the note in my pocket to myself, with the intention of getting more answers.

At least I had gained back some of Laina's trust.

That night, Laina sat amongst us at dinner while we continued to sail north, our course set for a small island just past the border of the Brannish Sea. There was a port there where we could dock and further repair the ship, but all things considered, the *Raider* was sailing just fine.

We sat at the long table on the quarter deck, which was only used for special occasions. Malin sat at the head, with Jenkins and Stratford on either side of him. Watson's seat beside Jenkins was left empty out of respect. I sat beside Laina towards the other end of the table, Grey, Briggs, and Kamau around us, with the rest of the crew filling in the middle.

Peel had killed one of his goats and made a wine sauce and potatoes with it. It was a way to celebrate our near-death experience and to honor Watson's memory.

"Watson joined this crew thirty years ago," Malin told us, swirling his glass of wine, looking thoughtfully at it. "He was a hell of a sailor and warrior before he took on his role as sailing master. He took manning his post literally, hardly ever coming down from that damned crow's nest, up until the very end."

Some of the crew chuckled, not to mock the sailing master, but in their nostalgia.

"I can say with certainty that he went out of this world exactly how he intended to. Watson is irreplaceable. He is the heretic of what it is to be loyal to this crew. We are in a new age of the *Raider*. Many of the men who were once the backbone of this ship and all that she stands for have passed onwards. I had a vision when I was a boy that I would stand at the helm amongst men with golden hearts. Watson was undeniably one of these men whose print rests on my very soul. He, and Cane and Angus and Alfie and Starky."

His eyes swept over the table, sliding passed Briggs's who did not seem to be emotional, but thoughtful.

"I can only pray that their deaths meant something and that they were released from the madness of this world and led to paradise. In this new age, I cling to those who have sworn me their oaths and offer their golden hearts. It is my life's mission to remain faithful to this ship, to the men of this crew, and to our combined efforts in securing all that is rightfully ours. Our bounty is waiting, gents. I know Watson would only wish for us to continue on."

Malin raised his glass. "Loyal 'til Death."

"Loyal 'til Death," the rest of the crew called back, raising their glasses to Watson.

I had not spoken. I drank to Watson, but my mouth soured at the captain's sentiment. Loyal 'til Death was beginning to feel like a much heavier burden.

Stratford cleared his throat. "I gotta say, as battle master, also with a few years under my belt, I 'ave seen o' lot of things. A giant squid isn't one of 'em. We were unprepared and I can't hold my men at fault. But I do feel the need to acknowledge someone who might be the very reason we're almost all still here." His eyes twinkled at me. "Finn, it was yer lion's heart that allowed us to get out of the beast's clutches, and to that, we all owe you our lives," he lifted his goblet.

The entire crew lifted theirs too. Even Briggs.

"To Fearless Finn!" Stratford belted in a war cry.

"Fearless Finn!"

Malin remained silent, sipping from his cup with his eyes boring into me. A chill went through me and the pocket that held his note burned against my thigh.

XVI: A Moment of Bliss

I had never known such conflicted happiness like I knew the night that the kraken had been killed. Since leaving home, all I wanted was to be taken seriously despite the circumstances of my birth and my gender. I knew it would take a miraculous feat to accomplish that, but I never expected this.

Regardless, I found myself sitting amongst my crew, drinking with them as brothers, with Laina's pretty head resting on my shoulder, while Jagged Everett led us through shanties.

"Do you know *Blow the Man Down*?" he asked.

"The version you sing, or the real one?" Jenkins asked.

"Whatchu mean? Mine is the right version," Everett shot back.

"Och, no it ain't. You have two songs mixed up." Jenkins cleared his throat, obviously needing to give an example.

As I was a walking down Paradise Street
Way aye blow the man down
A pretty young damsel I chanced to meet.
Give me some time to blow the man down!

Several others joined in at this point:

She was round in the counter and bluff in the bow,
Way aye blow the man down
So I took in all sail and cried, "Way enough now."
Give me some time to blow the man down!

Everett offered his mixed-up lyrics. From the combatting tunes I learned the next verse was:

So I tailed her my flipper and took her in tow

Way aye blow the man down
And yardarm to yardarm away we did go.
Give me some time to blow the man down!

Meanwhile Everett insisted on singing:

A pretty young eel with a slippery tail
Way aye blow the man down
She climbs up the loft and she reefs the top sail
Give me some time to blow the man down!

"Jagged!" Jenkins interjected, throwing the rest of the men off the melody. "You're getting the songs mixed up. That's the one about the fishes. This is the one about the mutiny."

"Well, it's the same damn tune," Everett grumbled.

That could have been argued about almost all the songs the crew sang aboard the ship, but I did not offer anything to this conversation. I just watched as Laina giggled at the exchange and a part of my heart fluttered at finally seeing her free and at ease.

She was quiet, at first, trying to observe rather than participate. She was suddenly around the men who had captured her, whom

I had gotten to know well over the last six months, but they were still practically strangers to her. The awkwardness of their relationship was not brought up though, and as the night went on, she opened up more, reassuming the position of the outspoken tavern maid I had been dazzled by weeks before.

"I bet I can drink you under this table," Laina shot at Briggs who had the gall to suggest Laina could not handle her drink which was why she sipped so politely.

"Oh, the lass thinks she can compete with the sailor." Briggs rolled his eyes.

"You get weepy when you're drunk," Grey said, sipping from his own cup.

"Weepy?" Briggs scoffed. "I'm not a child any longer."

That was true. Briggs celebrated his eighteenth birthday a few weeks before, but he would always be seen as the Kid to his crewmates.

"I lived in a tavern for two years," Laina challenged, "and you think I can't drink more than you can?"

I'm not sure if Laina knew that challenging Briggs would result in a competition, as it always did, but she soon learned when Kamau brought over one of the wooden tables and five tankards of beer were lined up in front of each of them.

"You don't have to, you know?" I whispered to her when no one could hear, not wanting to embarrass her in front of the crew.

She raised an eyebrow at me. "Do you have little faith in me as well?"

Of course I didn't. But I knew Briggs had at least fifty pounds on Laina and was a dirty cheat, but I was not about to fight her battles for her. "Of course not, but be sure to play as dirty as him." She kissed my nose and met my gaze with a sly grin.

"On your marks," Kamau called. The crew gathered around the table, watching Briggs and Laina as they got in crouching poses, ready to snatch up their pints. "Get set. Go!"

Laina snatched up the pint before Briggs could and gulped it down in four sips. She was on the second, but so was Briggs. The cups were the metal tankards so no one could see the second-by-second progress, but Kamau eyed each empty cup to make sure every sip was taken. They moved on to the third and that was when the crew made sure to make it more of a challenge.

"Yer guzzlin' the ale deeper than a sailor's cock," Stratford whistled at Briggs.

Briggs sputtered a bit but powered through. They were on their fourth and I watched Briggs go a bit cross eyed as he breathlessly grabbed for the cup. Laina had slowed down as well, but still sipped expressionless.

"Too bad the lass prefers honeypot," Everett said without discretion.

The ale pushed her belly out over her skirts, but the fifth drink still made it down her throat before Briggs could finish and she raised her hands after she slammed down the empty cup.

Briggs had clearly lost, without any way to deny it or win by default and the crew clearly accepted Laina now that she had shown up the Kid. But to his credit, perhaps turning into a man had raised his maturity enough to not sulk at losing. Instead, Laina received all their compliments on her handling her drink and having the gut of a sailor. She smiled, but once I had gotten her alone, I found out her secret.

I had laid out a blanket up in the mended crow's nest. We could have gone to her cell, now left unlocked where there was a bed. But I couldn't imagine making her go back there after being locked away for days. I wanted her to be able to sleep under the sky and not fear her freedom would be taken away again.

"Fae don't get drunk off that stuff," she said, belching from the gasses. "The stuff we drink would knock you right under the table. Fae wine is at least triple what that dirty water is."

I laughed. "Oh man, but it is a good trick to gain a sailor's confidence."

She smirked. "And it gets the loud mouthed one to shut up."

As happy as I was to finally have the freedom to show Laina affection around the crew, I was happier to finally have the night for the two of us alone. I held her and kissed her for the first time since the night at the tavern. That first night had been about me, her giving me the best first experience I could have ever dreamed of. I could not be patient and wait, easing into her pleasure. Following the battle and following her release, all I wanted was to devour her.

She lay out on the blanket, her dress still on, but her undergarments removed. I remembered all she had done to me that first night, and I worked to mirror her expert moves, albeit clumsily. But I must have done something right, as her toes curled when my tongue danced over the bud between her legs. I was enchanted with the look on her face, the way her brow crinkled and the heavenly sigh that escaped her lips. I was hardly experienced in the art of pleasing a woman, and worried I would be inadequate in bringing her pleasure. But I could feel her growing slick and the tension in her legs told me she was getting close. I buried my fingers inside of her as my tongue continued its teasing play.

There was a moment of silence, both from her breath and from the world around us. I had grown uncaring of anything that lay beyond the realm of the crow's nest. All that mattered was the woman who tasted like honey and smelled of dahlias. I felt her shatter into a million pieces as she moaned my name, making my need for her grow. Yet, I felt a release in knowing I had given her what she had once given me—that feeling of being on another plane of existence, anchored only by the person who brought me there.

We lay on the hard deck beneath the blanket. Her arms were wrapped around my neck, her breasts still bare from where I had pulled down her dress to taste the supple peaks. I wished to touch them more, but also knew we needed rest. We could have both slept, but instead we continued to whisper and look up at the stars.

We had spoken simply for a while. Of the calmness of the sea after our encounter of the kraken, and how delicious dinner was, and how Briggs seemed a bit more humble after being bested by two women. But I could not contain myself much longer, holding onto the question that burned in me.

"Do you still hate us for it?" I asked her.

"Hate you for what?"

"Locking you away."

Laina turned over to face me, tucking her breasts back into her dress. Her green eyes found mine and I admired their reclaimed vibrancy. "No. Malin can go throw himself to the sea for all I care, but I knew you and the crew were just following orders."

"It doesn't make it right," I said, still disappointed in myself. "I think the crew also is just prone to the skepticism surrounding Spriggan," I said. It was no excuse, but I was beginning to believe that people were followers and followed what they knew to be safe. Humans did not know much about the fae except in folklore which often told of them being spiteful and mischievous. If they got the chance to speak with them, like the crew had with Laina, maybe they wouldn't be so skeptical.

"I'm used to that. That's why I almost didn't tell Max what I was. I planned to never use magic again."

"Really?"

She nodded. Her brow furrowed before continuing to speak, considering what to tell me. "My people were killed for what we are. All of them. I'm supposed to be dead and for a while I thought if I used magic, I was dishonoring their memory.

"The Wastes are supposed to be impenetrable. I've thought a lot over these past few years if they somehow got someone from the inside or another magic being to aid them, but they shattered the shield that has protected my people for two hundred years, since my ancestors sailed from Brannland.

"My mother sensed it. She could feel the shield breaking, as did many of the other more powerful fae. Their powers were linked to the shield's magic, and it struck terror within them. They knew it was coming down. She brought me to the edge and forced me out before the attackers got in and they slaughtered them all. I was miles away, but I heard the gunfire and the screams. When the shield went down, something happened to our magic and it... changed. I still had my magic, but it took a long time to force it out of me again. I think whatever they did stopped it for a while, so they had time to kill my family. Just like when Malin bound my magic."

I held her tight, not wanting to interrupt her or make her carry on if she didn't wish to. I could feel her shoulders shake a bit.

"I just..." Laina's voice broke. "I don't want to hate. But how can I not? After what Prath did to me. And Malin. I don't see how helping rebuild the ship changes how he feels towards my kind."

"He promised you'd be free," I told her.

"I don't trust his word," she said, her voice sturdy again.

Neither do I, I thought, but I didn't say it, knowing it wasn't the right thing to say. Admitting to what I knew about him would spark her well-deserved anger. I didn't want to do anything that would shatter this moment. All I wanted was to keep Laina in my arms as long as possible.

"I won't let anything happen to you," I said instead. "You'll be safe as long as you're with me."

She nodded and nestled into my chest.

I felt guilty then, not telling her of what I knew of the captain's plan. But I had not figured out what I was to do about it, and I feared I would fill her with rage before I could find my footing. These were problems we could solve in the coming days. I would tell her. I could maybe tell my trusted crew mates too. I just had to figure out how to not let the captain on to my plotting.

When I woke up a few hours later, she was gone, as was the note in my pocket.

XVII: The Incident

Laina wasn't at breakfast, nor was she wandering around the ship. I had assumed that perhaps she had found some remote corner to sleep. The crow's nest was private, but not necessarily the most comfortable place to rest our heads. I tried not to be disappointed that she didn't stay, but who was I to rob her of a good night's sleep?

I had made the mistake once of assuming she was being well-treated with Malin. I didn't make the same mistake and went to his quarters.

"Good afternoon, Finn," Malin said, unsurprised when I came in without knocking.

"Good performance yesterday. The men will be talking about it for years to come."

"Where's Laina?" I asked, fearing the answer I was to receive.

Malin frowned at me, displeased that I didn't partake in his meaningless small talk. "The girl definitely has left her mark on your mind. There was an incident last night. The fae slipped into my quarters and held a knife to my throat. She meant to kill me. Thankfully, I anticipated such and I was able to bind her magic again and get her back to her cell."

Horror struck me. It couldn't possibly be true. Laina had every reason to be upset. And the note in my pocket was now with her. She would have known of Malin's schemes.

"You were with her last night," Malin said, reading my expression. "Did she say anything that would suggest that she planned on committing this crime?"

I hesitated. I knew she was angry. She had said she wouldn't forgive Malin, but she did not say anything about murder. Though, if she had seen my note, it would definitely explain why.

"Sir," I croaked, unsure if I should be telling him, but the burden weighed on me. "I—" I nearly confessed to the note, but realized that would have been foolish. It was the only bargaining chip I had, even if it was now on Laina's person. But I still needed answers. "Do you mean to kill her? The legend... and the memo I translated about needing blood... do you mean to kill Laina to get the treasure?"

"I was told by the apothecary that I would need a sacrifice. Not the fae though," he explained. "A simple sheep or goat would do. Just something to offer the northern pagan gods."

I met his eyes. "Swear?" The word slipped out before I could stop it.

"Do you have reason to mistrust me?" Malin asked. I could think of many, but I waited for him to finish. "I allowed you to join my crew and to prove yourself as a worthy sailor. You were nothing more than a lady waiting to be wed and bred before you joined us. Now you are one of the crew, respected by all. You were instrumental in killing the kraken. You learned to fight for us all. I see all that you are, Mayra. And I see a member of the crew that will continue to bring us glory, but don't let the ways of that fae bring you down. She means to do me harm and sees you as the easiest way. She could have chosen Briggs, Grey, or Kamau, but they are all strong with loyalty. You, being young and naïve are an easy target. You see that, don't you?"

Did I see that? She had taken me to her bed. She had made me feel ultimate pleasure. But that was all that was. I did not know if she shared my affections. She had never said so much.

He nodded, though there was still a cloud of disappointment above him. "In her cell she will remain until we are to Brannland. And Pax and Briggs will look after her. You are not to see her."

"What?" I asked. "But sir—"

"She was in your bed, Mayra," Malin told me. "I trust your loyalty. I trust that you wouldn't lie to me. But it is clear that you are capable of being manipulated by the fae and I can't risk my life again."

There was nothing to argue. As much as I hated it, as much as I wished it wasn't true, Laina had fooled me.

"It happens to the best of us, lass" he told me, his expression softening. "I realize this is an act of young love and many of us go blind when a temptress gets her clutches on us. The important thing is to remember who you are to this ship. In fact, I have some good news through this. Would you go fetch Loverboy?"

I wasn't sure what kind of good news could honestly be brought about in light of recent events, but I did as I was told. Grey was at the helm with a far-off gaze.

"Malin would like to see us both," I told him.

He turned my way, taking in my expression. "What happened?"

"It's Laina," I said quietly. "Malin says she slipped in his quarters and attempted to kill him."

Grey looked surprised. "I mean... 'spose we did capture her. I just wouldn't have thought."

I shrugged. "It's what Malin says."

Neither of us said it, because of the oath we swore to be loyal to the *Raider*, but I hoped Grey was thinking what I was thinking: perhaps the captain's word wasn't as pure as we were meant to believe.

The two of us soon sat across from Malin at his desk and he carefully looked us over. It was like a merchant appraising a vase for sale.

"I am in need of a sailing master," he explained, his finger rubbing over his chin.

"And Watson's shoes will be quite large to fill. He was a keen navigator, reader, and had great intuition. I believe either one of you could do his job with time, but for now, I would like you to split his duties. Grey, you have been aboard this ship for five years now, and I know you know a bit about each position aboard. You have led the helm well and I think you would make an adequate sailing master.

"Mayra, you have proven that you absorb information like a sponge and have a knack for picking things up. You can also interpret texts and analyze maps with the same careful eye Watson once had.

"With time, I believe one of you could take on this position independently, but for now, I think the two of you combined will be an impenetrable force."

Neither of us said anything. I was conflicted with the promotion. It should have been a good thing. I should have been happy that my efforts had been recognized and I was being compared to Grey who had given five years of his life to this ship. But part of me was unsettled with the offer. The captain had just told me I was easily manipulated, and that Laina had gotten in my head. I was certain

Malin had greater motives for this. I just couldn't place them yet.

We were dismissed and I followed Grey back to the helm. He seemed troubled in his own way. The days following our talk in Astreim were more solemn than I was used to with him. I hated that our relationship had changed.

"So, we are to be co-sailing masters," Grey finally said when I had not built up the courage to say anything at all.

I nodded. "I hope that didn't insult you. I don't mean to overstep."

"Overstep?" he asked with a smirk.

"You've been here a lot longer. You deserve the position over me."

"You killed a kraken. I think that deserves something," he reminded me.

I shrugged. "I could take over the helm for you, but I don't deserve to be an officer."

"Don't turn down a position for the sake of my feelings," he told me, though I noted a bite of bitterness in his tone. It made me think of how I'd feel if I'd devoted my time and energy to this ship for years only to have to share a promotion with a newcomer.

"I'm not sure I want to be an officer for him," I said, shrugging.

"I know you're conflicted about Laina, but she made her choice. And I know what love can do to one's heart, but you must remember your goals. I don't want to see them stifled because of her."

I bristled at his words, wanting to fight for her honor. To say that my heart wasn't blocking my journey. But I couldn't argue with Grey when I had no proof of the contrary. Everything seemed to point that my affection for Laina was the thing holding me back. Dedicating myself to this crew and exceeding their expectations had gotten me a lot farther than love ever could.

"Think they'll start calling me Lovergirl?" I asked, hoping to lighten things between us.

He smirked. "Don't go stealing my name, sailing master."

"Fearless Finn to you," I winked.

That should have settled my feelings, but I was still in a state of unrest. I wanted to simply commence with my duties aboard the ship as a newly appointed officer. But I couldn't let things go. I had grown tired of speculating about what she had done and why. I needed to speak with her once more before I could put my feelings behind me and move on. It was probably foolish and furthered my behavior of the love-dumb sailor, but if I never spoke to her, I would never feel as though things were settled between us.

Malin had forbidden me from speaking to her, but my need for closure won out. I didn't tell Grey. I did not want our friendship to become so secretive, but I was finding that the trust we once had, and the comradery was not so transcendent when it came to my relationship with Laina.

Briggs had been set to watch her, but he was not very attentive. He was off playing cards with the others so I could easily slip into the room where she was being held.

It had only been a day, but her eyes were like mud, her hair like straw. She looked up when I walked in and I could see the dark circles that shadowed her face.

"I didn't do it," she whispered before I could ask her anything.

"That's not what Malin says," I replied. I wanted to trust her, but she had already searched my pockets, stealing that note. I could not allow myself to be played like a fool.

If she really attacked Malin, of course she would deny it. But then how could I trust her word?

"Mayra, he's using you. He's needing a key to Brannland and you have connections. How can you not see that?"

I didn't deny that. I knew I was a tool. My heritage was too convenient. It felt as though I was being played on all sides. "I don't know my family there," I admitted. "I didn't write that I was coming. I don't see how that makes him more able to cross their border." I had never told Malin as much. All he knew was my heritage and my knowledge of the language.

"Brannland does not believe in punishing my kind and they know that the southern pirates will do anything to get that treasure. He means to earn their trust by using you."

I thought about the promotion. He said it was to reward my bravery but nothing Malin did was for the benefit of others. Laina was certainly right, that I was being used as a tool. But despite our nights together, and the sweet words she had told me when all was peaceful, I could not find it in me to fully trust her either.

"But did you try to kill him?" I asked.

"Mayra, you have to hear me out," Laina sighed. "I was trying to find his plans. I thought if I could see the rest of his notes I would know if my life was at risk. He saw me digging through the pages and he pinned me to the wall. I did what I had to protect myself."

"So, you did try to kill him?" I asked. "After you dug through my pockets?"

"I tried to defend myself," she said through her teeth.

I looked in her eyes, searching for the truth. It wasn't just that I had shared her bed. She had shared pieces of herself to make me believe I knew her down to her soul. I had found her with a knife to her throat, held by a beast of a man who was better off dead. She had told me of her people, all destroyed by the monsters from Aldina. I believed her. I could sense no falsity within her. And she may have threatened Malin, but only after he had taken her from the tavern, where she had been safe for a while and locked her away as if she was a villain. She did what she had to survive, just as I had done since my mother had been burned on the stake.

But she was fae, the very being so many were afraid of. Did they have good reason? My mother was hung for the crimes of people like her, simply for sharing some of the same non-magical tradition through her healing and herbal medicine. She was either suspected of being fae, or consorting with fae.

My mother had not consorted with any fae. However, I wondered what she would think about Laina. She would have liked her, I was sure. She would have thought she was charming and elegant and stubborn as iron, but in the best way. She would have thought she was beautiful and funny. And she would have thought Malin was the monster for keeping her locked away, robbing her of her magic.

"I believe you," I whispered, reaching for her hands through the bars. She laced her fingers with mine and the faintest bit of light returned to her irises. "But I can't turn my back on my crew. That risks both of our lives. I need to stick by them a little longer. I've been promoted which will give me more opportunities to figure out what Malin is up to. And when I do, I can find our best chance to escape."

I meant it, too. I had nothing more to gain here. I could have been a pirate the rest of my life, but we were approaching Brannland where I could take Laina, and we could make our escape.

"Is that so?"

I whipped around to find Jenkins standing above us.

"I—"

He was back up the steps before I could defend the treasonous things I had just said. I had just put Laina and myself in that much more danger.

XVIII: The Whipping

Retribution did not take long. Jenkins had heard us speak before, but this time was different. He had heard my explicit declaration to follow Laina and work against Malin. I ran up to the main deck, hoping I could stop him from telling—

"Finn!" Malin's voice bellowed across the deck.

It is hard to achieve absolute silence on a ship while waves crash into the creaking wood. But in that moment, anyone could hear my unsteady breath on the other end of the ship as I stood to face Malin.

"Yes, Captain?"

He beckoned to me and I was side eyed as I climbed the steps to the upper deck. I knew what was coming. I'd be a fool to think I was safe from the captain's justice.

"You broke our code," he told me, loud enough for the entire crew to see my shame. "You aided the Spriggan which allows me and the entire crew to question your loyalty to the *Raider*. I sentence thee to ten lashes, to be delivered at present."

My stomach dropped. The crew had all turned, paused all chores, to see my face glow scarlet. There had not been a whipping since I had been on the *Raider*, so surely there was a thirst for entertainment. I had actually believed that Malin was above such barbaric forms of punishment. But of course, reality cured my naïveté.

"Jenkins!" Malin called.

The first mate came from the captain's quarters, wielding the weapon that would be used to flog my back. It was a sturdy rod with nine strips of leather hanging from it. I had watched men and even women be flogged by church officials for crimes that went against morality set by religion. But that whip had only one rope, and most still walked away weeping.

I did not try to feign bravery because I knew there was no way out of this. Either I begged on my knees and looked pitiful in front of the men that I had only recently gained respect from, or I bore my punishment, and could preserve that respect for another day.

I shuffled to the post where my hands would be tied, turning my back to Jenkins. I was ready to grit my teeth and take the flogging for realizing who was the true villain between the captain and the fae.

"Shirt off!" Malin called.

I turned, my jaw hanging. He meant to humiliate me and show just how damaging my turn of loyalty was. I looked at the other men. I was sure by now everyone knew my gender. I had stopped hiding it after I had killed Prath. Some of them wore the same look of shock I did. Others, like Grover and Stratford, looked almost intrigued by the command.

This punishment was more than just a lashing. It was taking away my safety. I could not reveal my breasts in front of the desperate men I had caught countless times lingering near Laina's door, trying to work out if they had a chance to have their way with her. Her lock kept her safe. I would be exposed amongst the wolves.

I was not about to cry, so I swallowed the lump in my throat and moved to remove my shirt.

"I'll take Finn's lashing!" a voice rang from the crew.

I turned to see Grey climbing the steps. He did so without hesitation. Malin's gaze turned sour.

"It is *Finn's* punishment to bear."

"Ay," Grey nodded, "but the code also says an able man can take his spot, should he not be able to receive the punishment."

"And why would Finn be unable?" Malin inquired.

"He fought the kraken just yesterday. I watched the cannon recoil and blow his shoulder out of socket. Put it back myself."

Malin looked at me. "Is this true?"

I nodded to the captain. The truth was that I pulled a muscle at most, and while it might still have been sore when I extended my arm, it did not prohibit me from taking a lashing. But I knew Grey was doing his best to protect my dignity.

"Well, the code also says you must deliver the punishment, to see the weight of your wrong-doing." He raised his eyebrow. "Think you're capable of doing it left-handed?"

I glanced at Grey who gave me quiet reassurance. It was what must be done, as much as I didn't want to. Either I was to whip my friend or bare my breasts for thirty men to see. I put the whip in my left hand though, being that the right was the one claimed to be out of socket.

Grey was bound to the post, his bare back facing me. My stomach was in knots. I knew Grey was up there by his own autonomy, but nothing about this felt right. If I took the whipping, even exposed, I could preserve a bit of respect. Grey had everyone's respect, and he was meant to be my co-sailing master. That title was his now, I decided. If Malin did not strip the title from me, I would eagerly pass it to the least cowardly of the pair of us.

"You will not hold back," Malin warned me. Doing so would likely end up with us both flogged and Grey's sacrifice would be for nothing.

It truly was still a punishment being made to whip my closest friend aboard the ship in front of men who were meant to fight alongside me. I would not watch their faith in me fade as I delivered the lashes with my left hand.

The whip slapped Grey's back and he tensed at the blow. The first delivery didn't draw blood, but the crack was like a gunshot. I felt struck down to my core by the blow. Even delivering it with my unaffected arm brought me pain. But I could not stop. Not without risking everything. I could only hope that it inflicted less pain that it would have had I done it right-handed.

The second lash slapped over the rising pink welts. The third lash began to bring blood to the surface of his pale skin. To his credit, Grey hardly flinched as I delivered each blow. Perhaps I did not have the strength Jenkins would have had he been chosen to give the whipping, but there was not a way to be delicate with nine strips of knotted leather. The pink and red of his back told me I had still done enough harm to allow him to regret his decision to protect me.

"Again!" Malin called.

My hand still gripped the whip, but I had paused when I saw the blood begin to seep from his back. I couldn't see his face, to see if he hated that I allowed him to be whipped in my place.

By lash seven, I could see the splits in his flesh. And as I continued to whip over those, the wounds deepened. By the tenth, Grey was shaking, and sunk to the deck when he was released from the pole.

I wanted to run to him, but I was frozen on my whipping stage. Malin took the cat from my hand.

"That'll do, Mayra," he whispered. While he kept the same neutral frown to his lips, a hint of a smile twinkled in his eyes.

"Grey," I whispered as Pierce applied the balm to his slashed back. Many of the lashes had resulted in vibrant welts. Some of them oozed with blood. Grey winced as Pierce dabbed them with the balm covered cloth.

"Not now," he groaned.

I lingered by the door and watched Pierce work, attempting to soothe the pain I had inflicted. I couldn't stand to walk away. Not when this was all my fault.

Pierce finished and left us alone without a word. I did not know who the surgeon was loyal to. I'd been assessing everyone this way.

If I were to work against Malin, would Pierce be on the side throwing me into the ocean?

I needed to know where Grey stood. I feared that the whip had shattered all that was once between us.

"I am so sorry," I whispered. I sat beside him.

"It's not like I haven't been flogged before," he said, shrugging his shirt back on. "I wouldn't have taken your punishment if I didn't think I could take it."

"I could have refused."

"At that point we would have both been flogged. There was nothing you could have done."

"He meant to humiliate me. And isolate me," I said, bitterly.

"He meant to make certain he still had your unwavering loyalty. You make him question who you're fighting for."

"Am I supposed to sit idle while he locks up innocent people to use their blood for his gain?"

Grey shrugged. "That's what the rest of us are doing."

"Do you approve of what he's doing to Laina?" I shot back. I feared his answer. If he was stuck on being loyal to Malin, there would be no hope in stopping the captain on my own. Grey was my only chance.

"Of course not," he said. "It's brutish, but are you willing to put your life on the line for someone you just met? Over your crew?"

"Over men who tried to drown me?" I laughed. "Over a captain who wanted me to strip naked to put me in my place? That same captain wishes to kill someone because it's believed her blood is cursed. I lived beneath that logic for far too long. I can't accept it and I can't let it go on. You are the only one here who has had my back and I need to know if it came to it, would you stand behind me, should I try to raise forces?"

I hadn't meant to ask so bluntly, but my very blood seethed at the thought of what Malin had done to this crew. These were good men, throwing away all their ideals for his mountain of riches. I had been paid pennies since boarding. There was a place to sleep at night and a way to get away from home, but I couldn't tell what drew the men to be so tightly bound by Malin.

Grey blinked at me, taking in what I was asking. "You mean to fight Malin?"

"If I had to—to free Laina and us all—yes."

"Mayra, you understand what you're asking? These men have been bonded by brotherhood beneath Malin. They've fought alongside each other since before you were born. You can't divide them. Especially being a woman. I'm sorry to be so plain, but none of them will listen to you."

"I can if I just get a few others to question his methods. You, maybe Kamau. Even Briggs. And I have a gut feeling that there are more men than you think who question him. I just need to shine a light on it all."

"You may be right. But not one of those men would hold a pistol to Malin."

"Maybe if someone like you were to show them it's possible."

"I wouldn't hold a pistol to Malin."

"What?"

"I understand your cause, but even that could get my throat slit. I have pledged my loyalty to Malin. Written in my own blood. 'Til death. That means something."

"I swore no such oath."

"There's a reason," he said, gravely. "You were never truly one of us."

My stomach hollowed. I had thought I had become part of the brotherhood. I actually thought I had achieved something when I slayed the kraken. When I jumped into the ocean. When I laid my body across Laina and shot Prath. I thought it all meant something. Like I finally belonged to something bigger than me. But through it all, the one person who I had once thought respected me, valued me even, still saw me as an outcast. Suddenly, I seemed to shrink away from Fearless Finn back into Mayra Hidalgo, the bastard from Playada.

"You don't see the monster that he is," I whispered.

"It doesn't matter," Grey shot back. "My bond to this ship and this crew runs deep. For many of us, the *Raider* and the sea will be our final resting place. The whole crew has accepted that and it doesn't matter what Malin is, because we pledged our loyalty."

"But he means to kill Laina!"

"I won't give up my destiny for your love." Disdain drenched his voice.

"But I thought—"

"You're wrong." He turned away from me. "You're a woman and I did what I did because of my own code of honor. Not because I choose you over my crew."

"What about Starky?"

The question threw him and his eyes narrowed. "What about Starky?"

I pursed my lips. "No one has their story straight. He was either ill or he died in battle. Something happened and everyone is trying to cover it up. What happened to him?"

Grey just shook his head and turned from me.

Perhaps he was right. Perhaps I never belonged on this ship amongst these men. It did not matter that I looked the part. It certainly didn't matter that I renounced my life as el Don Hidalgo's bastard. I was the outlander. The one of impure blood playing a fool in the pursuit of finding a true home. That place was not aboard this ship. I couldn't even say if that place was in Brannland.

But I still needed to get north. Because that was the only place there was any chance that Laina and I could be free. It could end up being another dead end, but I had to try.

I left him in the surgeon's quarters, alone. I was unable to confide my feelings to my friend. And I was unable to go to Laina in her cell. I had thought Grey, of all people, would understand. He would know that this was more than just pining over some girl. It was saving the life of someone who I believed was destined to share my fate. Whose life would be interwoven with mine. And maybe Grey would have shared his place in that.

But he made it clear that wasn't the case. His blood oath to the ship came before doing what was right. I wondered, fearfully, if he had a hand in his uncle's death for the sake of his loyalty to Malin.

I had already decided that without him, I wasn't going to give up. I needed to find a way to free Laina, as well as myself.

XIX. Transcribing

I was never foolish enough to think that my punishment was over once I was made to whip Grey.

I wasn't kept in the cell with Laina. Not at first. That would have been seen as a reward for all my disloyalty that I had committed over the past few weeks. It started with the silence. I was not acknowledged by my crew mates except for their spiteful stares. There was no obvious hostility. Not even the continuance of Briggs's pranks. That was almost worse. I was just a shadow looming over them.

Grey's words rang in my ears. "You were never one of us." I was no longer Fearless Finn.

I was just Mayra. Sometimes I didn't even feel like that much. Often, I felt like a ghost amongst them. I was reminded of how distant I was that first day aboard. I had been separated from my family and had not yet bound myself to the crew. I was the loner just trying to find my way. And after the whipping, it was as if nothing had ever changed.

For a full day, I was left out to sit with this feeling. I got my own meals. I slept in the quarters. I watched them play games from the railing, but I did not engage with them and they looked through me.

At the end of the second day, I went up to the captain's quarters, wondering what he meant to do with me. My title had been stripped, obviously. I was moments away from giving it up, but Malin was sure to make the first move.

And after twenty-four hours of silence from the crew, I was locked in the officers' quarters, guarded day and night while I transcribed countless Brannish texts. It could have been worse. I was not so proud to think I could not be shamed further. But the question remained: why was this how Malin wished for me to spend my captive time?

Long hours of pen strokes, translating the Captain Lars's log, the map notes, the historical texts ripped from books. My hand felt like it was going to fall off, but I persisted. I didn't want to know what would happen should I not comply with Malin's simple requests.

Briggs brought my supper, leaving it on the desk without a word.

"No quip for me?" I asked, tired of the silence and the feeling like I had disappeared.

He looked over his shoulder at me, shook his head, and left me to my thoughts.

Three days of this. The writing. The brief encounters with Briggs around mealtimes. I slept on a threadbare blanket and my cloak on the floor. Stratford, Jenkins, and Watson each had beds in here, but even though they moved to the crew's quarters to allow me the isolation, I did not feel right sleeping in any of their beds.

Avoiding Stratford's cot was mostly out of apprehension as to what lay in his blankets. He was a pervert with no outlet for his less desirable thoughts.

Jenkins's was because I felt inadequate. He was the beacon of this crew, representing all that a good sailor should be.

And perhaps, logically, Watson's bed was the safest. But I could not bring myself to lie where the dead man never laid himself.

As I translated, my mind grew numb to the information I was writing. None of it seemed useful. It wasn't anything that would aid them on the search. Some were as simple as a captain of a Brannish ship reporting on the weather for that day, or that Davey's hand had grown inflamed from an untreated splinter.

My mind detached from the information, and I occupied it with as many good thoughts as I could muster. I thought of Laina's hands. Her soft perfect hands running down my back, cupping my cheeks, and cradling my breasts. I thought of her lips and of her voice. I thought of her eyes when they were vibrant and full of life. I tried not to think of her condition, sitting in the cell, thinking about how I had failed her.

I thought of any good memory I could conjure up about being home. The days Mateo and I spent on his boat. The times we'd laugh as we swapped stories of the gossip the town was circling around for the week. I even thought of Lupe. I thought of the time between my mother's death and his betrothal to Carla. We were never necessarily happy together, but I remembered a feeling of contentment when the initial grief had passed and we had settled into this new version of our lives. Knowing what I knew then, about how Lupe was not my real father, and had taken me in as a good deed for my mother, I knew he did his best through that time.

There was an evening that I sat on the porch, looking at the stars. The stars were a reminder of her because I knew she was among them in eternal bliss.

Lupe came out of the house, taking a seat beside me, directly on the wood. Words escaped me. Lupe and I did not spend quality time together. Nothing was said between us, both of us unsure how to navigate our shared space, so we continued to look at the stars in silence. I felt as though Lupe tried to think of something to say. Many times, he licked his lips, or opened his mouth, only to close it and continue to exist beside me without breaking the silence.

I had initially been curious about his starts and stops but grew weary of the game. I finally ended it when I got up to leave for bed.

"Goodnight," he said behind me.

"Goodnight, Papa," I replied.

As distant as we were, as much as I had craved for him to be more of a father to me, I knew he did his best, and the memory of staring at the stars was oddly comforting.

I finished the stack of notes I transcribed, but there was a piece of parchment at the bottom of the stack, already in the Common Tongue.

I got a prickle on my neck, knowing I wasn't meant to see this. The letter was from a Mr. Rowan, and he informed Malin that he agreed to his terms:

1000 gold for the ship and crew for transport to the Westlands for five years of indentured service. Their release is reliant on the quality of work performed and behavior whilst in custody.

I read it again and again. Of course it didn't say as much, but I could see Malin's intention. He meant to sell the ship and crew. A thousand gold was a small fortune for one man. That and what was promised from the dwarf's treasure. He did not mean to split it amongst the crew. He meant to hoard it, give up pirating, and leave the crew to be slaves in the Westlands.

Malin was more of a monster than I thought. If anything, Laina's treatment was his reasoning for getting the treasure to pay out his crew. But no. Loyalty didn't matter to him. Only wealth.

I had to tell someone. But I never saw anyone aside from Briggs.

I couldn't accept that Malin had won. But I was locked away and Laina was in a cell. The crew hated me and still believed the captain had their best interest in mind. It was hard not to feel hopeless that everything was for nothing.

After I had fallen asleep on the floor on the fifth night, the note crumbled beneath my head on the pillow, I was awoken to Jenkins and Malin pulling me to my feet towards the door.

"What's going on?" I asked, nearly shrieking.

"Hush," Malin spat back.

"Where are you taking me?" I asked. I didn't think they would throw me overboard, but the longer I was on this ship, the more I saw Malin's true cruelness. The cordial captain who had treated me softly the first half of this trip was no more.

We were still in the middle of the ocean, but I could see the hooded sailors waiting on their boat, the plank laid across so they could pass me to their hands.

"I suggest you don't struggle," Malin said in my ear as soon as I began to kick, "unless you want to go for a swim. They are taking you back to Playada."

Through their hoods I could see they had the same copper skin I did. I didn't know these men, but they were unmistakably Playadan. My heart sank. All these months only to return where I started.

I had no choice in the matter but to let my ex-captain pass me to these strangers' hands and hope to whatever god existed they wouldn't treat me worse than Malin. That thought was fleeting when I thought of Laina in her cell. I did not know how she fared. I couldn't even ask Grey to ensure she came out of this okay. My soul told me that he wouldn't stand for torture or cruelty, despite his obvious allegiance to the crew over me. I hoped it was all just words because I had challenged his way of life. I had to hope he would do what was right, because I wouldn't be there to save her anymore.

As the men took me into their custody, binding my hands so I would not thrash, I knew I would not be in Playada long. They could take me back to Villaviciosa, but I would find a way back north. This ship would also certainly make port before then. I would find a way to escape. My only fear was I wouldn't be in time to save Laina.

"It was a pleasure to work with you, Mayra," Malin said, tipping his hat at me as the ships parted ways. "Laina will see her people again soon."

"Fucking bastard!" I screamed, only for the men to gag me. "He means to sell you out!" I yelled to Jenkins. "He means to hoard the whole damned lot of treasure!"

Jenkins did not acknowledge me. I deflated at the realization that he had probably cut a deal with Malin to ensure his own benefit from the arrangement.

"Still speaks like a sailor," Malin laughed. "Good luck to the man who tries to make a lady out of you."

I watched as the *Raider* slid past us. I tried to scream, tried to get just one of the crewmates to come up and see that Malin was giving me away. Surely, they didn't hate me enough to let him get away with this. Just days ago I was being congratulated for killing a kraken, and now I was being passed off to strangers to be returned to the place that wanted to see me hung and burned.

Everything was hopeless. But I would get north. I would. I would escape these men, return to Laina, see to it that Malin died and the crew was freed. There was no longer conflict within me about where my loyalties lay. All along he meant to harm them all. Laina was the distraction while he plotted to rid himself of the crew and ship. I knew they were all in danger, but what was I to do about it?

The hooded sailors left me tied on the deck, not addressing me. I still had the gag on, but I had given up making any kind of noise. The *Raider* was out of ear shot, and yelling wouldn't help my circumstances here. If I was compliant enough, maybe they would let me loose and I could escape.

I heard footsteps approaching me. I could feel their hands cut me loose, then removed the gag. I whipped around, ready to strike if he made a move on me. But I found myself staring at a familiar face.

"Mateo," I whispered.

"Hi Mayra," he smiled. He was dressed in formal coats and wore a tricorn hat. He had a patch pinned to his breast: Capitán Ries.

XX. The Other Captain

"How— But— What—" I couldn't form sentences. Why was he here? How did he come to command this ship? But the sentence that finally fell from my mouth was neither of those. "Do you really mean to bring me home?"

"Of course not," he said. "You're not safe there." Before we spoke any further, he took me to his quarters. I looked at the men who had tied me and recognized Jorge, Daniel, and Hugo. There were other village boys, but this wasn't a ship meant for fishing.

"What business are you in, Mateo?" I asked as he led me up the steps.

He took in a breath and replied with a smirk. "Smuggling."

I was in no place to judge, having just spent the last six months amongst pirates, but it was an understatement to say I was surprised.

"Your father's fishing business?"

"Demolished," he replied. "Here come sit. Let us reacquaint."

He gestured to the desk that was in his quarters. It was modest compared to Malin's but still impressive, being that months ago he was to work as a sailor for his father. I knew it would be quite the story I was to be told.

"I don't know quite where to begin," he admitted as he felt my gaze on him.

"I feel as though congratulations are in order," I replied, putting my boots up on his desk. "Capitán Ries. How in the hell did that come about?"

He smiled, sheepishly. "Well, that requires me to tell you what came about back home since you left."

My gaze darkened. I had thought everything would be as it always was: oppressive and stagnant. I did not think my absence would change anything. I thought of

Lupe though. There would be questions about where his daughter went.

"There was an uprising," Mateo told me. "Carla made quite the spectacle of herself when you turned up missing. She claimed Malin stole you and called to overturn the treaty. She got Don and Dona Alvarez to back her, and even worked on my mother as well. But Pa and Lupe made it clear of their opposition. For once, my mother was on Pa's side. Lupe made it clear that the agreement was consensual to send you away, to get you passage to Brannland. And Carla was quick to spin that story.

"Carla assumed it was a plot to steal her unborn baby's heirship. She got the church involved. And others in the town joined her propaganda. It became religious as well as political. She went so far as to say that Lupe aided the Spriggan by sending you to Brannland with Playadan secrets."

The narrative was both incredulous and not. Carla had been told by both Lupe and Malin that sending me away was an agreement. But that was of no concern to her. It became clear that her marriage to Lupe had nothing to do with love and all to do with political power. If she got the church to back her, and the other lords, and made Lupe out to be a traitor, she and her child would take over the lordship. The vileness and cunningness of her was impressive.

"To my surprise, as well as our fathers—," Mateo started, then wiped his brow. "Sorry, I mean your uncle."

"He raised me. He's more of a father to me than anyone," I replied.

Mateo nodded. "Right. Well, they got some of the other townsfolk together and it turned out many were sick of the church's overarching rule. Not everyone wanted to see you suffer. A lot of the working men: Pa's crew, the farmhands, the smiths, the butchers and most of their wives too—they all backed our fathers. The town was divided. The church closed off the ports and only received resources from their connections to the Aldinian church, which they rationed off to their followers. They meant to starve them out.

"Pa had the idea to send us out on his boat to intercept those ships and snatch whatever we could. We were able to overtake one of them completely, leaving the crew on a small island outside of Port Napol which is how we got this beauty. I call her the *Rebelde*." He gestured around us.

"Tomas overtook one too, taking some of the other working men on that crew. Between the two of us we're able to get resources to our fathers and keep their cause alive. We've also cut off communication between the church and Aldina."

That explained how Mateo had become captain. But I still had questions.

"But why are you this far north?"

"To get you of course," he replied.

"What?"

"We received a message. Anonymous, but a hawk came to us, letting us know that you were being held captive and needed aid."

An anonymous message? It must have been Grey. But I thought of our last talk and how he told me he couldn't join me. There was no way he'd risk interception of a message to reveal allegiance away from Malin.

He dug out the parchment and handed it across to me.

Mayra Hidalgo is in trouble. The captain means to kill her when we make it to Brannland. Send help.

— B

No. It couldn't be. B. That would mean—

"That sneaky bastard."

"You know who it was?" Mateo asked.

I nodded. "Briggs. He and I have a complicated relationship."

"Ah," he replied, clarity pouring to his face.

"No, not like that," I said quickly. "He hazed me for being the newest on the crew. Almost drowned me once. But we became friends later on. I just never thought he would ever defend me." This brought me to what I really needed to talk to Mateo about.

"We have to go after Malin's ship."

"The *Raider*?" Mateo asked.

"What other ship would I be talking about?"

"It can't be done."

"But he's holding Laina captive," I said firmly.

"Who's Laina?"

It was my turn to tell him of what I had been up to since we last saw each other. I told him of my position aboard, of learning the ship, of the raid, of earning the crew's trust. I told him about Malin's plot to capture a Spriggan. Which led us to the tavern where I met Laina. I told him of her hair, of her eyes, of her boldness. I left out the intimate bits, but

I'm sure he caught on to the intensity of our interactions. And then to her capture, to my betrayal of the captain, to my realization of what was to become of the crew, leading up to the present.

Mateo didn't speak when I had finished, and I waited anxiously. His rebellion with our fathers told me he was not opposed to a relationship with a Spriggan, but there were other things in play. My relationship with a woman. Our parting ways and my refusal of his betrothal. I was losing faith that he'd help me get to the north in time to save her.

"You're in love with her?" His face was neutral. I couldn't tell if he asked out of jealousy or curiosity.

I hesitated, because I feared his opinion, and because I didn't know the truthful answer to such a question. "I admire her and I wish her safe."

Mateo was my only chance of saving her. Fear stifled me as I thought of the risk of losing both my oldest friend and the girl who held my affections. The crew as well for that matter. Grey had been my friend. So had Kamau, Everett, Hagley, Peel, and Grover and Stratford in their own way. Even Briggs had proved to be an ally. Perhaps my biggest ally now that I knew what he had done for me. I didn't feel right abandoning them now when I knew Malin would stop at nothing to get that treasure. This was not just about freeing Laina. This was about freeing them all from the false cloth of loyalty Malin gagged them with.

"Then let's go save your lady."

We could not ride the *Raider's* tail should they become aware that we followed and blow us out of the water. It was Mateo who suggested we give them a six-hour lead.

Six hours.

That was six hours longer that Malin had to turn the crew over to his buyer. That was six hours he had to torture Laina and slit her throat over the treasure. But we could do no better if we were killed, so I agreed.

The *Raider* had long ago hit the horizon before we started to sail.

"We're a light ship," Mateo assured me. "We'll likely make up two hours before we meet them in Brannland."

Because I had been privy to Malin's maps and notes, I assisted Mateo's sailing master, Hugo, in tracking our course to Devil's Rock. I had known Hugo from Villaviciosa. He played cards with Mateo sometimes. He nodded at me if our paths crossed. While I helped set our course, he spoke to me with a level of respect, making me wonder if he recognized me.

"We are set west now. If we continue due west for three more leagues, we can travel up the coast as we drive closer, coming at them from the south undetected."

"Have you accounted for the northward wind, Señorita Hidalgo?"

He did know me.

"Luff up the mainsail and heave to before reefing. It may lose us a knot or two, but we'll be in more control."

He gave me a quick nod, approving my assessment.

It was hard not to be in disbelief at their compliance. Months ago, these men would not have looked in my direction, let alone take orders from me. Their mothers probably told stories of my wickedness to ensure none of them tried to take me as a wife.

"Don't go near the Hidalgo girl for she has Spriggan blood running through her veins and will turn your cock small and blue."

Little did they know, their cocks did nothing for me.

"You had a talk with them, didn't you?" I asked Mateo as he manned the helm. He was a much more hands-on captain than Malin.

He shrugged. "I told them I would not hear of any Spriggan bullshit and they would keep a civil tongue. But you've also done well enough to prove your nautical knowledge."

I knew Mateo was doing his best to protect me, but I hoped he saw I no longer needed protection. I thought I had proven to both him, his men, and my former crew that I was just as capable as each one of them.

There was a day and a half of sailing ahead of us in addition to the protected space we kept between us and the *Raider*. Being a smaller ship quickened our pace. We had to stop all together sometimes to leave the distance between us.

Night fell and we blew out all the lights to remain unseen. Mateo and I sat on the foredeck with Daniel at the helm. I could not see the *Raider* on the horizon, but I could feel her.

"Tell me of your travels." I attempted to distract myself from both the thought of Laina and of the dark open water. Six months at sea did not soften my apprehension of what lay beyond my sphere of sight.

"Well, you know how I acquired the ship," he said, sipping the wine from his cup.

"Yes, but surely something else of note has happened these past six months," I said, sipping from my own. I had grown a taste for ale and rum during my time on the *Raider,* but I took what was given to me. "Did you have a run in with the kraken at the northern border?"

"Kraken?"

I had been raised a lady, but my best friend had always been Mateo, who I talked to openly, who I could strive to impress with the tricks I could do and the stories of outlandish experiences. And I had lived amongst men these past six months where the only way to impress them was to compete with their stories. And my story of defeating the kraken was the best of all. I told him of our encounter with the sea beast, down to the details of each of the suckers spurting out blood.

Mateo looked a bit overwhelmed after I finished my tale.

"Fae and krakens," he shook his head. "And here I thought all this time that the church spoke of Spriggan as propaganda."

"They did," I said. "My mother was not fae. She simply knew how to heal with herbs and prayed to different gods."

"I know," Mateo said. "I was not trying to say your mother wasn't good. Just that I never truly believed in fairytales."

Had I? Did I truly believe that the fae folk and sea monsters of my mother's world existed? I remember being a dreamy eyed girl hoping they did. But before I met Laina, it all seemed like fantasy and make-believe. My mother and I had painted our dream world, where we returned to the snowy north and lived amongst the creatures of stories. It was all a romantic notion, but I was sad to say that I did not have faith in its reality. Not until Laina.

"I met a girl," Mateo admitted, seeming almost embarrassed at his confession.

"Why didn't you tell me sooner?" I asked, clapping my hand on his back.

He shrugged. "I didn't think it was the most important thing to discuss."

"Tell me about her," I urged. The last time Mateo and I had been together he proposed marriage. I could feel that in both of our minds, but neither of us wished to bring it up. He seemed guilty about meeting someone, even as I had also moved in a different direction. Six months ago, everything was different and we had lived within another life.

"We were docked at an island just off the northern tip of Playada, at Bonaire. It's the last port of Playada to restock before entering into Aldinian waters. We used Pa's seal to obtain supplies. The man who ran their docks, George Maduro, had a younger sister, Yara. She kept up on his books and inventoried the stock. She's about twenty, has long dark hair, and bright green eyes. The greenest I have ever seen."

Mateo's eyes went glossy as he spoke of her. I was not compelled to compare my lady's eyes when his affection for Yara was so clear. It warmed me to see him so taken by her.

"We meant to sleep on the ship during our time there, being that the island did not have a proper inn, but a storm passed through. It became so strong that George and Yara insisted that the crew and I stay at their residence. Their father, an Aldinian lord, left them a massive estate. The entire island was theirs, so that he could keep eyes on the south. But when he died and the war ended, they pledged their allegiance to Playada. Their mother came from a small Playadan village. I reckon he also meant to pay them off to keep them quiet, with them being bastards and all. But he didn't have any other children that they knew of.

"We stayed in bungalows outside of their home, grouping in fours, taking any cot or piece of floor offered. The storm lasted seven days and did not let up. It broke several of the roofs in the village. Even the Maduros's house was hit. We helped repair the best we could. The ceiling split in Yara's bed chamber and I went up to help her. George was away, tending to an elderly woman's hut near the dock. I made sure her virtue would not be questioned. Her maid was nearby and we did not shut the door. But her affection for me and mine for her could not be denied. There were moments of temptation but we overcame them. But she's so smart and beautiful. And she is a well-bred lady of the house, taking an active part in her and her brother's estate. I realized that I wish to marry her.

"I asked George for her hand, but he was weary of me. He had seen our ship and knew we were smugglers. I understood. We were strangers in his house and he did not know my intentions. If I had a sister, I imagine I would be just as suspicious of a stranger around her. But there was a day when a child had gotten swept in the sea. The mother screamed and I immediately dove in. It could have killed us both. There were rocks everywhere, but I wasn't thinking about that when I heard the child yell then go under. I grabbed her and pulled her to shore. She was okay, thank goodness, and the mother thanked me. George was there to see and said he would be honored if I married Yara." Mateo smiled, reaching into his pocket. "So I will give her this when I return," he pulled out a small black box and showed me the dazzling emerald ring.

"It's beautiful," I said, taking it into my hands. It had a silver band, coiled to look like vines. The emerald was a deep green, and I knew it was meant to compliment her eyes. "Why didn't you ask her before you left?"

"I received the message of your safety and left that night. It didn't seem right to leave a fiancé, so I left the girl I had been courting."

Guilt hit my stomach. It was because of me that he left his love. "I'm sorry, Mateo."

He shook his head. "Don't be. I know she is waiting for me."

"How do you know?"

He twisted his mouth. "I may have stayed the night with her right before I left."

I could not contain my amusement. "So much for her virtue."

He chuckled. "Well, I intend to marry her, so she is not ruined for me."

I knew Mateo would be a good husband, even if some of his ideals were still so rooted in the culture I had left behind. Perhaps they would find somewhere else to settle, since his older brother would be Don of Villaviciosa and her brother was lord of Bonaire.

I was given a cabin below Mateo's quarters to sleep that night. I curled in a ball on the thin mattress, grateful I had been rescued but with the quiet and empty space around me, I was no longer able to hide from my anxious thoughts.

Most of them were for Laina. I didn't think Malin would kill her, but I did not trust anything about him anymore. He had shown me his intentions, his note still burning in my pocket. And now I knew that the crew was also in danger.

I thought of Grey and how we left things. He may not know Malin's plan yet, but he would when they were put on the market. And as much as I did not want pride to come between us, perhaps then he would see that I had been right.

I shook my head at myself. I cared for his life more than being right. All of their lives. His. Kamau's. Stratford's. Even Briggs—Briggs who had been my greatest ally all along.

I needed to get to them. I didn't sleep well that night. I was tormented by dreams of blood and betrayal. I would not sleep well until I saw that they were all safe. We saw the tip of the Devil's Rock and the *Raider* docked there two days later.

XXI: The Devil's Rock

"What are we to anticipate from the Raiders at the Devil's Rock?" Daniel asked me.

Mateo had called us all to the main deck after we weighed anchor off the shore, out of sight from the *Raider*. We had scouted while night still covered us and we didn't see any lights or movement on the ship, meaning the crew had already gone to shore. They were presumably within the caverns, seeking out the lost treasure. Our time was almost out, but we could not go in after them without a plan.

I had told Mateo's crew all that I knew of Malin's plan numerous times:

He sought after the dwarf's lost treasure. The apothecary in Astreim had told him it was hidden in the Devil's Rock. She also confirmed that fae blood was needed to open the chest. He also needed a sacrifice. I did not know if that was Laina or an animal or some other unlucky victim. That made Laina the key to the treasure and once Malin got it, both she and the crew would be sold or killed and he would escape to the unclaimed islands south of Playada with his riches and build his empire.

Coming from my mouth, it all sounded like nonsense. Stories of fae and dwarves and greedy pirates. I felt foolish as I said it, but Mateo urged everyone to have an open mind. None of them had seen the kraken or Laina perform magic. To the minds of these novice sailors, the retelling of my past six months seemed intangible. They hadn't seen anything like this before, having never left the village before they joined Mateo's ranks. But I was sure if they had enough faith to follow me, they would soon see for themselves that I spoke the truth.

But had I said enough to convince them? And if so, what would we find once we reached

Devil's Rock? I did not know with certainty that the treasure would be there, though I was certain we would find Malin and Laina. If we did not stop him, Malin's crew would be sold to slavery.

"So we wait for night?" Jorge asked.

I shook my head. "No, that's too long. That gives them twelve hours to find the treasure and for Malin to finish off anyone who is no longer useful for him. It also gives them enough time to get back to the ship, and I'm sorry but this ship cannot compete with them if it were to come to cannon fire."

Mateo nodded. "You're right, but can we also compete with a whole crew of experienced fighters? I've seen these men. They've seen a lot more battle than we have."

I hesitated. He was right of course. Hand to hand, the boys of my village could not compete with the Raiders. "If I can get to Grey or Stratford or Briggs, I could convince them not to fight us. Then it would be us against Malin."

Everything relied on both crews having faith in me. Something I had lacked days before, but before the sun was high, we tied *Rebelde* to the broken dock beside the *Wind*

Raider and began our climb up the Devil's Rock.

Our plan was mostly improvisation. We hoped we would not meet the crew all at once and they had split to find the treasure. I had the notes in my pocket, both Malin's and Briggs's. If we ran into anyone, I would speak and convince them to lead me to Malin. I needed as many of the Raiders on our side as possible. Mateo had ten green boys who had only stolen and dealt in self-defense combat. They had not been involved in standoffs with pirates. And if it came to that, I wasn't even sure I could handle it. My friends were on both sides of the fight, even if at one point or another they had all believed me wicked. But I was certain that I was doing the right thing. I couldn't let myself dwell on even the possibility that this didn't work. I would be leaving this rock with my crew and with Laina.

Laina would be with Malin. I knew he would not trust her to leave his side and that he would still have her drugged to diminish her magic. I did not know how to solve that. Her magic would make this all so much easier, but perhaps Malin would have the antidote on his person. A thought occurred to me as we began to ascend the cliffs to the cavern opening.

"We have to board the *Raider*," I told Mateo.

"Are you crazy?" he asked.

"Possibly, but Malin will have an antidote for Laina in his cabin. If we get it to her, we have her magic and that will give us more of a chance to escape with her and the crew."

I could tell Mateo was on the edge of his faith in me, but he and I went alone to the *Raider*. We approached carefully, viewing from Mateo's spyglass often to see if anyone was keeping watch. I knew someone would have to be on the ship. Malin was not foolish enough to leave it unattended, but the Crow's Nest was empty, as was the foredeck and the visible spots of the main deck.

We climbed the rope that dangled over the side. He wouldn't have left his first mate or battle master. Kamau, Briggs, and Grover were his main combatants so they would be on the mission as well. That left—

"Grey," I said as we climbed over the edge.

He sat across the deck at the card's table, unmoving as he watched us climb aboard. His skin was covered in black soot and there were several burns and scrapes along his arms.

"Hi Mayra," he said.

"You don't seem surprised to see us," I noted. I had been tense and on guard, but my muscles released when I saw Grey.

"Your stealth skills need some work," he retorted. "Would have alerted the whole bay of your arrival had there been anyone around here."

Mateo touched the pistol at his side, but I shook my head. "He's a friend. I think." The last part I whispered but knew he could still hear me.

"How is—"

"She's fine," he said. "For now. But Malin and the crew will be killed before the moon rises."

My heart fluttered. "What?"

"They've been captured," he told me. He didn't look fearful, but I knew Grey enough to know he still quaked within. He was trained by his lordly father to not show such things on his face. "I meant to sail, to find help, but then I saw you make port. Figured help was coming to us."

"Help?" I asked incredulously. There were many questions on my mind that I hoped would be answered, but this was the first. "Why on earth would I help save Malin?"

Grey shook his head. "I don't mean to save his life, but to give him a better death. It's not good Mayra."

"What happened?"

"They found the Dwarf's Treasure. It's in the rock. But they also found the dwarf."

I cocked my head. "From the story?"

"He guards it and tortures any who touch it. I got away, but the rest of the crew is locked away and Malin is paying the price."

"And Laina?"

"He sees she holds Spriggan magic so she's safe for now."

"We came to get her antidote," I told him. "And we'll have to go in after them."

All our plans were meaningless now. Mateo's crew would never follow us knowing that a dwarf, or any Spriggan creature, was on the other side waiting for them.

"I'll gather the men," Mateo told me, as if reading my mind.

"Do you really think they'll go?"

Mateo sighed. "Many of them owe me for their lives. I have to hope that's enough."

He left the ship while Grey and I went to Malin's cabin to look for the antidote.

"Mayra, I'm sorry," Grey said, turning to me as we crossed the threshold. More emotions flooded to his face in the absence of the men I came with. "I thought you were lying, but everything you said was true. Malin was playing us all. I don't know what he's up to, but I know now, he doesn't give a damn about this crew."

"What did you find out?" I asked.

"After you disappeared, I went to Malin," Grey said. "I asked if he killed you. He denied it of course, saying you left of your own accord, to go back to Playada. That's what he told us all. That you, a lady, could not stand to be at sea any longer. I don't think any of us believed it. It was Briggs who told me what he found out.

"He told me of Malin's initial plan to kill you outright, but that when the Playadan ship arrived Briggs had suggested to just release you, and you'd be too far to do anything anyway."

I suddenly owed that bastard more than I wanted to stomach.

"I cleaned out the officer's quarters, taking my place as the Sailing Master. And I found a missed pile of your notes. I didn't find anything too strange. Just transcribed entries regarding his treasure. But on one of the pages, you had written coordinates of a captain in the Western Ocean. Does he mean to sail us West after all this?"

I shook my head. "He means to sell you all at the end. Once he gets the treasure, he will sell you to a slave master and sail off to the unclaimed lands."

I unfolded the note, in Malin's distinctive script and Grey nodded. "I was an ass. My own blind loyalty made me do foolish things, putting you and everybody else at risk. He meant to use Briggs, you know."

"Briggs?"

"As his sacrifice."

My stomach hollowed. "But why?"

Grey looked out at the sea. "Uncle Starky did not die an honorable death. He died because he got in Malin's way. There was a mission a few years back to go into the Wastes. Watson and Starky said it was nonsense. There was no going into the Wastes and making it out again. They both thought this, and for months, they argued with Malin's motives. Malin threatened them both. Said if they pushed further, they would be deranked, and left at the next port.

"Watson stood down. Starky did not. It wasn't immediate. Malin did some digging. He found out that Starky had played around with a lass along the Wastes. Briggs's mother. And Malin came to believe that Briggs had some kind of fae blood. He told Starky that he'd be testing Briggs to see if he held any kind of magic. Starky forbade it. Yes. He died in battle. But it was Malin who shot him.

"Briggs didn't know. He suspected. We had talks of what could have happened, but he thought Malin would never kill his father because of how much respect he had for him. All the while Malin was watching Briggs. I don't think he has any sort of magic in his blood. His mother may have been magical but it did not get passed to him. But he's the sacrifice the treasure would need to be activated, and then he could keep Laina and use her magic."

I was speechless. The whole story had my head spinning. Briggs had some connection to the Spriggan, and Malin meant to kill him for the treasure.

"I was a fool, Mayra," Grey continued. "I denied for years what happened to Starky. I thought the same as Briggs. Until you came along. Until you translated all those texts and filled Malin's ideas with these ideas of Spriggan. I realize now, he will do anything, even kill his best officers, if they get in the way of getting this damned treasure."

"Then why save him?"

"I mean to save the crew," Grey said. "They're all innocent in this. Malin doesn't deserve to drag everyone down with him."

I nodded. I finally knew enough to convince me that Malin was evil. And Grey was right. The crew did not deserve the same fate.

"Mayra, I'm so sorry about how I treated you. You didn't deserve any of this."

I shook my head. "I'm sorry too. I let my feelings for Laina overpower me."

He smiled. "You love her. You do anything for the people you love." He looked at me with soft blue eyes and I felt a flutter in my gut. His fingers found mine.

"I do love you, Grey," I told him, keeping my hand in his. "But I love you in a different way than I love Laina. You feel like a piece of me. You feel like home. You feel like a missing part that helps keep me moving. But I can never be your woman. I cannot give you the companionship another woman could give you. But I can give you brotherhood and camaraderie and fight beside you until the very end."

He gave my hand a squeeze and nodded, releasing me. "That's all I could ever hope for. Now, let's go save your faerie."

When we were little, Mateo and I would look for secret beaches outside of town, to be out of the fishermen and our fathers' watchful eyes. With Villaviciosa being a trading post, most of our coast consisted of the docks. But we were willing to walk a few miles down the road to where the cliffs got too unforgiving for the merchant ships. There, we would climb down, and enjoy the vacant beach and the view of the ships passing from afar.

Those cliffs were maybe fifteen feet high. At the worst, a fall would result in a nasty bruise and some taunting from the others, but nothing permanent. The Devil's Rock was not so kind.

The cliffs, with sloping sides and footholds, stretched to the sky, at least fifty feet above us. A fall would be the end. The Devil's Rock was the name of the entire island, which was almost entirely made of rock. We had docked at a small outstretch of the stone, and walked up a gravel beach. Now, we looked up at the cliffs that made up the rest of the island. It was a wall of black and gray swirled rock, without obvious places to grip onto and climb up.

Winter may have passed, with spring blooming by that time in the south, but its hold had not released the north. I tugged my cloak tighter. My southern companions shivered in their linen shirts. From where we stood, I could see at the top the formations of caves and caverns. The crew and Laina had to be within them. But first, we had to figure out how we were to get eight men and me up the cliffs.

"How did the crew climb this?" I asked Grey.

"Laina."

"She has magic?"

"Malin left her with enough to help get them over the cliff, but not enough to harm him."

It infuriated me that Malin used Laina's magic when he had no rights to it. Still, I longed for our own faerie magic as I looked up at the rocky monolith before us. How would we manage on our own?

Mateo came out from behind us, carrying a burlap sack full of rope and grapples. He was more prepared than I was, but I still questioned whether or not it would matter when I could see pieces of rocks shifting with each gust of wind.

He sent up a grapple several times, only for it to skid down the cliff, bringing down pieces of rock with it. Each time he failed to get a hold, I felt a little more defeated. Looking around, I winced at the doubtful looks the crew exchanged with each other. Which is why it was no surprise when Daniel put a hand on my shoulder, a heavy sigh escaping his lips.

"This isn't our fight."

Mateo turned to face him. "Any man who cowers now is not a part of my crew."

Daniel shook his head. "I agreed to smugglin'. I did not agree to falling to my death trying to save pirates and faeries."

"I didn't agree to sit with you when you had the bloody flux, but I did that, didn't I?" Mateo ground out. "Even when you were cryin' and shittin' every which way."

"And I thank you for that, el capitán," Daniel tipped his hat, "but I was not asking you to risk your life for strangers and thieves and Spriggan."

Mateo took a step forward, but I put myself between them. "Let him go. He's right. This isn't his fight."

And it wasn't the fight for four other men either. That left me, Grey, Mateo, and Jorge.

"Don't you want to leave too?" Mateo asked Jorge.

He shook his head. "If you or la señorita Hidalgo were to die and I wasn't there to prevent it, I could never forgive myself."

And that's how I ended up climbing a cliff with the three most honorable men I had ever known waiting to catch me if I fell.

Of all the things I had done to be known as Fearless Finn, I thought this deserved to be at the top of that list. I tried not to think of how the grapple shifted on the cliff or that if I fell, three men were not likely to break my fall without injury. But if I got up, there was a good chance the rock could hold at least one other man, and then we could secure the rope above and be more helpful to the two men who remained below.

I gripped the rope with most of my strength and balanced myself with the rest. My palms screamed as the rope dug into them. I could feel my skin opening and stretching. I had no choice but to bite through it. If I allowed that bit of pain to stun me, I would be dead.

I tried not to think of the space between myself and the ground, but when my hands threatened to give out, I dared to look. I was only ten feet above where I started.

"Don't look down!" Grey scolded me. "Just work through the pain."

It was just a bit of blistering, I reminded myself. There would be worse pains in my life. There had been worse pains. But while all the skin was peeled back from my hand, I could not think of a single one.

I put one boot above the other, scaling the cliff, feeling my feet slide against the brittle rock.

Since thinking of other pains was not helping, I tried to get my mind away from the cliff some other way. I thought of sailing. Of our days of being on the open water. I remembered when we first set sail and the thought of being in the water without a single piece of land to look at had frightened me. But after these months, it had become a comfort. There were the quiet nights, when we were a day's journey from any kind of land. I could hear splashes of the larger animals coming up to breathe every now and then. They did not frighten me because I knew they wanted nothing to do with us. (This was before we had met the kraken). I would sit on the main deck and feel peace with being alone.

I thought of the hills of Villaviciosa above my father's house. At dusk, when all the farmhands had gone home and Papa was not around, long before Carla darkened our doorstep, I would go up and sit. I'd watch the sun dip down below the sea, always wishing I was out in those waters. This thought gave me the relief to keep going. Years ago, I had felt all was hopeless, like my wishes would never be granted. Even under the circumstances, even though my captain was a selfish bastard who had kidnapped Laina and my entire crew was being held captive by some unknown legendary creature, I still had all that I had wished for when I was in grief.

The opening to the cavern was right above me, which meant thirty feet falling was beneath me. I couldn't think of that. If I fell now, we would never save Laina and the crew. I tugged hard on the rope, hoping to steady myself so I could place my hand on the ledge and pull myself up the rest of the way. Foolish move. My hand broke off a piece of the cliff and the rope and bits of the cliff went falling down. I was now hanging from the cliff with blistered hands and not enough strength to keep going.

I tried to pull myself up, but my muscles were giving out.

"It's okay Mayra," Mateo called up, "we'll throw back up the grapple."

I shook my head. There wasn't a secure place for it, and by the time they found one, my body would have given out and I would be on the rocky bottom of the cliff. But they didn't see me giving up. They tried to work quickly, but it wasn't quick enough.

They hadn't even thrown up the rope by the time my fingers slipped off the cliff side.

XXII: The Draugr

I had been expecting to fall, so when I didn't, I was mildly confused. But I was so tired that I allowed whatever force had stopped my fall to continue its work. It brought me up the cliff side, laying me on the most solid part of the rock so the risk of falling was gone. Finally, I looked up and saw Briggs with a pompous grin.

"Saved your life, didn't I?"

Of course, the bastard would be cheeky at a time like this. I found it in me to hug him.

"Oh, come off it," he said, but he hugged me back.

He threw a rope down and pulled up the three that waited below.

I looked down at my hands. Skin hung off, and the pink skin underneath oozed clear liquid. Should I need to fight anyone off, even by holding a pistol, it wouldn't come without that stinging pain. I tried to remember all my moves from that moment until we got out of the rock were to prevent mine and everyone else's death. Blistered hands could not stifle me.

"How'd you get away?" Grey asked Briggs when he climbed up.

"The crew cut me loose because I was smallest," Briggs said. "It was between me and Monk but he's caught the fear."

Grey nodded. "How's Malin?"

"Barely holding on," he said gravely. There was no humor left in the boy who always had a remark.

"And Laina?" I asked.

"She's the only reason he's not dead yet."

"What exactly are we up against?"

Briggs seemed at a loss for words. "I don't really know. All I know is it smells like death and it moves, but I can't say for certain that it's alive. He's a wee fellow though."

"Wee as in fae folk? Or wee as in small?"

"Both."

We were after the dwarf's treasure, so it went without saying this was likely a dwarf. But the legend was from hundreds of years before. Dwarves were said to live much longer than humans, but from Briggs's description, this dwarf wasn't alive in the same way he had once been.

"What's it doing to Malin?" I asked.

"Torturing him," Briggs said, "for touching the treasure. Laina's keeping him calm enough not to kill him outright."

I recalled the legend I had read to the captain. Could this be the same dwarf from the story?

"Is there a tomb or a casket in the cavern?" I asked.

Briggs shrugged. "The cavern is somewhat of a maze. There could be along one of the other tunnels."

"I think I know what it is."

I told them an abridged version of the legend of the dwarf's treasure, being that our time was running out. I also told them of the creature my mother had once told me stories of.

"A draugr attaches its spirit to objects that were meaningful in its life," I explained. "So even in death, it will protect that which was most precious to it."

"So, how do we stop it?" Grey asked.

"We get it back in its tomb and lay it to rest. Then we burn the remains of its bones."

It was not a simple process, and I had not yet seen the creature. And all that I knew about the creature and the treasure were from fables. I did not know if it would truly work, but for now it was all we had to go from.

Briggs led us through the cavern towards where the dwarf kept Malin and the crew.

Like he had said, the cavern was built in a maze, with the tunnels winding around and branching off. But Briggs had marked his way with white chalk, and we followed a winding path, each turn marked with an arrow. After three right turns and down a large straight stretch of cave, Briggs stopped us, placing a finger to his lips, even though no one spoke.

The cave opened to a large room and I saw the crew behind bars divided into two small holding cells below a platform. And I saw the wee man Briggs had warned us of. I could smell the stench of death and could see how he stumbled about clumsily. His skin was slightly blue and swollen and ghastly to look at. It was definitely a draugr. He was marching around a wooden table where Malin was pinned down.

Malin's groans echoed across the walls of the cave, and it stunned me to see him this way. He was unclothed except for his undergarments. There were pins nailed through his wrists and a rope around his neck. He was still breathing, but just barely. His face grew purple with the strain.

And beside the torture table, was Laina, speaking to the dwarf in a soothing voice.

"It's okay, my love," she murmured. "He didn't mean it."

"Took the treasure," he spoke in Brannish. "Took the treasure and harmed my lady."

"It's alright," she replied. "I'm okay."

"What's he saying?" Mateo asked in my ear.

"The treasure. Malin touched the treasure and he's being punished for it."

We hid behind a rock, looking at the scene, and I could see all our brains trying to work out what we could possibly do. I knew I needed to get the draugr back to its grave, but where was the grave?

I looked at the crew in their cells, also looking bloody, dirty, and hopeless. But they appeared to all be alive, and that added to our numbers.

"We need to free the rest of the crew," I told Briggs.

He shook his head. "The thing will get mad."

If only I could get Laina's attention so that she could distract the draugr from looking our way.

The draugr moved around Malin's body, circling him like a wolf circles its prey. There were stories of draugr feeding on its victims or just outright killing them. I wasn't sure what we dealt with. Malin still had all his limbs, but the thing seemed to enjoy slowly inflicting pain on him. The draugr gripped the pin that was in Malin's left wrist and twisted it. Malin's body stiffened and he let out a scream.

"Please!" he wept. "Please, I'll leave. I'll leave the treasure. Just—please." He sobbed for his life.

"You tried to take my treasure," the creature said in its hoarse voice.

"Let him go, my love," Laina urged him. "Let him and the crew go. Then we can be alone together again."

"But he took the treasure," the draugr insisted, very much like a toddler. His bulbous face scrunched up in a pout with his bottom lip protruding over his top lip.

"And we must find it in our hearts to forgive, just like we forgave that wretched girl."

"We killed the girl," he replied. If he was alive, perhaps this would have been a humorous retort. But being a corpse, he said so without any emotion.

Malin stood stiff again. "Just do it," he whispered.

Laina eyed Malin and I knew she was thinking what I was thinking. Perhaps a swift death would be more merciful. But she couldn't do it. If she did, she could anger the draugr and break the illusion that she was his love from the story—the Sjöfru.

The draugr stuck another pin in Malin's foot and his screams got louder. We could not just stand by and watch. It was crazy and irrational, but I jumped from the rock and went straight to the cells to free the crew first,

Malin's screams drowning out the sounds of my feet.

Mateo and Jorge exhaled quickly when I left my hiding place. But Grey was right beside me, seeing what I aimed to do. I took the iron knife he gave to me and began to work on one of the locks while he worked on the other. I saw the surprised faces of my crew. Grover, the Monk, Kamau, and Stratford clutched the bars of the cage. There was a simultaneous inhale as I began to work on the lock. The metal was old, probably close to a thousand years, and it didn't take much to pop the lock and open the door with an incredibly loud creak.

Each sound, the clinking of the lock, and the footsteps of the men, was like thunder and I waited for the draugr to be alarmed, but Laina had his back turned to us as she spoke more in the voice of his long-dead lover.

"We can go back to our cottage in the countryside. I miss the sun. I don't wish to remain in this cave."

"The treasure. I must guard our treasure."

Of course, the draugr would not survive beyond this cave, let alone in the sun, but

Laina spoke to him as if he was still alive, giving the crew a chance to run for it.

A few of them clapped me on the back as they passed. Stratford stopped and hugged me.

"I'm sorry, Finn—"

"Later," I snapped in a hushed whisper. But I was happy to see them. Stratford, Jenkins, Kamau, Everett, Hagley, Peel. They started to climb the rocks, making quite a bit of noise while they did so. The creature must have been mostly deaf, being that he didn't hear beyond Malin's pleas and Laina's comforting words.

Briggs, Jorge, and Mateo helped the crewmates climb up to where they had hidden, leading them out of the cavern. I did not want any of them to stay and fight. I wanted to ensure they all made it out with their lives.

As the last of them wriggled their way up on the ledge and made their way out, I searched the cave for any sign of a tomb. Laina continued to distract the draugr and I wished to free him before finding it, but I couldn't do so without alerting the creature.

I needed to know where the creature slept.

"Do you see a tomb?" I whispered to Grey.

He shook his head. "The treasure is down that tunnel though." He pointed his dagger to the tunnel behind the platform. There would be no way to go down it without exposing our location. I wasn't truly concerned with the treasure. I was more focused on getting Laina and the crew out of here.

Laina tried her best not to look at us, but I could see her nodding her head towards the tunnel, signaling to us where we should take it to end this. On her thigh, she rested her hand, five fingers at the ready. A countdown. I nudged Grey and made sure he got the message.

Four.

Three.

Two.

One.

I ran for the tomb and Grey ran straight for the draugr, his dagger at the ready to strike him in the back. He aimed right for the center of its spine, and while it seemed to alert the creature, it did not bring him down. He whipped around, and with impressive force for the dwarf, swiped Grey from the platform so he made a *thud* on the cave floor.

I almost reacted—going down to shield Grey from further blows from the draugr, but I couldn't let my emotions distract me. Saving his life before slaying the creature would increase our peril.

But instead of finding the tomb, I had an idea.

Grey's knife was steel and mine was iron. I had once thought he gave it to me because the metal was less sharp and strong and wouldn't do as much damage. But for an old Spriggan creature, it was just what I needed.

I brought my blade down into his side. It did not re-kill the undead, but it did stun him long enough for me to toss Laina the antidote, bringing magic back to her hands. She took the potion, her whole body radiating as her magic returned. For a moment, I was breathless at the purity of her skin, the way she lifted her face to the heavens, power flowing through her in a way even I could see. Then, just as quickly, she faced her hands toward the draugr, binding him with her power. He seized, his body snapping to rigidity like invisible ropes cinched him tight. All he could move was his head, which he whipped in her direction, pure rage in his clouded eyes.

"You aren't my woman."

She shook her head and in perfect Brannish said, "It is time for your poor old soul to rest." She nodded towards the hall. With her magic and my iron remaining in his side, we dragged him toward his tomb. A stone door was dragged to the side, revealing an uncovered coffin. I'd adjusted to his death smell, but the pungent room made me turn my head and shallow my breath. Scattered around his coffin were the remnants of his treasure, carelessly strewn by Malin. He was the one who likely freed the draugr, opening the coffin to search for more treasure.

Laina confined the draugr to his coffin, keeping her magic's hold on him as Grey came to us, carrying a lit torch. He touched the draugr with the fire and the creature burst into flames, his flesh disintegrated in the box, along with the ash of his bones. He would never rise again, but even still, Laina collected the remains in a pouch she carried.

"It's customary to spread their ashes on the ocean, to ensure they never return," she explained. "Besides, he'll get to be with his sea nymph again."

Having just defeated the beast, I wanted nothing more than to hug my lady and be free of this place, but there was one matter to resolve.

Malin gasped for breath as he lay flat on the torture table. I cut the rope and moved to remove the pins, but he shook his head.

"It'll hurt more, lass," he murmured, his voice so weak. "Just let me be."

I looked at Grey and Laina. Laina looked away, walking off the platform, allowing Grey and I to decide the fate of her captor. I would not force her to use magic to save him. Besides, by the look of his wounds, he was too far gone. No magic could save an already claimed life. Death took Malin and Watson in much the same way.

"What would you like me to do, Captain?" Grey spoke up. His brow was furrowed, and he clutched Malin's hand, keeping him in this world a few moments longer.

"Jenkins knows his duty," Malin told him. "You know yours. Carry on. Take the treasure if you must. But I am no longer captain of the *Wind Raider*."

Grey nodded, taking his pistol from his belt.

"Wait," I told him. I went to Malin's head, where he looked up at me with strained eyes. "I need to know one thing before you get your peace. Did you really mean to kill Briggs and sell the crew?"

There was nothing left for him to lie about. He was fading. But I wished for him to clear his conscience so he could be remembered well.

"Yes," Malin said. "But I always meant to buy them back. It was a way to get us the island and start a pirate empire. Jenkins knew."

His breath shook.

I stepped away, turning as Grey pulled the trigger, putting Captain Charles Malin to rest as the pathetic, greedy bastard he had always been.

XXIII: Skarn

The *Wind Raider*'s crew had seen what remained of Captain Malin when they had made their escape, so it did not come as a surprise when Grey, Mateo, Jorge, and I carried his poorly wrapped body from the Devil's Rock. They took off their hats and touched the corpse that had once been their captain.

Everyone learned of Malin's plan to sell the ship and crew. Briggs did not go near the body, and I didn't blame him. Malin had taken him under his wing after what had happened to his father, and after all those years of manipulation had only meant to do away with him.

"Did you know?" I asked Jenkins.

He nodded. "I did. I meant to protect Briggs. I knew he had fae blood, but tried to convince Malin to get his sacrifice elsewhere. I could only do so much though without making him think I also doubted him. I didn't want to end up like Starky."

That was fair. I couldn't blame the first mate from protecting his own skin.

"Briggs told me of what Malin planned to do with you though and I helped get it in Malin's head that it was better to send you back to Playada. I knew you'd be determined enough to get back in the end."

I cocked my head. The first mate hadn't sold me out the first time he heard Laina and I talking. And he had the second time after he found out what was to happen to Briggs. Everything lined up. And here we were, saved because Mateo's ship was alerted and Briggs and I no longer threatened to be killed by Malin.

The captain, despite his treachery, was given a sailor's burial, letting his body drift on a raft out to sea. Many of the men spoke kindly of the memory of him. Afterall, for many of them, Malin had been their leader for the last twenty years. He could even be considered a friend to many of the older officers.

I chose not to speak. I did not hate him, but I could not find it in me to speak kindly to his memory. I did not have the history the others had. I had six months of feeling his loyalty to his crew, and six months of questioning his motives and his integrity. It was better that the crew speak of him only in the light. And I chose to let go of the darkness that clouded Malin's character in my mind. No man deserves to go to his grave so gruesomely. Not even Malin.

I sat on the beach after the ceremony, watching the raft drift off towards the horizon. Laina sat beside me, her head resting on my shoulder.

"What now?" she asked after we had been quiet for what seemed like hours. Our reunion was not one of passion, but of comfort. Our clutched hands were bound in a way that I never wished to break.

"We go to Brannland," I said. "That was always the plan, right?"

She nodded. "What of the crew? Of Grey? Mateo? The treasure?"

These were all good questions, but nothing I had answers for. All I had was what I had control over, which was getting Laina and I safely to Brannland so we would not have to suffer any longer in the lower world.

"Let me have this moment," I told her. "Let me have you a moment longer before we have to face the real world again."

"You have me," she whispered into my neck.

I wrapped my arms around her, hugging her tight, rocking our bodies slowly. My head was in the heavens to finally have her. To not fear she would be taken away. To feel as though we were both safe now after all that had once threatened us. "Do you remember when we first met?" I asked into her red curls. "When you said you wouldn't settle until you found someone who cherishes all that you are?"

I felt her nod into my breast.

I tilted her chin up so I could look in her green eyes while I spoke to her. "I want to be that person for you, Laina. Since the day we met, even before you took me to your bed, I felt as though I knew you to your core. I did not know you were fae, but I knew you had a past that haunted you, and I knew you wished to run. And I would run with you anywhere. That's how I've always felt. But what if we found a place to be safe together?"

The corners of her mouth picked up, and she pressed a soft kiss to my lips, parting to tell me, "I'm yours, Mayra Hidalgo."

Stratford, Jenkins, Grey, the surviving officers of the *Raider*, convened on ship when the full moon rose, ready to discuss the next important move. Laina, Briggs, and I were invited to join them.

"There will be a vote," Jenkins said, "to accept me in Malin's place. That is always how it's been. I may be first mate, but I don't mean to step into a position until I've properly earned it."

None of us thought the position belonged to anyone else. Jenkins had held many of Malin's secrets, but I trusted him to have our best interest. He had shown me enough that he was both loyal to his former captain, but always more loyal to his ship and crew.

"What of the treasure?" Stratford asked.

The matter stumped us all. It was likely cursed. The dwarf was gone, his body burned and ashes drowned. Superstitions kept us from going back into the rock to collect it.

"We need some currency for the next few months," Jenkins said. "We could take the smaller stuff. The coins and jewels. But the four items—the dagger, the ring, the armor, and the amulet—I want nothing to do with them."

I remembered something Starky had told me, back all those years before. "You know Bjorn in Brannland, yes?"

Stratford and Jenkins nodded, recalling the Brannish chieftain.

"We should bring them the treasure," I offered. "Sell it so that it does not go to waste. I'm certain Laina can make sure it does not harm us to take it."

No one wished to leave riches for someone else to find, so it wasn't hard to convince the crew to carefully take the treasure aboard the ship, secured in a chest, and locked in the cell that once held Laina.

"It is not inherently cursed," Laina said. "It was the dwarf that was cursed to guard it."

But superstitious pirates would not hear of it. They would not go near the room as we made preparations to sail to Brannland.

"Will you come with us?" I asked Mateo, knowing his answer before he spoke.

He shook his head. "My bride has been waiting long enough."

I hugged him tight and wished him well on his journey.

"Will you ever return?"

I shrugged. "I may, but if I do not, you know where I'll be," I looked over my shoulder at Laina, who played cards with Grey and Kamau.

"I'm glad you've found your happiness," he told me.

"And you as well."

I watched as his ship left Devil's Rock, feeling both wistful and happy for my longtime friend. It was more than likely we'd never see each other again. But anything was possible. I'd thought that our last goodbye was months ago, and look what happened. I was at least glad his pockets were filled with coin from the dwarf's treasure. Before he'd left, I'd urged him to split it with Jorge and deny his disloyal crew. But telling Mateo to be selfish, even rightfully so, was like shouting into the wind.

Our voyage from the Devil's Rock to Bjorn's village was only a few days, but with all that had happened, it seemed to last ages. We were eager to get off the water and pursue our next step. But we were also anxious at the repercussions of what had happened in the rock.

Jenkins had explained to me that a ship was always subject to scrutiny when a captain turned up dead. Even more so since Malin's name was known from Playada to Brannland. Bjorn was the chieftain of the village and much of the business conducted there was done through Malin.

"But surely he'll know you as the dutiful first mate?" I asked, hoping to encourage him.

He remained grim. "Almost all first mates who superseded their captains did so intentionally."

In a lot of ways, nothing had changed. Most of the men had resumed their posts and duties. The treasure and all its so-called curses remained locked away, but Jenkins made sure the crew was paid for their loyalty.

Jenkins was a much more proactive captain than Malin ever was. Stratford, filling in his shoes as first mate, did not need to conduct the ship with the same heavy hand Jenkins had. Jenkins continued to be the loudest and most authoritative voice. His transition into captain-hood was accepted without question from the crew, already having their respect.

Captain Jenkins did not remain behind a door and a desk, plotting his next move. More often, he was on the main deck or behind the helm. If a rope needed tightening it, he tightened it. If a sail needed to be mended, he mended it. No one was assigned to bring him his meals. Instead, he sat with the crew and entertained us with his stories and banter just as he always had.

Grey was promoted to battle master, and I was offered the position of sailing master.

"It should be you," I told Briggs.

He raised an eyebrow. "You were the one chosen to be Grey's second."

"But your father was sailing master before Watson. You should fill his place."

"Da would be proud," he smiled. "I know what Malin did," he told me without me asking. "I've known a while. But... I didn't want it to be true. Now I know."

"I didn't want to think he was that evil either," I admitted.

"Will you stay?"

I simply shrugged. I had not made a decision yet. I did not know what waited for me in Brannland.

The men were in solemn spirits. For months, it seemed even at our worse, everyone found it in them to play a game of dice or sing a shanty. We had all seen things these past few months and now had to deal with it in our own ways. The ale barrels were running dry from the men dealing with their problems.

I leaned on Laina, not to talk things through, but to distract myself from the future. I didn't want to admit how nervous I was to return to my mother's homeland. But I was also scared at how torn I was between staying as part of the crew or staying in Brannland and leaving this life behind. Our hiding place from these problems became the crow's nest, being that Grey remained down in the bunks.

It may have been cold, but her fae blood ran hot and she kept me warm with her touches and kisses. I could not think to mind the cold as her lips traveled down my navel, below my waistline, and she inched down my breeches to feast on me.

Laina had a way of knowing that the comforts she provided me helped ease my mind through all the turmoil. And I allowed myself to forget while she edged pleasure out of me.

"Oh gods," I gasped, tilting my head back as I breathed through those waves of pleasure. "I love you."

Her red curls bounced as she stopped what she was doing to look at me. "What?"

I went scarlet. It was a silly thing to say. I knew that, but I couldn't take it back once I'd said it.

"I'm sorry," I said, the pleasure burning off much more quickly than usual. "I just meant—"

She smiled. "Sometimes we say things when we're overcome. It's okay."

She was right. I was overcome, which was why I was feeling things so quickly, and needing her closer and desiring to never leave her side despite my love for the ship, crew, and the sea. That had to be it.

The Brannish coastline was a boneyard compared to Playada. In the south, the water gently rode up the land, gently caressed the fine sands, and receded out in a whisper. Everything in Brannland was harsh, rugged, jagged, and sharp. There were no sand beaches, but rocks and cliffs and ice.

Even as we approached the landing spot for Skarn, we could not see any impression of a settlement behind the tall cliffs. But Jenkins guided the ship into a small bay, unseen until we were within it, and up a narrow strip of water. We docked there, still below a cliff, but tied to a sturdy dock.

The Brannish men were there within minutes, dressed in furs and armor, all holding swords and spears. They had the lunar skin and sapphire eyes of the north, some with hair like straw and some with jet black hair. Some even had bright red hair like Laina.

"Raiders," the one in front, who happened to be the tallest of them, said as greeting.

Jenkins approached him, his hand outstretched. I guessed that it had to be Bjorn. They spoke for a while, Bjorn looking at our crew with suspicion. Jenkins had been right:

without Malin, we were held with much less trust. Still, the tall, broad men began to lead us up the hill to their settlement.

The springtime sun did not shine in the north and I held my cloak close to me. Many of my crewmates had brought blankets from the ship, looking envious of my wool cloak that provided as much heat as the warriors' furs. Laina stayed close to me, and I wrapped some of it around her as well.

The village was through the hills, and many of Bjorn's people were out and watched us approach. There were perhaps thirty or so people outside the log cabins and canvas huts. A mixture of men and women tended to the fires and their children. They cooked on the fires, even though it was freezing. They had houses behind them, but my mother said that her people liked being below the sky whenever possible.

They whispered in Brannish, but I could pick up much of what they said.

"Strangers?"

"No, that dirty captain's men."

"Where's the dirty captain?"

"Seems like they got a new one."

"Probably killed the bastard. Serves him right."

They may have been suspicious towards us, but it didn't seem like they looked at us hostilely. Bjorn led us to what I perceived as their village's center and in Brannish spoke to his people:

"The Raiders have returned at the demise of their captain. He was subject to darkness and has faced justice. We treat them as guests."

There were exchanges of agreement with their chief.

We were given food and shown to a place to lodge while we remained there. Bjorn allowed Laina and me to sleep amongst the other women, away from the crew, which they found curious.

"I didn't know southern girls could be pirates. Always thought the Aldinians frowned upon women in power," a blonde woman told some of her companions. She was in warriors' furs. I had not noticed before, but not all those who greeted us had been men. Many of the women had knives on their sides and carried swords.

"They certainly do," I replied back in Brannish.

This startled those who were in the quarters.

The warrior woman spoke to me. "You speak Brannish?"

"My mother taught me."

Her blue eyes looked me up and down, likely not seeing my Brannish ancestry, as my Playadan heritage overpowered me. "Who was your mother?"

"Vivanka Ogden," I replied. A spark of excitement awakened in my chest to speak her name.

A hand gripped my shoulder from behind. I turned to face a tall woman, six inches taller than I was. She had long black hair, braided in a crown. Her eyes were icy blue, and she had high cheekbones. She wasn't in furs, but a simple green dress with golden thread on the edges, identical to my cloak.

When I saw her, my breath was caught in my chest, and I nearly fell, if it wasn't for her hand keeping me up. The vial under my shirt rattled against my chest.

"Mama?" I gasped.

Acknowledgements

This book started with an idea for a love story and my two main characters. I could see them so clearly: Mayra was rebellious, suffered from grief, felt doomed as a woman, and was still figuring out vital pieces of herself. And then she meets Laina, a free spirit with her own dark past she's running from. Many of the concepts that exist in this final product were also in this contemporary first draft. I wrote half of a novel, set in a small town based on my hometown, following the love story of these two characters. But I knew something was missing from this story.

I am a fantasy reader. I get caught up in stories of love, but only if there is also magic and dragons and kingdom-based politics. So, I started from scratch, breathing new life into these characters. I added pirates, faeries, took away the reality and laid out a fantasy realm. I added a bunch of new side characters and gave them as much personality as I could. And I suddenly found the words pouring out of me. I was excited to live in this world of fae and piracy because those were the stories that kept me up late turning the pages when I was a kid (and even now). This enthusiasm meant that despite that I am a full-time student working two jobs, there is a finished product to share with all of you.

And none of this would have been possible had it not also been for a few special people.

First, and most importantly, to my wonderful mother, Crissi Langwell. My thanks goes beyond the tremendous support for this book—which included editing, formatting, cover conception, beta reading, and constant words of encouragement. My mother also gifted me with a love of reading. She was the one who first read me stories about princesses saving princes and fighting dragons. I would not be half the writer I am now if she didn't instill in me an excitement for reading and language. Thank you for molding me as a writer and for helping me make this book all that it is.

I also owe a special thank you to Alberto Melendez, who saw the beginning of the fantasy draft of this book and offered gentle nudges to bring my characters more life.

Also to Jesse Osman who's love of reading matches mine, and who's advice also set me on track to finish this book.

And to Shannon Bayley who saw a close to finished product and helped me smooth out some of the edges.

And thank you to my bountiful community of friends and family who have encouraged me on the journey to get here. Thank you Dad, Liz, Shawn, Haley, Jordan, Joe, Liam, Anne, Pam, Grandma Nancy, and to my siblings, Lucas, Amara, Kaya, and Shiloh. You all make my world that much brighter.

About the Author

Summer Raine McLerran is an author in Northern California, where the big redwoods and beautiful coastline fueled an early love of storytelling. Writing since the age of seven, Summer has always been drawn to tales of adventure, fantasy, and the allure of the high seas. While she wrote entries in private journals and short stories in spiral bound notebooks, Summer also wrote a collection of short stories her senior year of high school that incorporated the history and ghost stories of the summer sleep-away camp she attended. *A Drop of Faerie's Blood* is her debut novel.

Summer earned her Bachelor of the Arts Degree from Sonoma State University in English and Creative Writing and continues to dream up imaginative worlds full of rich history and pirate adventures.

When she's not writing, Summer attends Renaissance Faires, plays Dungeons and Dragons, and is a speech pathology student with the hope of becoming a licensed Speech-Language Pathologist working with elementary aged students.

Find her at summerrainemclerran.com.

www.ingramcontent.com/pod-product-compliance
Lightning Source LLC
Chambersburg PA
CBHW021842010726
47493CB00005B/1516

* 9 7 8 1 9 6 1 2 4 0 0 6 3 *